MURDER ON THE MENU

KATIE MARSH

Boldwood

First published in Great Britain in 2025 by Boldwood Books Ltd.

Copyright © Katie Marsh, 2025

Cover Design by Head Design Ltd

Cover Images: Shutterstock

The moral right of Katie Marsh to be identified as the author of this work has been asserted in accordance with the Copyright, Designs and Patents Act 1988.

All rights reserved. No part of this book may be reproduced in any form or by any electronic or mechanical means, including information storage and retrieval systems, without written permission from the author, except for the use of brief quotations in a book review. This book is a work of fiction and, except in the case of historical fact, any resemblance to actual persons, living or dead, is purely coincidental.

Every effort has been made to obtain the necessary permissions with reference to copyright material, both illustrative and quoted. We apologise for any omissions in this respect and will be pleased to make the appropriate acknowledgements in any future edition.

A CIP catalogue record for this book is available from the British Library.

Paperback ISBN 978-1-78513-929-1

Large Print ISBN 978-1-78513-930-7

Hardback ISBN 978-1-78513-928-4

Ebook ISBN 978-1-78513-931-4

Kindle ISBN 978-1-78513-932-1

Audio CD ISBN 978-1-78513-923-9

MP3 CD ISBN 978-1-78513-924-6

Digital audio download ISBN 978-1-78513-925-3

This book is printed on certified sustainable paper. Boldwood Books is dedicated to putting sustainability at the heart of our business. For more information please visit https://www.boldwoodbooks.com/about-us/sustainability/

Boldwood Books Ltd, 23 Bowerdean Street, London, SW6 3TN

www.boldwoodbooks.com

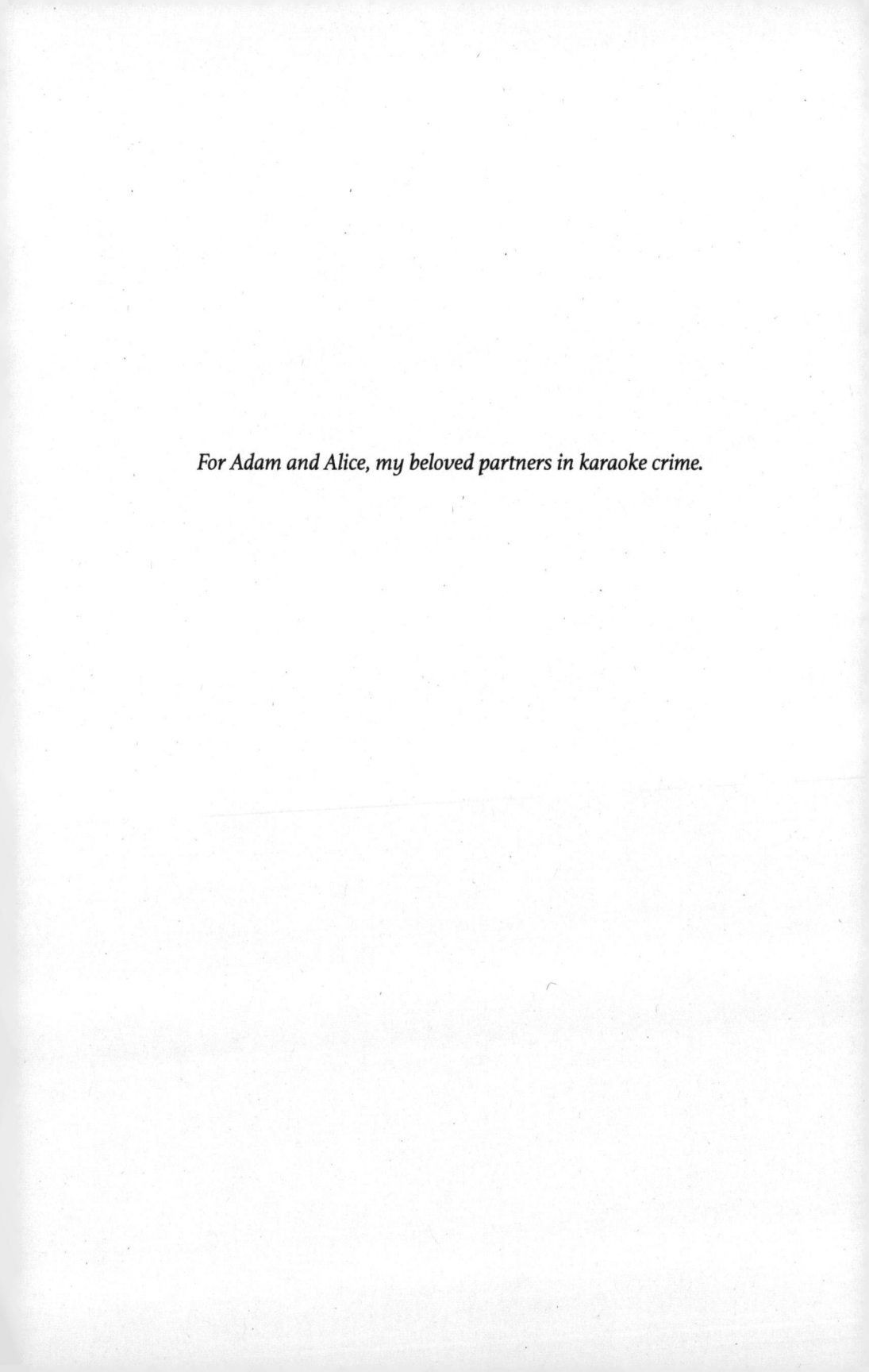

For Adam and Alice, my beloved partners in karaoke crime.

PROLOGUE

The gun went off as soon as Amber stepped into the forest. She turned and dived into the trees, knowing only that she must keep moving, praying she could outpace whoever was behind her.

As she forced her way through branches and over bumpy tree roots, her sodden trainers weren't even pretending to grip the rough path beneath her feet. She caught a flash of movement to her left, before tripping on a root and falling forwards. Rain poured down her face as she flew through the air, arms flailing in a desperate bid to avoid crash-landing into a tree.

Too late. Her face slammed against the rough bark and she fell down, winded. For a second, she lay, rain or possibly blood blurring her vision, her hamstring screaming at her for landing so hard. Then she heard footsteps behind her, closer now. She pushed herself up, ignoring the buzzing in her head. She had to get moving. She had to get back to the castle.

Amber bargained with the heavens as she ran. If she got out of this alive, she would never go away again. She would stay at home, safe with her true crime podcasts and her punchbag. Her best friend was the reason she was on this supposedly relaxing and luxurious weekend away, and now – nearly twelve hours in – there were three dead bodies and a killer on her tail. Amber had felt more relaxed the last time she had gone for a root canal.

She put her aching head down, leaning into the wind, and started to run as fast as the weather would allow. Her feet slid on moss and snagged on stones, but still she increased her speed as she heard boots drumming behind her.

The killer was coming, so Amber ran, the rain penetrating every last inch of her, wishing that her Stormwear coat actually lived up to its name. She looked down the slope at the edge of the forest, seeing the dark grey shape of the castle walls rising below her. She had to get inside before it was too late. She pushed her wet hair from her face as trees lashed above her, the storm raging. Her heart was pounding but she was close now. She could do this. Speed. And silence. That was all she needed. She had to be as silent as the grave.

'*Clio to Amber, over.*' The walkie-talkie on her belt crackled into life.

Amber jumped, hearing the boots behind her changing direction, starting to veer her way now. She reached for the off switch on her walkie-talkie, but couldn't find it, her cold fingers scrabbling over the plastic.

'*Are you alive, Amber? Over!*'

Amber ducked behind a tree before cutting down to the right. She was running the wrong way now, but at least she might have put the killer off the scent. She tried to detach the walkie-talkie from her belt, but her fingers were too cold. She bent over awkwardly, pressing the comms button, speaking in a whisper. 'Clio, shut up.'

'*We've found something. Over.*'

Amber's head hit a branch and she reeled, struggling for balance.

'*Amber? Are you dead? We've found something. Over!*'

Amber permitted herself a silent swear as she once again tried to remove the damn thing from her belt. No luck. She gritted her teeth, whispering again. 'Clio, stop talking. Now.' Amber saw a movement to her right and raised her fists. Fat lot of use they would be against a gun, but they were all she had.

'*Oh thank God you're alive. I was so worried. Over.*'

Swearing, Amber bent down, pressing the comms button again. 'I won't be for much longer, if you keep talking, Clio. The killer is chasing me. Now. With a gun. Shut up. Please. Over.'

At last, the penny dropped. '*Oh God. Got it. Over.*'

Where was the killer? Amber stared frantically around her, before darting left, cutting down a steep slope towards the castle. Just a few more metres. Just a few more—

The walkie-talkie squealed, feedback cutting through the air.

'Clio!'

'Sorry. Dropped it. Over.' More feedback, followed by the familiar sound of Clio shrieking four-letter words. 'Can't. Find. The. Off. Switch.'

Amber started to sprint. The killer must be about to catch her now. Any second she expected to feel hands around her throat, or a gun jabbing her spine. Her only option was to keep moving. The castle loomed above her, turrets steadfast, immune to the storm. If Amber took enough twists and turns, maybe she could still make it.

She turned as she came out onto the gravel drive, her trainers skidding as they hit the sharp stones. But she didn't break her stride, determined to get inside, to get to the rifle store, to get her hands on a weapon that could protect her. She was nearly there. Just a few more metres.

But then, just as Amber was reaching for the heavy metal door handle, somebody grabbed her. Now she was being wrenched off her feet, falling backwards, powerless. She crashed against the gravel, all the breath knocked from her body. She looked up, eyes blurring, knowing that this was it. She did the only thing she could do. She pressed the comms button on her walkie-talkie. Maybe her friends would find her. Maybe this wouldn't be the end.

Amber closed her eyes. It was official. Relaxing weekends away were not her thing.

TWELVE HOURS EARLIER...

1

AMBER

As a woman who didn't like surprises, Amber was very proud of how well she was coping with her current situation. She was even managing to smile as she clung to the handrail of the rickety boat which seemed destined to sink before it reached the remote island that was the weekend destination for Amber and her two best friends.

'It's so exciting, isn't it?' Her friend Clio flung out a hand, only just saving herself from falling as a huge wave crashed over the bow of the boat. She pulled herself back up, beaming, her recently bleached white-blonde hair slick with rain, her cheeks flushed by the gale-force wind that seemed to be doing its best to stop them from arriving.

'So exciting! Thank you so much for inviting me.' Amber would rather be at home trying to get her company accounts to balance, but she couldn't let Clio down by showing it. Her friend had been obsessed with getting into the brand-new Chateau la Fontaine retreat ever since she had heard that it was coming to the south coast, and had been entering competitions for months in a bid to win a spot at the soft launch this weekend.

The original Chateau la Fontaine, in Palm Springs, was the stuff of legend. Exclusive enough to ban smartphones, it was set in 200 acres of grounds, boasting three infinity pools, a spa, firepits, a fragrance concierge and the kind of celebrities who only travelled by private jet. As it was owned by chef Valerie la Fontaine, so famous that even Amber had heard of her, the food was, of course, beyond compare. As local chatter grew about the new Chateau, located on an island only a few miles from their hometown of Sunshine Sands, Clio had grown more and more determined to be one of the first guests. Last night she had got the call to say she had won a weekend there for herself and two friends, and now here they all were.

'Who else would I have invited? It's the ultimate birthday present for you, isn't it?' Clio nudged Amber. 'Happy birthday! It's a bit of a surprise, eh? I hope all our clients were okay with us disappearing so suddenly?'

'They were fine. And it's only a weekend.' Amber wasn't keen to share that the detective agency didn't really have that many clients at the moment. She had been paying Clio and Jeanie, her other employee, out of her savings for the past two months. She would have to talk to them soon, but for now she forced a smile. 'The last time you won a competition was at school, wasn't it?'

'Yes!' Clio grinned as another wave hit the boat and sprayed them both with copious amounts of salt water. 'I won that awful pink Tampax dispenser and the cassette tape Walkman! God, I loved that thing.'

'Until it ate your *Starlight Express* album.' Amber felt herself start to relax. A weekend away with Clio and Jeanie, the best friends who were her family. Maybe it was just what she needed. A weekend away from being their boss at the agency – a chance to just be one of three; one of the girls on tour.

'Oh yes! I bloody loved that album.' Clio knelt down on the heaving deck and unzipped her large pink suitcase, only for a pair of bright turquoise knickers to be whipped away by the wind. She stuck a hand out, trying to catch them. 'Damn. Those were my favourites.'

A deep voice came from behind them. 'I can see why.' Amber looked round. A man with thick blond hair and stubble that belonged in a Gillette commercial was grinning at Clio, head on one side, his blue eyes glinting suggestively.

He held out a hand. 'Kieran Anderson, showbiz reporter for the *Daily Herald*.'

'I'm Clio. Clio Lawrence.' Clio's hand was still down on the deck, rummaging in her case. 'I'm trying to find my waterproof... But it's a bit late now, I suppose,' she sighed, scrambling up, indicating her sodden red jumpsuit. She peered up at Kieran in the manner of a midlife woman who was in denial about needing glasses. 'Haven't I seen you on...?'

'The telly? You might have done.' He gave a short chuckle that was presumably meant to sound modest. He shoved his hands deep into the pockets of his battered leather jacket. 'I pop up here and there. I have a podcast too, of course.'

'Of course you do,' Amber muttered under her breath.

He turned towards her, palm already outstretched. 'And you are...?'

'Amber.' She let go of his hand as soon as she could, hoping he would leave them alone.

'She's not just any Amber.' Clio lost her balance as the boat battled another massive wave. Naturally Kieran was there to catch her. 'She's Amber Nagra – *the* Amber Nagra. She runs a local detective agency – you've probably heard of it. We've been headline news around here. The Bad Girls Detective Agency?'

'Um...' Kieran clearly had no idea what she was talking about. His blue eyes roved over Clio's body and Amber wondered whether he was busy guessing her bra size. 'You'll have to enlighten me. I love the sound of the Bad Girls.'

Amber's nausea was rising and she wasn't entirely sure it was due to seasickness.

Clio bubbled on. 'We've solved two murders so far.'

'Murders?' That got his attention. He caught Clio by the elbow as the boat dived again. Amber was left to flail alone.

'Yes.' Clio tucked a strand of hair winningly behind her ear, in a move Amber knew to be a first step to flirtation. Oh God. Now Amber wanted even more to be back at home with her accounts. 'We beat the police to the killer both times.'

'I bet you did.' Kieran took a step closer to Clio and Amber could practically see her friend melting. Clio had a thing about men in leather jackets, even when they were stupid enough to wear them in the worst storm so far this year.

It was time for Amber to intervene. 'Are you here covering the opening of the Chateau, Kieran?'

'Yes. I am.' He nodded, running a hand through his hair just as the boat rocked again, hit sideways by the vicious wind. Amber wasn't entirely sure that Kieran scooting into Clio was an accident, especially given how long his hand rested on her waist while he steadied himself.

He gave her a toothy grin. 'Valerie invited me to the launch. I did a piece on her a while ago for a major Sunday paper. An in-depth interview about her move over to the UK. Nice photos. You know the sort of thing.'

'Valerie la Fontaine?' Clio looked like she might explode. 'You've met her?'

'A few times, yes.' He shrugged. 'I meet a lot of celebrities in my line of work.'

Clio was lapping this up. 'Is she amazing? I bet she's amazing. And her food just sounds divine.'

'Oh, it is.' Kieran was all systems charm, but there was something about him that told Amber trusting him would be a mistake. She turned away, hoping Clio saw through him before she started on the champagne that would probably be waiting when they finally made it to the island.

Amber staggered across to Jeanie, the third member of their trio. She was standing with the captain of the boat – a tall man with a gold chain showing beneath the unzipped V of his navy waterproof. Thin strands of long sandy hair flailed around his head, which domed above sharp brown eyes surrounded by smile lines. His feet were in big black boots and his legs were encased in what looked like blue overalls.

Jeanie smiled at Amber. 'Are you okay?'

Amber nodded as the boat creaked and jerked. 'Yes. I don't get seasick, luckily.'

Jeanie shook her head, pushing her long blonde curls back off her face. They trailed wetly down her back. 'Not the boat – the surprise!'

'Oh.' Amber arched an eyebrow. 'I'm holding up. Just.'

'If you say so.' Jeanie moved with the boat as it dropped and rose, her childhood sailing trips with her dad showing in every confident move she made. 'This is Ray.'

'Hi Ray.' Amber raised a hand before grasping a handrail to rebalance herself.

Ray gave a rasping laugh. 'I bet you're wondering what you've got yourself into. The proper Chateau boat has been delayed at the shipyard – it's still being painted, apparently, so I had to borrow this off one of the hire companies back in Sunshine Sands.' He turned the ship's wheel with a tanned hand that bore a Knebworth tattoo. This man was clearly a rocker. His eyes twinkled at Amber. 'I'm sorry it's not quite the glamorous crossing you might have been expecting to the new Chateau la Fontaine.' He scraped his fingers over his greying stubble. 'We're ironing out a few things this weekend.'

Jeanie shook her head. 'It's a free weekend away. We're not going to complain about anything, are we?'

'No way!' Amber raised her voice to be heard over the wind. 'No complaining here!'

Ray eyed her sympathetically. 'You look like you're wondering if I know what I'm doing.'

'No, not at all.' Amber inhaled deeply. 'I was actually thinking I'm happy you're in charge of the boat, not me, or we'd all be at the bottom of the ocean by now.'

He threw his head back and laughed. 'Well, I'm glad you approve. I'm meant to go back to the mainland straight after we arrive. There's supposed to be another party of guests coming later, down from London.' He reduced the speed of the motor as they approached the island. 'But the trains are being cancelled so I'm not sure they're going to make it, let alone whether I can sail back to the mainland to collect them if they do. So it might just be the five of you at the new Chateau for the weekend.'

'We'll make it work.' Amber was flung forwards as the wind whipped above them.

'I bet you will.' He gave a slow smile. 'A lot of the new staff are stuck in London too, so it should all be in proportion, shouldn't it?'

'I suppose so.' Seawater sprayed Amber's face and she tasted salt on her lips. 'We are going to make it, aren't we?'

'Of course.' His confidence was reassuring. 'I've been here two months and I haven't sunk a boat yet.'

'That's good to know.' Amber braced herself as another wave smashed across the bow. 'So, what do you do at the new Chateau, apart from getting people there?'

'I'm the head groundskeeper. I joined the team in the first wave – hand-picked by Valerie la Fontaine herself, no less.' Amber was thrown towards him by another gust of wind. He smelt of sweat and tobacco and she spotted some leather bracelets around his wrist, peeking out from beneath the waterproof.

'What's Valerie like to work for?' Jeanie blinked up at him while Amber peered ahead. A grey, rocky mass rose in front of them. If this was the island then it wasn't giving out welcoming vibes either.

Ray beamed. 'She's a great lady, Valerie. No one like her. I've only met her on Zoom – she arrived this morning, apparently – but I like what I see.' He swung the boat's wheel and it tacked across towards land. 'A great lady.'

'So I hear,' a voice piped up from down below them. Amber looked down but couldn't see anyone.

'Hello! Down here!'

Amber peered over the railing, to see a woman in a wheelchair parked beneath the awning, smiling up at her. She had long grey hair, red lipstick and a large birthmark on her cheek. She was wearing an all-body water-proof that obscured everything else about her and an enormous black handbag lay on her lap. 'Hi.' Amber waved. 'I didn't see you come on board.'

'It's easier to get on board first, when you're stuck in one of these. Bloody ankle.' The woman indicated her wheelchair. Her left foot was encased in a cast with a plastic bag over it, presumably to try to keep it dry. 'I'm Jocelyn and I'm a Valerie la Fontaine superfan.' She declaimed her words as clearly as an actor taking to the stage, waving a bony hand, smiling with snaggled yellow teeth. Her face was a mass of lines and wrinkles, but she was as excited as a puppy who had just spotted a bag of treats. 'It's lovely to meet you.'

The boat lurched and Amber's legs went out from under her. Her chin clanged against the handrail. 'Shit.' She put her hand to the point of impact and it came away red.

'First blood, hey?' Kieran was above her, holding out his hand to pull her up. Nothing in Amber wanted to take it, but it was that or communing with the deck until they got to dry land.

'I've got plasters.' Jeanie was rifling through the navy bag that seemed able to produce everything from TCP to hand cream to shortbread to – once upon a long ago – a pair of stilettos. 'Wait a second.' She pulled out a small jar of peanut butter. 'Oh, that's where that went.' She dived back in.

By the time Amber was patched up they were nearly there. Even here, close to the rocky shore, the wind was howling and the sky was the depressing grey of Amber's eye bags. Ahead, the narrow stone jetty was framed by looming pine trees as far as the eye could see, topped by lowering storm clouds that obscured the chateau itself. Amber sighed inwardly. Here she was, on her first relaxing weekend away for decades, and she was on an island that looked like a breeding ground for serial killers.

But her friends were at her side and that made today a very good day indeed.

'Are you ready for this?' Amber looked at Clio and Jeanie.

'Of course!' Clio couldn't keep still, like a Labrador about to be let off the lead.

Jeanie nodded in agreement. 'Ready? For a luxury holiday where I don't have to cook or clean or get woken at 2 a.m. because the twins have decided that it *is* morning now?' Her face lit up. 'I was born ready!'

Amber nodded. 'Okay then. Let's do this. A weekend with no crimes, no dodgy husbands, no surveillance, no fraudsters – just face packs, thick white robes, gourmet food and giggles.'

'*Yes.*' They all beamed at each other. Amber noticed that Clio was also smiling at Kieran, but she could worry about that later.

The boat had reached the jetty and Amber stepped onto the shore.

It was time for the relaxation to begin.

2

AMBER

'Hi, Amber! Welcome to Chateau la Fontaine! I'm Melissa, the manager. Let me lead you through to the Red Room, where we have welcome drinks ready for you.'

Amber did her best to wipe the water out of her eyes as she followed Melissa through the cavernous entrance hall of the castle, past a gilt mirror that told her she was most definitely not looking her best, into a high-ceilinged room with red walls and floor-to-ceiling windows at one end, facing the sweeping gravel drive. As they came to a halt, the manager turned towards her.

Amber saw bright brown eyes on an exact level with her own long, dark hair swept back into a tight chignon, full lips painted the same shade as an immaculate red suit. The woman held out a hand, complete with gold nails that matched the word *'Melissa'* on her elegant black name badge. Her smile was so #blessed it was blinding and her husky American accent was straight out of the US workout channel that Amber had unsuccessfully campaigned to ban from the gym.

'It is Amber...' A crease appeared between Melissa's perfectly arched eyebrows. 'Isn't it?'

'Yes. I'm Amber.' Amber looked down. Her black jeans were soaked through and water dripped from her cagoule onto the polished wooden floor. She looked around at the gleaming silverware piled on the long table in the corner, at the glittering champagne flutes arranged on golden trays, and felt a twist of discomfort. She was out of place here.

Melissa took a step towards her, her stare intense. Amber started worrying she had a spot on her chin. 'I gather it's your birthday, Amber?'

'Yes.'

'Oh, wow, that is awesome!' Melissa seemed a little too excited about this news. 'Happy birthday, Amber! We're so happy to have you here.' Melissa's smile could light the magnificent pyre of sticks and logs that lay waiting in the grate to Amber's left. The broad fireplace was embossed with marble angels and golden clouds were scattered across the mantelpiece. Whoever had designed this castle, subtlety had not been their MO.

'Thanks. It's lovely to be here.' Amber was rather hoping Melissa was going to mention their rooms soon. She desperately needed a hot shower and the golf carts that had transported them up to the castle from the jetty had been bone-crunching to say the least. Amber knew that as competition winners they were guinea pigs – testing the venue before the official launch later in the year – but given how cold they were she was surprised that the fire wasn't even lit yet.

She stared at the manager expectantly, head on one side.

Melissa clapped her hands together. 'Of course! Silly me.'

Amber relaxed. Huge piles of the softest white towels, a rainforest shower, maybe even a jacuzzi in her room. She was ready.

'How about some champagne?' Melissa gestured to a server standing quietly in the corner, dressed all in black. 'To celebrate?' He stepped forward bearing a tray of flutes filled with foaming liquid.

Amber tried to speak, her teeth chattering now. Clio and Jeanie appeared beside her, drawn from their admiration of the ceiling, which was painted with stars and dazzling comets, all in brand la Fontaine golds and reds. Amber joined them in reaching out and taking a glass, before tipping her head back and downing it. It was delicious, sweet, the bubbles popping on her tongue.

Before realising what she was doing, she had finished it. She felt a bit warmer, so held her glass out for a refill. The server wordlessly filled it up and she lifted it back to her lips, as if to the manor born. Inside however, she was struggling. She didn't do luxury. She didn't do relaxing. She didn't do chilling out or massages or swanking around in expensive Red Rooms, lit by scented candles that probably cost more than Amber's car. Instead, Amber structured her days carefully, keeping herself busy, going from workouts to the office, to client meetings, spending hours on surveillance in her car or writing up client reports.

Clio's eyes sparkled. 'Isn't it great here?'

'Incredible.' Jeanie held up her glass. 'Cheers!'

Amber looked at her friends, her heart squeezing tight. She couldn't let them down. She had made that promise years ago, and she hadn't broken it yet.

'Cheers.' She emptied her second glass and focused on her friends. She loved spending time with them and they knew how much she hated her birthday – which was not surprising given she didn't actually know when it was. Every year she felt the same pinch of sadness as the birth date she had been assigned by social services came around, wishing despite herself that her mum had bothered to leave a birth certificate in the basket with her when she had abandoned her on a bus.

Usually, Amber shut herself away until it was over but maybe this would be the birthday that changed everything? The one where she actually had a good time. She wasn't locked in a children's home that smelt of despair and Clio and Jeanie were here with her. Recently the three of them had only really talked about work. This weekend was a chance to escape all that.

Amber inhaled. She had come a long way. She could relax. Smile. Make the most of this time with the friends who were now her chosen family. She smiled at the server, reading his name badge. A diamond stud gleamed in his ear. 'More champagne please, Angelo.'

'Of course.' He filled up their glasses again and Amber felt her shoulders start to descend.

Jeanie smiled. 'I could get used to this! Much as I miss one twin climbing the curtains while the other one tries to get into the oven.'

'They're still doing that?' Amber grimaced. She had babysat Jeanie's two-year-old twins a couple of months before, and had aged a decade in four hours.

'They are.' Jeanie sighed. 'I'm one *PAW Patrol* plaster away from the apocalypse.'

'Me too. Only in my case it's the financial apocalypse. I've got noooo money. Thank God it's payday – Nina's next uni accommodation payment is due.' Clio's face drooped. 'I haven't paid rent to Bez for months, and I still can't afford Nina's tuition fees. Some mum I am.'

'Hey, you're doing your best.' Amber wondered for a second if she could increase Clio's pay so that she could keep her daughter's university education on track, but knew deep down that she couldn't afford her salary as it was. 'And let's face it, you've had a bit of a year, what with Gary and everything.'

Clio sighed. 'Yes. I can't say finding my ex dead on my doorstep was a highlight.'

'And being accused of his murder?' Jeanie sipped her champagne.

Clio rolled her eyes. 'Worse.' Her tone was light but Amber had seen how much she had struggled. A smile tugged at the corner of Clio's mouth. 'I loved the bit where we caught the killer though.'

'Me too.' Jeanie raised her glass and they all chinked.

'Me three.' Amber turned to see that Melissa was somehow beside them again. As a gay woman, Amber was used to female attention, but this was something else. She felt a strange prickling sensation and turned away.

Clio was still talking. 'That moment when you leapt in front of the bullet, Jeanie. Amazing.'

'Ladies!' Kieran appeared beside them. 'Bullets? Tell me more. You three really do have all the drama going on.' Somehow, he had got changed and was now in an emerald-green shirt and tight jeans, his aftershave an eye-watering cloud around him.

'Hi, Kieran.' Clio gazed up at him, batting her eyelashes in a manner that told Amber the champagne was taking effect. The canapés were arriving on a silver trolley, and Amber moved towards them, drawn by the delicious aromas. A chef with caramel-coloured hair and a spotless white uniform was arranging them on a long oak table that ran along one side of the room. His name badge said *'Henri'* and he looked clean and fresh, someone who would always use alcohol gel after going to a shop and who would never pass up a chance to use a bidet.

His ferocious expression, however, was far from welcoming. He slammed down plate after plate, taking them off the trolley with the jerky speed of someone who is not enjoying their job. Melissa strode towards him, putting her hand on his arm. His chin jerked up and he spat words in her direction in a furious hiss that was easily loud enough for the guests to hear.

'This is not my job.' His French accent lent the words an extra venom. 'This is for servers, not chefs. I am meant to be cooking the dinner!'

Melissa kept her voice low as she remonstrated with him, until he put the last platter down and stormed off into the hall, still mouthing expletives. Ray passed him at the door, his long sandy hair now tied back, carrying a pile of kindling in his hands. He knelt down by the huge fireplace and pulled a box of matches from the back pocket of his blue overalls.

'Sorry about that.' Melissa grinned apologetically. 'We are still recruiting, but a number of our support staff couldn't get here, so we're all having to be a little bit flexible. The rest of our guests may be stuck too, apparently! If Ray can't get the boat back to the mainland.' Her laugh had an edge of hysteria. 'Damn storm. And Valerie's desk has been put in the conservatory instead of her snug. And the Wi-Fi is down.' Everyone instantly got out their phones to check this and yes – it was indeed down.

Melissa collected herself. 'I'm so sorry. We just have a few teething troubles.' She started to arrange the platters in rows and Amber saw a whole baked camembert with tiny balls of downy bread to dip inside, huge langoustines next to delicate round cakes, asparagus tips surrounded by dipping sauces and even a dressed crab on a golden platter. She found she was salivating as the room was suffused with the smell of bread, garlic and fried meat.

'Oh, wow!' Jeanie followed Amber to the table. 'Who needs Wi-Fi? I'm going in.' She put her glass down and picked up a gold-rimmed la Fontaine plate from the pile at the end of the table.

Jocelyn rolled into view in her chair, the white cast on her left foot propped up in front of her. She had removed her waterproof and was wearing a tartan dress with a huge bow at the collar. Her cheeks were flushed and she had balanced an empty champagne glass on her lap. 'Goodness, this looks wonderful.' She clapped her hands together. 'What a treat. I can't believe I'm about to taste Valerie la Fontaine's canapés. My friends will be so jealous.'

'I know!' Clio followed suit. 'I can't believe the prize includes all our food and drinks.'

'All the drinks, hey? Dangerous.' Amber had a flashback to their first all-inclusive package holiday in Zakynthos, back when they were nineteen. Thanks to Clio's commitment to cocktails, Amber had been forced to extract them from a nasty nightclub incident involving a podium dancer, a fire alarm and three very angry bouncers.

At the far end of the room Ray threw some more logs on the fire. One landed with a loud bang on the hearth, making them all jump.

'Well before I tuck in, I think I need a trip to the little girls' room.' Jocelyn eyed them hopefully. 'I'm so sorry to bother you, but could someone help me to get there?' She coughed apologetically. 'This bloody chair is so hard to move around in and I have already had rather a lot of champagne.'

Clio jumped in, used to wheelchairs from the old people's home where she volunteered. 'Of course!' She took control, pushing Jocelyn away towards the door. 'Which way is it?'

The old lady gestured left with a crutch. 'That way, I think...' Clio pushed the chair out into the hall. A second later Amber saw them going the other way and could hear Jocelyn apologising. 'So sorry, I haven't got my bearings yet. This place is so vast, isn't it?'

Amber turned back to the food, only to find Melissa at her elbow, her eyes trained on Amber's face. 'Shall I let you know what we have here?'

'Um. Okay.' Amber took a step backwards.

'Here we have some balsamic pearls with *Tomates à la Paris*.' Melissa indicated a tower of tiny white spheres topped by flecks of red and green. 'And here are Valerie's famous Pepper Cakes with langoustines – they are to die for!' She smiled at Amber, her eyes lingering a little too long. 'And—'

'*Bonsoir!*' A woman entered the room, sleek and tall in a tight-fitting black jumpsuit.

Jeanie froze, an exquisitely small blini halfway to her mouth. 'Is that her?'

'Who?' Amber was still wondering what she had done to deserve Melissa's attention.

'Valerie!' Jeanie blinked. 'Oh no, Clio will be so gutted she missed her!'

Amber nodded. 'Hopefully she'll be back in a minute.'

'*Bonsoir*, everyone.' Valerie spoke in a husky French accent. 'I got in early this morning, and I thought I'd come and say hello to my first ever guests in this castle.'

She clapped her hands together. Her long dark hair flowed down her back, her skin glowed and even in a room as lavish as this, she eclipsed her surroundings. Her long nails were red with gold tips. She was brand la Fontaine to her core.

Kieran stepped forwards. 'Hi, Valerie. Good to see you again. It's been a while.' He opened his arms as if to hug her, but Valerie stiffened as soon as she saw him. She went into reverse so fast that she collided with a chair, and Melissa stepped forward to help her to disentangle herself. Valerie leant down, muttering something into Melissa's ear. Melissa nodded rapidly, eyes widening with concern.

Valerie stood straight again, chin up, eyes flicking back to Kieran and then away. 'Welcome to the chateau, *tout le monde*. I am sorry that we are still under construction a little bit... The forest lodges are not quite finished, the boat is not ready, half the staff are not here, the Wi-Fi does not seem to be working properly yet.'

She pushed a lock of her dark hair out of her eyes. 'I am so sorry for all this, but I beg you for your understanding.' She put her palms together as if in prayer. 'And I can promise you that the kitchens are *magnifique* and we are ready to give you the finest food and wine while you stay here with us.

'Tonight, you will be in the excellent hands of my right-hand woman, Melissa here, and my brilliant sous chef, Henri, and server extraordinaire, Angelo. And you have already met Ray, *non*? Your captain? He is about to try to get another boatload of guests to the castle in this terrible weather. Maybe he can work miracles, *non*?'

'Not sure about that.' By the fireplace, Ray shook his head.

Valerie gave a forced laugh. 'I hope they can make it, but if not then with only five of you this really is a very, very soft launch, is it not?'

Amber noticed the way Valerie's nails drummed against her leg, the way her eyes darted towards Kieran and then away. He was clearly unnerving her. Valerie's heavy silver watch glinted as she glanced at the time. 'I have to go and prepare my menus for tomorrow – I am going to try some new dishes on you all. Be ready!'

Kieran tried again. 'If I might have a word, Valerie. For the piece I'm working on...?' His voice was thick with subtext.

'*Non.*' Valerie held up a hand. 'Not now.' She didn't even look at him. 'So, tonight there will be canapés, champagne and then later some of our most famous *plat principals* and the bar will be open till midnight. And then tomorrow, we have a whole day of excitements for you. I can't wait. So, I will see you all tomorrow, yes? *Bon appétit.*'

She gestured towards the table with her head held high, but Amber could see that she was shaking. Why was Kieran so upsetting to her? What was he up to?

Once more he stepped forward, clearly unwilling to take no for an answer, muttering something into Valerie's ear, resting one hand on her arm, the other hovering around her waist. Melissa stepped smartly across and moved Valerie away. She whispered something into her ear.

'Oh yes!' Valerie turned back and smiled. 'One more thing!' This time her warmth seemed real. 'Happy birthday, Amber! I have made you a little something.'

Angelo brought in a birthday cake on a golden tray. Tiny pastel macarons, topped with Chantilly and melted chocolate. Amber's mouth watered. And fortunately Valerie's aesthetics meant that there was only one candle on top, rather than the full forty-six.

'Wow. Thank you so much.' Amber blew the candle out, trying to pre-empt the singing. Anything but the singing. 'There's no need to—'

'*Happy birthday to you...*'

Melissa had got them started. What was up with her? As everyone else joined in Amber was sorely tempted to crawl beneath the table, but instead picked up a bottle of champagne and emptied it into her own glass. Once several lifetimes had passed, the song came to an end.

Valerie leant forwards and kissed her on both cheeks. She smelt of cinnamon, her tanned skin glowing, her hair silky, brown eyes clear. 'Have a wonderful time.' Her eyes flicked towards Kieran and then she walked off.

As she did so, a door at the side of the room gave in to the howling gale and blew open, revealing a huge white banner pinned between two trees. The wind ripped and roared but the banner stood strong, seven words clearly depicted in red.

Kill our woods and we'll kill you.

'Melissa.' Valerie turned, pale beneath her tan. She clicked her fingers. 'Get rid of that now.'

Melissa stared, face stiffening. 'Oh man. Not again.'

Valerie's eyes had darkened. 'Now, please.'

'We're on it!' Melissa's voice had risen a tone. 'Ray. Get it taken down now.'

'Aren't I meant to be taking the boat and trying to get the rest of the guests?' Ray rose from his place by the fire, where the kindling was just starting to smoke, his boots leaving a muddy trail across the floor.

'Take it down first.' Melissa spoke through gritted teeth. 'I thought you said the protestors had all gone.'

'Well...' He held up his hands. 'It's not my fault if they choose to come back, is it?'

Melissa glared at him, before turning back to Valerie. 'Don't worry.' Her tone was pacifying, her hand on Valerie's arm. 'We'll...'

But Valerie had already turned back to her guests. 'I am so sorry about that. And I promise you that nothing else bad will be happening here.' She looked at Amber. 'Have the best of birthdays.' She turned and left the room.

Amber turned to Kieran. 'Did you know about the protestors? I haven't seen anything in the local press.'

He puffed up, clearly delighted to be asked. 'Well, when I interviewed Valerie, she did say that some locals clearly think the island belongs to them. Some druids or other – they think the trees in this forest are spiritual, or holy, or some such wafty crap. The castle used to belong to some old eccentric who holed up here for months on end, and let the locals come here to worship – fair game for anyone with a boat.' He popped another canapé into his mouth. 'Then he died and Valerie announced she had bought the place and that she was chopping down some trees to build the lodges, and all hell broke loose.'

Amber frowned. 'That's weird. Why haven't I heard about it?'

He popped a piece of bread into his mouth. 'Valerie didn't want to make a fuss, I guess. It would be bad for business, and she's all about peace and exclusivity, isn't she? Having protestors hardly screams "chillax in my luxury retreat" now, does it?'

'I suppose not.' Amber's brain was whirring. However hard she tried, she could never switch off her urge to get to the heart of things; to dig, to uncover the truth. And then, as she chewed on a delicious sliver of salmon marinaded in lemongrass, she remembered. The thing she hadn't done in the rush of coming here. The thing she had forgotten.

It was the first of the month and she had forgotten to pay Clio and Jeanie their monthly wages.

'Amber? What's wrong?'

Damn Jeanie's ability to read her so well.

'Nothing.' Amber flapped a hand. 'Just... Um... Excuse me a minute.' She tried to look relaxed as she made for the door, despite the fact that her heart was beating out of her chest. Nina's accommodation. She couldn't be responsible for Clio's daughter losing her digs.

As soon as she was outside the Red Room, she started to run. She crossed the darkness of the long hall, sprinting past a door that must lead to the kitchen, with sweet smells wafting out. She checked her phone. No signal. Damn the Wi-Fi being down. She would have to go higher and hope.

'Amber? Are you okay?' Jeanie must have followed her, but her friend's voice dwindled behind her as Amber sprinted past the *'No Access to the Public'* signs and launched herself up the wide stone steps of a spiral staircase. Supercilious ancestors eyed her suspiciously from their golden portrait frames. Frankly, they had every reason. She was a rubbish boss and a rubbish friend. Recently, money had been so tight she had been paying her friends manually every month, so that she could scrape the amount she needed together in advance. She had never forgotten until today.

Desperately, Amber pushed against the first door she found. A dark cupboard full of brooms and mops was all her reward. Sweat was breaking out on her forehead as she pulled the door closed and crouched down, hiding from everyone, just until she got it done.

No signal. Not even one bar.

'Shit.' She got up again, leaving the cupboard and running up the stairs. Another room. Another phone check. And this time, one bar of signal. She slid inside and sank to the floor, opening up her banking app. Minutes ticked by as the app loaded. As fast as she could, she set up the first payment, and then waited to see if she would be able to clear it. The wind whistled outside. Amber waited, gritting her teeth, not caring that she had now been up here for about a quarter of an hour. The girls need never know her mistake, if she could only get this done.

She transferred more money across from her dwindling savings to cover the second payment, and then hit 'complete transaction.' Her phone froze.

'*No.*' She narrowly refrained from throwing it across the room.

The bar of signal had gone.

'Nooooooo.' She regrouped. She would just have to go even higher.

She ran up another flight of steps. She was on the top floor of the tower now. The thick walls were made of honey stone, and a suit of armour stood beneath a small window, next to an arched black door.

The bar of signal was still absent.

'*No.*' Amber looked around. Maybe she could make the transfer from inside whatever room the door led into – maybe it had a staircase leading up to the turret? She could hear footsteps coming up behind her, so took a deep breath and turned the handle. It was locked.

'Damn.' She needed to get in there. She tried the handle again. Nothing.

Desperate, she hurled herself at the door. It didn't give. It must be locked from the inside. But Amber was determined. The turret must be up there and she had to pay her friends on time. She tried again, but it remained firmly locked.

She eyed the wood. Outside, thunder rumbled and roared.

She would give it one more try. She took a deep breath and ran towards the door, lowering her shoulder as if on one of the many police raids she had carried out in her twenty years on the force.

The lock gave way and she burst through. She was halfway into the room before she realised that something was lying on the carpet. She stopped.

Not something. Someone.

There she was: Valerie la Fontaine, a pool of blood by her head, her face as white as the huge sheepskin rug beneath her body, her brown eyes wide. Amber knelt down, hoping she wasn't too late. Some of Valerie's long nails were broken, fragments scattered on the carpet and papers had been thrown all over the floor by a table in the corner. A china vase lay on the rug and an emerald-green throw lay half-off the sofa, still clutched in Valerie's fingers. Maybe she had grabbed it as she fell. The room was full of candles, emitting such a strong smell that it made Amber's head throb and long rainbow matches stood in a glass jar on the mantelpiece over the fire.

Who could have done this? Amber pulled some latex gloves from her back pocket. She never left the house without them – her old detective habits died hard.

She felt for a pulse.

Nothing.

She bent over the body and started mouth to mouth as she had a hundred times before, on street corners, in front rooms, on sports fields. Then she got out her phone and dialled 999. No signal. She tried again. Nothing.

So, just her. She tried and tried, but Valerie was gone and as she worked Amber noticed that the chef had been hit several times in the head. She knelt back, swearing in frustration as lightning lit the sky outside the casement window.

Amber's mind raced. Valerie had been downstairs greeting them only recently, so the killer had been both quick and ruthless. Somehow, they had killed Valerie and escaped from a locked room, all in a fifteen-minute window.

Amber looked out at the furious sky as she reached for her phone to try dialling 999 again. Whoever had done this, they were also trapped here by the storm. And, for all Amber knew, they were planning to kill again.

SATURDAY – 6 P.M

TWELVE HOURS UNTIL THE POLICE CAN COME

One dead body

3

JEANIE

Jeanie was halfway through her third canapé when she realised she was alone. Ray had stamped outside, presumably to try to take the banner down or launch the boat, leaving the fire crackling in the hearth. Kieran had wandered out into the hall staring down at his phone, and Melissa and Angelo had asked her if she wanted anything and then excused themselves to go and help in the kitchen.

The Red Room felt huge without anyone else to share it with, so Jeanie decided to follow Amber and find out what was going on. She had heard her footsteps running upstairs when she had suddenly disappeared a few minutes ago, and so she headed up the curved stone steps to find her. She had seen the flash of panic on Amber's face just now and knew that something was wrong. Recently Jeanie had noticed the dark circles beneath her friend's eyes, had seen the way she closed her laptop whenever Jeanie or Clio came near, had heard her giving her punchbag even more hell than usual on the mornings she managed to get the twins organised and arrive early at work. Jeanie knew that trouble was brewing.

She kept climbing, breathless now. If only she hadn't been so distracted by everything that was happening at home. Or rather everything that *wasn't* happening, now her husband Tan had lost his job. He and Jeanie were so broke that they were squeezing their twins into increasingly tight second-hand shoes, and even feeding them was becoming a strain. But still, she should have taken the time to talk to Amber – she would put that right this weekend, starting right now.

Jeanie sweated up to the top of the staircase, the thick stone walls widening out into a small landing, a tiny window set high above a suit of armour. She looked around for Amber, her heart beating fast. As she took her hand off the banister, she heard the world outside crack. She suppressed a scream as high winds shrieked outside, so loudly it felt for a moment as if this tower might fall. A huge tree branch slammed against the window. Jeanie inhaled deeply, the skin on her neck prickling as she sensed someone behind her. She looked back but could see no one. She paused, listening hard. Was that... breathing? She put a hand on her heart, trying to calm herself.

Then she heard a tiny squeak. A creak.

Someone was close by. With her heart pounding, Jeanie eyed the suit of armour. Was there someone hiding inside it, waiting to pounce? She took a deep breath, steadying herself, before tiptoeing over to lift the visor. It rose one inch. Then two. Jeanie's jaw was clenched, as if she half expected some ghostly knight to fling his arms around her neck and strangle her.

But there was no one there, no face hidden inside the helmet. She was being silly. Weak with relief, Jeanie let the visor drop and headed up the next flight of stairs. Behind her, she could hear skittering footsteps – but it was probably Clio coming to find them, nothing to worry about.

She panted her way to the top, leaning against the wall, catching her breath before walking forwards towards the open door ahead. 'Amber?'

'Wait!'

Jeanie stopped in the doorway. Amber's voice came from the floor, from behind a low mahogany coffee table which had a peanut butter jar on top of it. 'Jeanie, stay there.'

A white plate with a golden crest was at one end, next to a pile of magazines. Half a sandwich rested on top, several bites taken out, below the initials *CLF* on its rim.

Amber held up a hand. 'Jeanie, there's...'

'What?' Jeanie looked around admiringly. The room was circular, nestling into the eaves of the tower. In one corner she could see a long red sofa with extra gold cushions at one end. A notebook lay open on the low, dark coffee table, a thick black fountain pen beside it.

Then Jeanie looked down. She froze. 'Oh God. *No.*'

'I just came up and found her here.' Amber pulled a pair of latex gloves from the back pocket of her jeans and threw them over to Jeanie.

'Wow, you really do go everywhere with those.' Jeanie fought down panic as she put them on. Her champagne flute seemed ridiculous and she was about to put it down when she remembered that this room was now a crime scene. She went back outside, placing the glass at the top of the stairs, wondering where Clio was. Still with Jocelyn, maybe. Then Jeanie stiffened. Could the breathing she had dismissed on the stairs have been real? The killer waiting for their chance to escape?

Amber spoke fast. 'I tried to resuscitate her, but I was too late. She died from her head wound, by the look of it.'

As ever, Amber's professionalism in the face of death was reassuring. Given the decades she had spent on the local police force, Amber had always been unusually comfortable with the darker side of life. But despite her friend's calm, Jeanie was spiralling, wanting to weep and swear, to ask why, whenever the three of them tried to step out of work for a weekend, someone inevitably died.

Her voice went up an octave. 'There's a kitchen knife over there.' Jeanie pointed a shaking finger at the floor by the sofa. A silver blade lay on the sheepskin rug. 'Who put that there?'

'I don't know.' Amber glanced towards it. 'It could be that Valerie tried to fight? Her nails have been ruined, so she may have scratched the killer, left a mark, maybe?' Amber looked around. 'Did you see anyone on your way up? Because the door was locked when I got here. And whoever killed her must have done it between us seeing Valerie downstairs and now. Which gives a window of about fifteen minutes. Who was in the Red Room when you left it?'

'No one. Just me.'

'So anyone could have done it?'

'Yes. I suppose so,' said Jeanie. 'And I didn't see anyone coming up here, no. But I thought I heard something. Heard someone, I mean. Breathing and a kind of squeaking sound, on the stairs.'

She examined the room, trying to slow her mind so she could think. The body of Valerie la Fontaine was stretched out on the thick white sheepskin rug in front of a cosy fireplace, which lay beneath the blank gaze of a black stag's head on the wall. A chef's hat hung from the creature's right antler at a jaunty angle that was totally out of keeping with the body lying on the floor. Low green lamps on golden pineapple bases glowed on dark brown coffee tables on either side of the fire, where red armchairs sat waiting for their owner to rest at the end of her shift. A piece of paper lay on top of one of the chairs. Jeanie moved across to look and saw a recent edition of a Sunday tabloid, opened to an article entitled '*Who is the real Valerie la Fontaine?*'

She saw the name below. 'Hey, this article is by that guy Kieran.'

Amber looked up. 'Interesting. Valerie seemed uncomfortable around him, didn't you think? I wonder what was going on there.'

'Yeah. And he left the Red Room just after you did, so...' As she surveyed the scene, Jeanie's mind was whirring into action, asking questions, hunting for clues. She had seen dead bodies before – once when Clio found her husband Gary dead on her doorstep and once on the dancefloor at Jeanie's own hen do. It would never feel normal, and she was dimly aware that she was starting to shake, but at the same time her brain was focusing on the hows and the whys, as well as feeling the chill of a murder taking place up here while she had been downstairs stuffing her face with canapés.

She made mental notes of what she saw. On the far side of the room was a huge black padlocked crate, embossed with golden suns, easily large enough for someone to hide inside. Jeanie walked over to it and tested the padlock. It was firmly shut. Next to it lay a broken wine bottle, its contents spilling onto the polished wooden floorboards.

'Can you turn the main lights on please?' Amber was searching around the body, her eyes missing nothing.

'Shouldn't we leave the scene untouched for when the police get here?'

'I tried dialling 999.' Amber frowned. 'But I can't get through. No Wi-Fi and no signal. So we just have to do the best we can.' Her voice came in staccato bursts. 'And I think it's worth us having a look, isn't it? Seeing as we're all stuck here with whoever did this.'

Jeanie's heart swooped down to her shoes as she digested this statement. Trapped in a castle with a killer. She swallowed, steeling herself. Amber was right, they should get to work. She flicked on the overhead light, leaping out of her skin as something scraped against the window. She relaxed as she realised it was only a tree branch flailing in the wind. She had to get a grip.

She forced herself to look down at the body. As Amber had told her on previous cases, this first sixty minutes was the golden hour – the time when everything was fresh, when discoveries could be made most easily. Valerie's lips were parted, and a vivid red scratch ran down her cheek, which had not been there when she had greeted them all downstairs. Her hair was pulled back from her face and her dark brown eyes were wide. Wordlessly, Amber reached down and closed them.

Jeanie felt nausea rising. 'So, not such a relaxing weekend, then.'

'No.' Amber was staring around the room. 'How about you take photos, while I search for clues?'

Jeanie nodded. 'Good idea.' She pulled out her phone and started work, snapping everything she could see.

As she was doing so, she spotted an old-fashioned phone on a table in the corner. It had a long cord and an antique golden receiver buried beneath a pile of folders. 'Look, there's a landline. On the table in the corner. Let's try using that to call the police.'

'Good idea.' Amber was already on her feet, moving towards it.

'It's got a dial tone.' Amber dialled a number, tapping her foot impatiently while it connected. It rang and rang. 'Marco's not answering.' She disconnected the call. 'I'll dial 999.'

'It might be for the best, Amber.' Jeanie knew that DI Marco Santini and Amber were currently in a hate-hate phase of their long relationship. Once Amber's boss, he had fired her last year, and was still sulking about the agency solving their last murder case before he did.

'True.' Amber sighed and dialled 999.

Jeanie quietly photographed the room as Amber talked to the responder. She snapped a footprint by the chest, an espresso cup with a spoon lying on its saucer. She also checked the bronze window catch, but it was firmly closed.

'I see.' Amber swallowed. 'And that's the earliest you can get here?' She nodded. 'Yes, we'll do our best. Thanks.'

She put the receiver down.

'Bad news.'

Jeanie waited. Fear started to creep through her.

Amber puffed her cheeks out as she exhaled. 'As I thought, the police can't get here in this weather.'

'Not at all? Not a helicopter, or something?'

'They can't come for twelve hours at least. The storm is too severe, and neither the speedboat nor the helicopter can get here.'

'But...' Jeanie gestured at the body. 'But someone's been murdered.'

'I know.' Amber was frowning now. 'They advised us to stay indoors, to all keep together, for us to keep the scene untouched – and to guard it so the killer can't come back and remove evidence. They also advised us to do a headcount and not to try to do any detective work – just to do our best to stay alive.'

'But the killer...' Jeanie stopped. She thought of her twins; heart-shaped faces smeared with jam, thick dark hair so soft. There was no way she was going to just sit here with a killer roaming the castle. She wanted to get back to them. She wanted to live.

Amber was staring at her. 'Yes?'

'Well, the killer is still here, aren't they? If no one can leave the island because of the storm – then they're stuck here too.' Jeanie felt a shiver down her spine. 'And...'

'And they might kill again?' Amber nodded. 'I know. And I don't think we can wait for the police. I think we have to try to catch whoever did this. Before they come for us.'

Jeanie took a deep breath. 'Okay. Then let's find Clio, make sure she's safe, and make a plan.'

'Deal.' Amber nodded as the wind whistled outside, and the two of them stood over the body, working out how not to get killed before morning.

4

CLIO

Clio was actually very much alive and *still* waiting outside the disabled loo for Jocelyn to come out. Having warned Clio about the state of her bowels in slightly too much detail, Jocelyn had then proceeded to sing a series of Gilbert and Sullivan songs while using the facilities. Clio had finished her champagne and was hoping there were still some canapés left as she leant against the wall at the far end of the hall. The castle had fallen silent, and all she could hear was the ticking of the grandfather clock that stood by the front door. She put her glass on the floor, realising that things had gone quiet in the loo.

'Are you okay in there, Jocelyn?'

'Yes, yes.' Jocelyn sounded testy, and Clio felt bad for interrupting her. 'It's not easy with this chair you know. I'm just coming out.'

Clio stepped back as the accessible door swung open, revealing Jocelyn sporting a new lipstick smile. She brushed a fleck of grey from her shoulders. 'Bloody dandruff, eh?'

Clio took the handles of the wheelchair and pushed Jocelyn back along the hall towards the Red Room. It was deserted, save for the server, Angelo, who was straightening the canapé platters on the long table.

'Where did my friends go, Angelo?' Clio picked up a fresh glass of champagne, smiling at Ray as he entered the room, his overalls soaked.

Clearly his attempt to go and get the other guests from the mainland had not gone well.

'Your friends went upstairs after Valerie came and spoke to everyone, I think. Maybe looking for you?' Angelo finished with the platters and started on the napkins, placing them at right angles to the corner of the table.

'*What*?' Clio nearly dropped her glass. 'You mean we missed her?'

'Oh, that is terrible news.' Jocelyn downed her glass in one. 'Do you think she'll come down again later, Angelo? Or tomorrow?'

'She said she would.' Angelo finished placing the final napkin.

'Oh, that is a relief.' Jocelyn held out her glass for more champagne. 'Might as well get a bit merry then, eh?' She chinked glasses with Clio.

'Cheers.' Clio wondered why her friends had gone upstairs. She wanted to go and find them – to hear what Valerie had been like in the flesh. She piled a plate high for Jocelyn – and for herself too – and made sure the old lady was comfortable by the fire. Then she walked out with her food and headed up the stairs. She could hear voices above her, so ignored the '*No Access*' signs and carried on up the winding staircase, chewing on a pillowy slice of baguette as she went.

Behind her, she heard a creak.

She stopped. 'Who's there?'

Silence. Clio's heart was racing and suddenly she felt very alone.

'Amber? Jeanie?'

Nothing.

As she started to walk upwards again, her footsteps sounded too loud and her pulse began to rise. She sprinted up the stairs far faster than her dodgy knee would have liked, tripping on the uneven steps, nearly dropping her food as she grabbed the iron railing for support.

'Amber? Jeanie?'

No answer. Fear was a rising tide inside her.

'*Amber?*'

'Clio?'

Oh, thank God. She launched herself into the doorway at the top of the stairs, very happy to see her friends.

But then she saw their serious faces, the way Jeanie was stepping forward to take her hand. And then the body.

It looked like...

'No.' Clio put a hand to her mouth. 'Valerie. No!'

Jeanie ran towards her. 'Clio.' Her arms were so warm, just as they always were, a port for Clio's many storms.

Amber took over. 'Clio. We're just working out what to do. I found her here – dead. The door was locked with the key inside, and there was no one here.'

Clio stood for a second, reeling. Then Jeanie hugged her again and something inside her steadied.

Jeanie spoke. 'We called the police on the landline. They can't come for hours, so because the killer's still here...'

'Because of the storm?' Clio's brain was struggling to keep up. 'That's why the police can't come?'

'Exactly.' Jeanie nodded. 'We're just having a look into what might have happened.'

Clio stared at the body, unable to believe that Valerie was dead. This was too much. Anger was rising inside her, and so she started to look, to search, to find answers.

She spotted the locked chest. 'Someone could have hidden inside here.' She walked across.

A pair of gloves landed at her feet.

'Put them on. Crime scene.' Amber went back to searching the fireplace.

Clio did as she was told as Jeanie shook her head. 'It's locked. So if they were hiding in there then they locked it back up before they left.'

Clio tapped her fingers against her leg, the questions starting to flood her brain. 'And how did they know she'd be up here?'

Amber considered this. 'Maybe she arranged to meet them?'

Jeanie frowned. 'Maybe. But everyone left the Red Room except me. How do we narrow it down?'

Amber stood, hands on hips. 'We need to find out where everyone has been since Valerie came and introduced herself to us all. We need to start interviewing.'

Jeanie stared at the stag on the wall. 'Ray went outside I think, probably to try to launch the boat? Or to sort the banner out.'

'Well, he didn't make it to the mainland.' Clio swallowed. 'I just saw him downstairs, absolutely soaked through.'

'Kieran's not in the Red Room any more either. Ditto Melissa.' Clio frowned as she tried to remember. 'Angelo was in there, though.'

'Well he left with Melissa earlier, so he's got to be a suspect.'

Amber cut in. 'Okay, so let's start with what we saw. And it seemed pretty clear that Valerie didn't like Kieran.' She was staring into the fire. 'So maybe we start with him. And then we'll need to construct a timeline. Who are the protestors, which staff Valerie got on with – who's new, and who has been with her for years, over in the States. And I just saw this.' She turned back to the body. 'Why does she have SC tattooed on her wrist?' She grimaced. 'This is getting more and more weird.'

'This is strange, too.' Clio gestured to a large Twirl sitting on the sideboard, next to a box of Yorkshire Tea. 'Why would a Parisian chef be drinking Yorkshire Tea or eating a Twirl?' She walked across to the small Smeg fridge in the corner. 'For a gourmet goddess, she had some very bizarre snacks.' She opened the door and peered inside to see a Fanta and a pork pie at the back. 'It's like she's classy France crossed with UK corner shop cuisine. You'd never know she flambées quails' eggs for a living. And her team must have set this up for her arrival today, so these snacks must be something she can't live without – all here waiting for her on the day she gets here.'

There was a crash from below them and all three ran to the window. A pine tree had been snapped in half by the wind.

Amber ran a hand through her hair. 'Okay, the most important thing is for us all to stick together.'

Clio looked at Jeanie, feeling a bolt of fear. Stuck in a castle, during a storm, not knowing who to trust, death around every corner. It was like a reality TV show without the enticing cash prize.

Amber picked up the key from the floor and assessed the state of the broken lock. 'Looks like I well and truly smashed that, so we'll use the deadbolt I spotted on the outside, okay? Hopefully it'll put people off going into the room and disturbing anything. We'll have to leave her here and start asking questions. We don't have any choice.'

'Okay.' Clio could hear the fear in her own voice. She fought to keep the panic down. They were so vulnerable. No weapons. No defences. No phones.

Amber took a deep breath. 'We need to be really careful.'

Clio had an idea. 'Should we talk to Melissa? She'll know everyone who's here. She may know why Valerie went upstairs too.'

A shadow crossed Amber's face and she shook her head. 'If I'm honest, I wonder if Melissa is involved.'

'What? Why?' Clio caught Jeanie's eye. 'She seems really nice.'

'She keeps – staring at me.' Amber shifted from foot to foot. 'It's a bit creepy.'

Clio blinked. 'Well, you are looking particularly gorgeous tonight, aren't you? You're rocking a drowned rat vibe.'

'No. It's not *that* kind of looking. It's kind of – hungry. Needy?' Amber shrugged. 'I don't know how to explain it.'

'But fixating on you wouldn't make her kill Valerie, would it?'

'No, but...' Amber ran a hand through her hair. 'I just don't trust her, okay?'

'Got it.' Clio didn't, but it was always best just to go along with Amber when she got hunches like this. She did her best to smile at her two best friends as they left the room, trying to ignore the fact that, with this storm trapping them inside the castle, they had absolutely nowhere to hide from the killer.

5

AMBER

Amber hesitated just outside the door of the snug. 'I can hear footsteps.'

Her two friends looked towards the stairs.

Clio put her head on one side, shoving her hands into her pockets. Her red jumpsuit was drying in patches now, the white blonde of her hair gleaming in the light. 'Let's lock the door behind us, quick.'

Amber drew the bolt across and it clanged into place. Leaving a crime scene accessible like this was far from ideal. The killer could easily come in and remove evidence, or tamper with the body in some way. She put her palm against her forehead, willing her brain to get into gear, trying to find another option.

The footsteps were getting nearer. She drew her friends close, dropping her voice to a whisper. 'Okay, so, we need to ask everyone where they were when this happened – see if we can spot anything.'

'Good idea.' Clio made for the stairs.

'Wait up!' Amber raised a finger. 'But before we do that, we need to agree to keep this death secret. That way, we can tell everyone all at once, and gauge their real reaction to the fact that Valerie is dead.'

Jeanie wound a soggy curl around her finger. 'Might they not suspect us of having killed her? If we cover it up? I mean, you found the body, and each of us was alone when the murder happened. The others will think we are suspects too.'

'Good point.' Amber weighed it up for a moment. 'But people's first reactions can be such a good indicator of guilt, so I think it's worth keeping it quiet, just to see what they do and say. So let's keep it a secret, yes?'

'Okay.' Jeanie nibbled her lower lip. 'It's just...'

'Yes?' Amber struggled for patience. The footsteps were just below them now. She spoke in a low whisper, leaning close. They had no time for debate. 'The killer clearly knows their way around the castle, and may kill again, so we just need to do something, anything, to identify them, in case they're looking for their next victim to pick off. Do you see?' Amber knew she needed to bring her friends along with her. 'Also *we* might end up on the killer's list, having found the body. You can bet they weren't counting on it being located so soon.'

'But hang on.' Clio held up a hand. 'We can't use mobiles as there's no Wi-Fi. So how are we going to work out who did it? We have no background on anyone. And we don't even know everyone who is here on the island, do we? There might be someone hiding out there, in the woods.' Her eyes were huge. 'One of the protestors. Or even someone else? Some total unknown?'

Amber opened her mouth and closed it again. There was no easy answer to this. The truth was that she had never worked a case like it. She had always been part of a police team, or safe in the knowledge that Clio and Jeanie were available via mobile phone, the entire planet at their fingertips. This time around, trapped here for the next twelve hours, there would be no DNA samples to guide them, no autopsy results to cast extra light, no CCTV.

'Well...' Jeanie began timidly. 'Melissa will have a list of all the guests, won't she? And as manager she would know most about who comes and goes on the island. So again, it seems like she's the best place to start, doesn't it?'

Amber knew Jeanie was right, but the thought of those bright brown eyes made her hesitate. If anyone was up to something, it was Melissa. Amber had a strong feeling that secrets were lurking beneath her glossy smile.

Amber compromised. 'How about all three of us round everyone up together first?'

'Okay.' Jeanie nodded. 'So, all we need to do is make sure no one finds out about...' She gestured towards the door. 'About Valerie?'

'Exactly.'

The footsteps were slowing now, and Amber could hear the laboured breathing of someone who had taken the stairs too fast. 'Who's there?'

'It's just me.' Kieran's aftershave preceded him. 'Thought I'd come up and find what you three ladies are doing up here – see if anything exciting is happening.' His eyes glinted with interest as he spotted the bolted door. 'Why have you decided to meet up here? Is something going on that you don't want us all to know about?'

'No.' Amber folded her arms, trying not to sound as defensive as she felt. 'I was just trying to get some signal. Turns out there is none to be found.' She shrugged. 'So it's time to head back down, isn't it girls?'

Clio and Jeanie nodded, but Kieran didn't take the hint.

'Is this Valerie's room?'

'How did you know that?' Clio watched him suspiciously, head on one side.

'Well...' He trailed off. Amber assessed him. Was that a hint of unease in his eye?

He shifted from one foot to the other. 'If it's like the first Chateau la Fontaine, then Valerie will have a snug in one of the towers – she told me it was one of the first things she set up over in Palm Springs, even before the pools or the guest suites.'

Amber shrugged. 'Well, we don't know what it is – we're about to head back down, so...'

'Why's the lock broken?' Kieran turned. 'Was that you?'

Amber knew that if she denied this it would come back to haunt her later. She was saved from answering by Ray, who rounded the curve of the staircase surprisingly quietly, face pink with exertion. 'Oh, hello.' He blinked. 'Can I escort you all back downstairs? This isn't an area for guests, so Melissa has sent me up to show you downstairs again.'

Melissa. Trying to get them all out of the way. Amber's suspicions about the manager grew.

'Would you like to come with me, everyone?' Ray gestured towards the stairs.

'Of course.' Amber gave him a smile.

He returned it, eyes glinting beneath bushy brows. 'This way please. Melissa's waiting.'

'I bet she is.' As they started to wind their way down the stairs, Amber noticed a red stain on his fingertips. He saw her peering closer.

'Cut it on a branch when I was getting that banner down.' He slid his hand away into his pocket.

Amber wondered if it were true, or if the blood had come from the scratch on Valerie's cheek, or even from one of her head wounds.

She took a deep breath as lightning flashed in the sky outside. For a moment it felt like the world was collapsing. The murder. The agency accounts. The lack of clients. Her unpaid friends. The killer on the loose.

'So, Ray.' Clio clapped her hands together and put on her best *Downton Abbey* voice as they reached the ground floor. 'Please could you gather everyone in the Red Room? I have a special announcement to make.'

'Of course, m'lady.' Ray gave a tight smile. 'Birthday karaoke, is it?'

How Amber wished it was. She wished she was back in Clio's caravan, pink microphone in hand, margaritas in the huge turquoise jug they had brought back from Greece nearly twenty years ago.

'What are you cooking up, ladies?' Kieran's wolfish smile made Amber suspect him too.

'Get me a drink and I'll tell you.' Clio put a persuasive hand on his arm.

'Your wish is my command.' He disappeared into the Red Room.

Clio leant towards Amber and Jeanie. 'So, are they our first two suspects?'

'Ssshhhhh.' Amber frowned at her. 'We don't know who's listening!'

'Sorry.' Clio shrugged. 'But wouldn't it be great if we could solve this?'

'Yes, but we have to stay safe.'

Clio sniffed dismissively. 'It's never safe, is it? Not really.' She brightened. 'And at least no one thinks I'm the murderer this time.'

Amber allowed herself a small grin. 'I suppose so.'

'You know...' Clio started walking again. 'If we solve it, it might be really good for the agency.'

Jeanie glanced back at Amber. 'Not now, Clio.'

Amber stopped. 'What?' She had made so sure that her friends wouldn't find out about the true state of the accounts, password-protecting files and always doing the accounts late at night when the others were back at home. 'What do you mean, "not now"?'

Clio shook her head. 'Nothing. But I reckon we can do this!'

'If you say so.'

'I do!'

Amber couldn't help but smile. 'Okay.' She nodded. 'Let's find our killer. We tell everyone together. We watch them, then we talk to them individually. It's not great, but it's the best we can do. The suspects so far are all the people who weren't accounted for in the fifteen minutes between Valerie's departure and her body being found – so that's everyone we've met here, basically. And in terms of clues, I'd like to understand more about the SC tattoo, the knife and the broken nails.'

Amber realised she had managed to sound like an actual detective. Relief surged through her.

They could do this. Just as long as the killer didn't strike again.

6
CLIO

Clio was rather enjoying being the centre of attention. She had once understudied Miss Marple in a touring production of *The Body in the Library* and had always been rather disappointed that the lead had never missed a show. Now, she paced in front of the fireplace in the Red Room, enjoying the click of her boots against the flagstones, keeping a covert eye on the people gathering in front of her.

'Henri. Just five minutes. Please!' Melissa was practically having to drag the chef in with her, with him protesting all the way. Clio wondered why he was so reluctant to join them – whether he really was devoted to producing the perfect dinner or whether he was in fact a killer trying to hide. He wiped something impatiently off his sculpted cheekbone and turned, his arms arcing through the air as he complained to Melissa about how all the food was going to spoil unless he could get back to the kitchen *tout de suite*. His extravagant gestures dislodged his white chef's hat and it fell to the floor, leaving his caramel hair to flop into his green eyes.

While it was tempting to look at Henri all day, instead Clio turned her attention to the server, Angelo, who was wheeling Jocelyn over to the fireplace. He muttered something under his breath as he grappled with the brake, and Jocelyn laughed, her lined face breaking into sunshine. Angelo went and got a padded velvet stool from beside the window and carried it back to her, placing her injured foot carefully on top of it.

Jocelyn grinned conspiratorially at Clio. 'It's bloody annoying, this ankle. This castle isn't exactly designed for a wheelchair. But it'll be worth it, to eat Valerie la Fontaine's delicious food.'

Clio nodded. 'Absolutely.' She thought of Valerie's prone body and shuddered.

Angelo fiddled with his diamond ear stud. 'Can I get you anything?' His voice had traces of the south London streets where Clio had spent her primary school years, and his forehead was entirely unlined. What was he – nineteen, twenty? Young enough to kill on impulse, maybe. Clio let the silent commentary run in her head, weighing up who could have done it, who looked as though they had a secret to keep. It helped her to feel like she had some power in this situation, despite the fact that she was trapped on this island with a killer.

'I don't want anything thank you, dear.' Jocelyn shook her head at Angelo, before turning back to Clio. 'What are you three up to then?' Her eyes snapped as she fiddled with the long string of beads around her neck. 'What's all this about? Another surprise for the birthday girl?'

'I'll tell you in a minute.' Clio made sure her face gave nothing away. She checked on Jeanie and Amber, who were watching from different positions in the room. Between the three of them they could see everyone's faces as Clio made the announcement. She liked feeling part of a team again. Normally at the agency they were all going in different directions and it was good to be back together, even in these circumstances.

Even better, she had a role to play and she was ready. She looked at Melissa, who nodded confirmation that everyone was in here now. They were all assembled: the three detectives; the staff: Melissa, Ray, Angelo, Henri; and the other two guests, Jocelyn and Kieran. The latter was by the window, standing to one side, grinning to himself. Why? Because he had just killed Valerie la Fontaine? Were all the questions he had fired at them at the top of the staircase simply a cover up for what he had done?

'Good evening, everyone.' Clio shivered slightly as the wind blew in from the fireplace behind her. 'I am sorry to say that I have some very bad news.'

'It's not the protestors again, is it?' Ray shoved his hands deep into the pockets of his boiler suit. 'Because no more Mr Nice Guy if it is.'

Clio held up a hand, unable to resist a dramatic pause.

'Just now Amber, Jeanie and I were up in Valerie's snug where...' Clio watched the faces in front of her carefully.

'You got into the snug? Like the one Valerie has in Palm Springs?' Jocelyn clapped her hands. 'I would *love* to do that. I—'

Clio held her hand up and Jocelyn piped down. Ray's lower jaw was jutting forwards, brows furrowed, while Henri was staring at the ceiling, looking as if he was seeking an escape hatch. Melissa was at the back of the group, arms folded, eyes sliding to Amber whenever they could. Clio could see Amber and Jeanie eyeing their subjects intently too and wondered what they were concluding.

She took a deep breath.

'What we found up there is that Valerie la Fontaine is dead.'

Jocelyn froze, Ray swore, and Henri was most definitely paying attention now.

'What?' Melissa's hand was over her mouth. 'Dead? How? When?'

Clio continued. 'She had been hit over the head. Her snug was locked from inside and the killer had left by the time we got there.'

'But...' A tear rolled down Melissa's cheek. 'She...'

Jeanie went across and put an arm around her as Melissa stood, sobs starting to shake her whole body. If Melissa was a killer, then she was a very good actress too. For a moment Melissa leant into Jeanie, a plant seeking water. Then she fiercely pulled away.

'Well, damn!' Melissa threw her arms wide. 'You three could have told me earlier, you know – given me a bit of a heads up. Come on! All that, "let's get everyone together Melissa, let's do it Melissa," and then this? Man alive. You three are a piece of work.' She stomped away to the far corner of the room, muttering what Clio strongly believed were swear words. Then Melissa turned, her bright eyes on Clio. 'And what the hell were you doing upstairs anyways? Clients are not meant to go up there. There are rules.'

Clio shrugged. 'Rules are made to be broken.'

'Not in Chateau la Fontaine they're not.' Melissa's brown eyes flashed, then she dropped into a chair and covered her face with her palms.

'Valerie... I can't believe it. Who would do this?' Clio was about to go across and comfort her when Melissa rose again. 'But seriously, you shouldn't go into staff quarters. There's no freaking way that's okay.'

Clio folded her arms defensively. 'I don't think that someone going up the stairs at the wrong moment is really the point here, do you? The point is that Valerie is dead.'

This time the information landed. Melissa's face stilled. 'Yes. Of course. Dead. Oh my God, what are we all going to do? She's the business, she *is* Chateau la Fontaine.' She stumbled over and collapsed on the edge of the sofa.

Jocelyn reached out and patted her on the shoulder, her face grey. 'This is terrible.' A tear rolled down her wrinkled face and she put a hand to her chest. 'Who...?' She looked around the group. 'And why?'

Kieran spoke from the window. 'She was famous. Weird people are always after celebrities, aren't they?' He ran a hand carelessly through his hair. 'I wonder if anyone saw anything – or heard anything...' He glanced at Melissa. 'Because it must have been one of the staff, yes?'

Melissa's eyes narrowed. 'Are you kidding me with this?'

'No.' He walked calmly over to the long table. 'Why would a guest kill her? We don't even know her.'

'You seemed fairly sure that you knew her earlier.' Melissa followed him, finding a target for her anger. She jabbed a finger at him. 'What's your problem, Kieran?'

'I haven't got a problem.' Kieran raised a canapé to his mouth. 'You're the one with the problem. What are you going to do with your guests now?' Melissa stood facing him, her face stone. He held out a hand, palm upwards. 'Refund time.'

A vein pulsed in Melissa's neck. 'You're here for free, you ass.'

Clio watched them. If Kieran was the killer, then he needed to up his acting skills. He looked like he couldn't care less that Valerie was dead. Jocelyn on the other hand was crying so hard she was in danger of dehydration. Jeanie went to her side, rubbing a hand on her back and passing her a tissue.

Kieran held the canapé to his mouth. 'Well, I'd better eat what I can now she's gone, hadn't I?'

Melissa struck the canapé out of Kieran's hand.

'What are you doing?' He grabbed another. 'I'm your guest.'

'You don't deserve her food.' Melissa stuck her chin out, in a gesture that was extremely familiar to Clio, though she couldn't work out why. Those delicate cheekbones, the dimple in the chin. The glossy black hair.

Jeanie stepped in between them, her back to Melissa. 'Kieran, Melissa has just lost a colleague and a friend. Let it go.'

Melissa sagged. 'We've put so much into this business, into setting up over here and now…' She trailed off.

Clio noticed how none of the staff went to comfort their boss. Instead, Angelo had retreated to a corner where he appeared to be trying to blend into the wall, Henri was swearing at the window and Ray was pacing up and down, long legs making quick work of this enormous room.

Melissa looked up. 'I need to see her. To say goodbye.'

'No.' Amber's voice was decisive. 'The police have asked us to keep the room locked until they can get here. No one is allowed to go in there.'

Melissa frowned. 'Except you three.'

'Exactly. Except us. I'm ex-police. They trust me.' Amber folded her arms. 'They know us – we've worked with them before. We're private detectives. The storm is too big for the police to get here, so they've asked us all to remain together to stay safe.'

'To stay safe? With this crowd?' Henri flung his arms out, indicating everyone in the room. 'What a joke.'

'What do you mean?' Clio walked towards him. 'Why aren't you safe with them?'

He tossed his head contemptuously. 'Like I'm going to tell you that.'

Ray laughed. 'As if you're whiter than white, lad.'

Henri rounded on him. 'What do you mean?'

'You know exactly what I mean.' Ray was now only two metres from Henri. 'I know…'

'*Mon dieu*. What do think you know, old man?'

Ray snapped back. 'I'm not old! And I know plenty.'

'*Merde alors*.' Henri jabbed his finger in Ray's face. 'You've only been working for Valerie for a month or two. You know nothing about her or any of us.'

Ray's eyes narrowed. 'Oh, I know plenty about you.'

Henri exhaled dismissively. 'You are full of shit.' He turned on his heel and marched across the room towards the hall.

Amber raised her voice. 'Henri. We all have to stay together. To stay safe.'

He glanced back. 'You do what you want. I am a big boy. I can look after myself.' And he stalked out, head held high.

'Good riddance.' Ray looked like he was about to punch the wood panelling. 'Now we can find the evidence to show he killed her.'

Clio approached him cautiously. 'So, will you help us, then?'

He frowned. 'Who put you in charge?'

Clio wondered where the jovial captain of the boat had gone. 'Like Amber said, we're detectives. It makes sense for us to lead the investigation and keep people safe until the police come. We want to talk to everyone, to find out where they were when Valerie was killed.'

Ray's mouth was a thin line. 'Why do I get the feeling you're just going to accuse me of killing her?'

Clio wondered why he was being so defensive. 'We're just trying to find out what happened so we can rule you out.'

'Or rule me in.' His dark eyes held hers.

Clio shook her head. 'I promise, we're just trying to work out who was where. We'll talk to everyone, okay?'

'Okay, okay.' He held up his hands. 'Sorry. Bit of a shock, all this. Let's see what I can remember. Before I saw you upstairs I was outside, taking the banner down, checking that all the protestors had gone. Then I was trying to launch the boat, but of course I couldn't because of the storm. Then I came back in and Melissa told me to go and look for Valerie.'

Melissa shook her head. 'Hell, no. I did not do that.'

Kieran interrupted, waving his phone. 'There's still no bloody Wi-Fi or signal. What the hell am I meant to do with no comms? I need to tell the world out there what's happening.'

'Typical. You're just after the story.' Melissa snickered loudly, a harsh, grating sound. 'Maybe you could help us try to catch the killer instead? Unless of course you're the one who did it?'

'Me?' Kieran rolled his eyes. 'Why the hell would I kill her?'

'I can think of a reason or two.' Melissa was squaring up to him now. She really was a tour de force. 'She knew things about you that might not have played well if they'd got out, didn't she?'

'Oh, screw you.'

'Yeah? Well, screw you too!'

Ray watched the show, a small smile playing on his lips. 'I *knew* Melissa was fiery. Always the quiet ones, isn't it?'

'Always the sexist ones, in my experience.' Clio swore beneath her breath. They didn't have time for this. 'Now, Ray, we need a way of communicating – the three of us – if we get split up. Does the team here have a back-up for when the Wi-Fi signal goes down?'

'We have some walkie-talkies.'

'Can you get some for us?'

'I need to…' He sank into a leather armchair. 'I mean, let me just take it in for a moment, yeah? I feel a bit weak.'

Clio felt frustration rise inside her. 'Fine, then where can we find them?'

'They're in my shed. Two minutes from that door.' He pointed his bony finger at the side door where the banner had been. 'Head right.'

Clio beckoned over Amber and Jeanie.

'I heard what he said. I'll go.' Jeanie visibly steeled herself. 'I think we'll need two of you in here to stop that pair from killing each other.' She gestured towards the canapé table where Melissa and Kieran were still competing to see who knew the most swear words. 'Maybe one of you can take on Jocelyn? I've run out of tissues and she's still crying.'

Wow. If Jeanie's famous handbag had run out of tissues, things must be bad.

'What if you meet the protestors?'

Ray gave a dry laugh. 'Those bloody tree-huggers. Maybe it *was* them. It wouldn't surprise me at all – they'd do anything to stop the lodges being built in their precious spiritual homeland. Weirdos.'

'I'll be fine.' Jeanie nervously headed for the door. Clio felt a clutch of panic, but they had no choice. If the three of them could communicate then they had some chance of staying on top of this situation.

'Right.' Clio hadn't finished with Ray. 'So, after taking the banner down and trying unsuccessfully to launch the boat, you came upstairs and saw us?'

'Yes.'

Clio's eyes met Amber's. No alibi.

'And where did you get the blood on your fingers?'

He looked downwards. 'I told you. It was probably a branch when I was getting the banner down. The wind's a bitch. And by the way, does it occur to anyone else that you three might have done it? And that you're asking all these questions to cover your tracks?'

Clio barked out a laugh. 'We're here for our first relaxing weekend away in years, why on earth would we murder the chef?'

'That's your story.' His mouth twisted. 'But for all we know you three are the killers. You might be trying to pick all of us off, one by one.'

'Oh, for God's sake.' Clio exhaled in exasperation. 'That is crazy.'

'No more crazy than your theory that I did it.'

'We never said you did it!' Clio threw up her hands. 'We're just asking a few questions! We're not trying to accuse anyone of anything – we're really just trying not to die.' She heard a loud noise and turned to see Jocelyn using the velvet curtains to blow her nose.

Ray was visibly unconvinced. 'So you say.'

'Yes. We do.'

Behind him, Kieran and Melissa looked like they were moving towards fisticuffs. Ray swore loudly and stood up. 'This is a madhouse. I'm getting out of here. Because I don't really see how three middle-aged women are going to keep me safe.' The contempt in his voice was so great that Clio was sorely tempted to show him how hard her right hook was.

Ray marched out into the hall, in the direction Henri had gone only minutes before. Clio sighed, walking over to the table, needing some food to eat as she and Amber talked things through. Everyone here had had opportunity. All they needed to work out was who had the means and the motive.

The three of them could do it. Clio dipped a tender piece of asparagus into an exquisite sauce béarnaise and chewed. She was just about to swallow when she heard a scream.

7

JEANIE

For someone who spent a lot of her life telling children to put their coats on, Jeanie was remarkably bad at remembering her own. As she ran along, she raised her hands in a futile attempt to create a barrier between herself and one of the fiercest storms she had ever experienced. The lowering sky rumbled above her and the pine trees that grew either side of the path that led away from the castle were doing nothing to protect her from the storm.

Her long curls were slick to her head so at least she could see properly for once. She just had to find the shed and get the walkie-talkies. Simple. She had done harder things. Back when Clio had been the prime suspect for the murder of her husband, Jeanie had faced her fears and jumped into the path of a bullet to protect her friend. Then, on her hen do, she had gone to the house of a suspect to challenge him about why he had committed murder. The thought of her mum busting into the house to save her still made Jeanie smile.

She wondered what her mum and her four sisters would think if they could see Jeanie now. They had loved being part of the murder investigation last year, clamouring for more responsibility, wanting to beat up the baddies themselves. Her little sister Penelope, a WSL footballer until injury had recently ended her career, was now seriously considering becoming a detective. Jeanie suspected Pen's total inability to follow any rules might hold her back, but then her eldest, and most rigid sister, Nicola, had taken up belly-dancing at the age of fifty, so you never knew.

She heard a loud crack behind her and whirled around. 'Who's there?'

Nobody answered. Jeanie gritted her teeth and started walking again. She had to get this done and stop letting her imagination run away with her. The killer was probably inside the castle putting on their finest innocent face, not out here with Jeanie. There was nothing to worry about. Jeanie just had to get to the shed. Above her, she could see strings of fairy lights that had been ripped from the trees. They were dangling, flapping in the wind, the ultimate sign that the party was over. To her left the castle walls rose high, the turrets barely visible in the whirling clouds. Once it had seemed like a safe haven – now it seemed more like a prison.

What was it Ray had said? The hut was… where?

Jeanie switched on the torch on her phone, only to see her battery was already very low. She had no choice. If she wanted to find the hut, she would have to run her phone down to zero. She switched on the torch and put her head down, leaning into the wind. She wasn't going to give up. At home she had two children and she wanted to live to see them read a book, swim a length, go a day without pulling each other's hair. She shivered as the rain started to penetrate her bra, trying to force her mind to focus on the events of the past few hours. Valerie's face freezing as she saw the protestors' banner. Kieran coming up the staircase. The broken nails, red and gold against the white rug. Jeanie had no idea how it all fitted together. And she was so busy trying to work it out that she didn't see the rope until it was too late.

'Oh God.' She was flying through the air, and grabbed the first thing she could find. It gave way in her hand and she landed hard on the ground, her hand clasping a guy rope.

She shone her torch around wildly, struggling to see. She felt wet canvas on her face. She appeared to have landed on top of a tent.

'What the hell…?'

By the sounds of it she had landed on top of someone inside the tent as well. A protestor? She looked around for a weapon.

'I'm armed.' She grabbed a twig, scrambling up to a sitting position, taking half the rope with her.

'Excuse me.' A voice came from beneath the canvas. 'You landed on my leg. Could you move please?'

Whoever it was, they were being remarkably polite, given the situation.

Jeanie responded in kind. 'Yes. Of course. I'm so sorry. I didn't see...' She was interrupted by a crack of thunder. She got to her feet, walking around to what she judged to be the front of the tent, and picking up what must be the flap.

'I'm so sorry.'

'It's fine, yeah?' The person speaking – a man by the sound of it – sounded like he wanted her to leave. Jeanie wondered why there was a tent out here, and what on earth he was doing inside it. Nerves whispered over her skin, but she had to check she hadn't done too much damage. Her older sister Charlotte called her 'terminally polite' and Jeanie knew it was true.

Jeanie took a breath, struggling to stay on her feet as another gust of wind tried to knock her over. Bracing herself, she shone the torch into the collapsed tent.

'Oh. Angelo. It's you.'

Angelo was shielding his face, but she would know that diamond stud anywhere.

'Why did you come out here, Angelo? You were inside a moment ago.'

'I got something on my waistcoat. I had to change it.'

Jeanie felt a jolt of nerves. Was it blood on his waistcoat? Was he the killer?

She started to back away, but the tent was doing its best to part ways with the ground. Only Angelo was keeping it in place as the wind whipped and roared around them.

'Why is your stuff out here?'

'I'm just...' Angelo sighed. 'I'm meant to get the boat back to the mainland after my shift, but tonight I'm staying in here.'

Jeanie felt her mouth fall open. 'What?'

Angelo fought his way out of the tent. 'Valerie doesn't want staff staying near the guests, and the staff quarters aren't ready yet, so there's nowhere else.' His face darkened. 'I thought she would treat us better, but we all had to sign NDAs before starting work here, so it's not like I can tell the press or anything.'

Jeanie stored this information away. Valerie keeping staff out of the castle surely meant she was trying to hide something – something that had got her killed. The place was huge – there must be enough space to accommodate all the staff here tonight, especially as so many of the guests and staff hadn't made it.

'But it's not safe out here, Angelo. Not with the storm and a killer on the loose.'

'Yeah, well.' His face was resigned. 'Just as well they pay us so much.'

'They do?'

'Yeah.' He nodded. 'More than twice the nearest local company. I'm saving for a round the world trip, yeah? It's going to be sick. Worth a night in a tent, I guess.'

On cue, the tent flew off in a flutter of sodden material to impale itself on a tree branch.

'Ah shit.' He kicked the ground with his black Nike trainer. 'Need a new plan, then.' He sagged, cheeks puffing out, and Jeanie could see how young he was.

She reached out. 'I'm sure they'll let you stay in the castle.'

'Maybe.' He straightened.

She took her chance. 'Can I ask where you were? When Valerie was killed.'

His eyes narrowed. 'Why?'

'Just a routine question.'

He was silent for a moment, and Jeanie felt a jolt of fear. He might be young but he looked strong and quick and he was way taller than her. She wouldn't stand a chance.

Then she relaxed as he started to talk. 'I went to the kitchen with Melissa, but then she went off to her room, I think, and I had a slash.'

'For fifteen minutes?'

'Nah. Course not. Then I went to polish the silver in the boot room, ready for tonight's dinner service.'

'Alone?'

'Yeah. Why?' His lips formed a thin line.

Jeanie knew it was time to stop. 'Nothing. Just wondering.'

'Okay.' He checked the time on his phone. 'I'd better get back. Find

Melissa. You know.' He nodded as if trying to convince himself, suddenly a teenager again. 'You should head inside, like, too? It's wet out here.'

Jeanie did her best to smile. 'I had noticed.'

'Okay. See you.' He turned away and headed down the path back towards the castle.

Jeanie wished she were going with him. 'Do you know where the shed is? Ray's shed?'

He yelled over his shoulder. 'That way.' He pointed in the opposite direction to the way Jeanie had been walking.

'Okay. Thanks.' She pivoted and started to run. Any longer out here and she would dissolve and she wanted to be back inside with her friends. She saw the shed looming ahead of her. Three walkie-talkies and out. That was all she needed to do.

She was nearly there. She reached the door and put her hand on the latch, lifting it up to let herself inside. Her torch faltered and died, so she reached into the pocket of her dress, remembering she had brought a packet of matches to light the candles on Amber's cake. Maybe they were still okay. Maybe.

She hoped so. She took one out and scraped it against the box.

Nothing.

She tried another.

Still nothing.

She became vaguely aware that she could hear breathing that wasn't her own.

One more match.

This time it sparked. Jeanie saw a pile of cake boxes, a flash of teeth, and the walkie-talkies hanging along one wall.

A hand clamped over her mouth as the match fizzled out.

She didn't even have time to scream.

8

AMBER

Back in the Red Room, Amber was embarrassed at herself for screaming. She never screamed. In all her years on the force she had prided herself on being the tough one, the hard one, the rock. It was the same with Clio and Jeanie – Amber was the one who looked out for them. She had started young, when Clio was being bullied and Amber and one of her foster brothers had waited outside the local Co-op to intimidate Clio's tormentors into stopping. That pattern had never changed. Amber didn't do self-analysis, didn't do trauma. She did pushing through, taking action, blocking introspection before it began.

But now a spider landing on her head had made her scream – one surprise too many – and on her birthday, too, which certainly wasn't redeeming itself this year. Childhood memories kept assailing her as they always did on this day, no matter how hard she tried to block them. Memories of doors opening after lights out, of bags being packed without her knowledge as she was once more shown the door. This was why she normally stayed at home with the door locked, working her way through *Wallander* episodes until the day was over.

But this year here she was, trapped in a castle with a killer. She shuddered, as Clio came sprinting towards her from the canapé table.

'Are you okay, Amber?' Her friend's eyes were full of a concern Amber normally saw aimed at other people. She felt herself squirm – concern was so close to pity, pity she had received from social workers, from teachers, from all the grown-ups who saw her as a child who had never had parents, rather than as the resilient fighter she knew she was inside. They hadn't known that she had never needed her parents. She had only ever needed her friends.

'I'm fine.' She wanted to switch off Clio's expression. To turn on the usual Clio, who talked about dating and cheese and why she was so angry that M&S had discontinued her favourite jeans.

'Are you sure?'

'Yes.'

'Okay, then.' Clio picked up a heavy gold pony ornament from the piano to her left. 'But for the record I don't believe you. I've never heard you scream before – something must have happened.'

Her lower lip jutted out, and Amber felt a pang of guilt. Amber never talked about her past with her friends, so they had no idea how dark things had been back then. The way she had felt as she was moved from foster home to foster home, each time hoping that this might be for ever, each time bitterly disappointed when it wasn't.

But now was not the time to start opening up. They had a murder to solve. 'It was just a spider. So, Clio, how about you talk to Jocelyn – see whether she's seen anything?' Kieran swept out of the room as she spoke, and Amber immediately wanted to see where he was going. She turned, nearly leaping out of her skin to see Melissa at her side.

'God! Where did you spring from?' She wondered if the manager had some kind of trapdoor.

'I just thought I'd come and see if...' Melissa's hand was reaching for Amber's arm. Amber stepped smartly away – she barely tolerated physical contact from her best friends, let alone strangers. '...if you were okay, Amber?'

'Well, I'm not the best, no.'

'Can I help with that?' Melissa was too eager. It set Amber's teeth on edge.

Clio hovered, picking up on Amber's discomfort. The two of them had always understood one another in the end, even back when they used to fight over Clio's terrible taste in men or over who was better at singing the theme tune to *Beverley Hills, 90210* (Amber, obviously).

'No, Melissa. I'm fine.' Amber moved towards the door.

'I can come with you if you want?' Melissa was still there at her side, still seemingly needing something from Amber. 'I could do with talking to you about...'

Amber shook her head. 'Safest if you stay in here. I won't be long.'

Walking fast, she followed Kieran silently down the shadowy hallway. The more Amber looked at this castle, the more she could see how far it had to go before being ready for its celebrity clientele. The state of the high ceilings out here was shambolic at best. It wasn't just the cobwebs hanging off the faded red lampshades, or the worn patches in the carpets beneath their feet, it was the mould blooming on the walls, appearing around the edge of the portraits of horses and hounds that were clearly well into a long residency. The golden sidelights flickered, and dark navy paint was flaking off the many doors she passed. Above her a light fitting had been taken out, showing a tangle of wires beneath.

This place must cost a fortune to maintain, let alone repair. Could money have been a factor in Valerie's death?

Ahead of her Kieran was still moving. Amber hid behind a grandfather clock as he stopped, trying a door to the left. It was cold at this end of the castle and her clothes were still too wet to be of any help. Kieran glanced backwards before entering the room and pulling the door shut behind him.

Amber didn't have time to waste. She followed him through the door, which sported a golden plaque telling her it was The Conservatory. She closed it silently behind her.

A dim glow came from a rickety chandelier in the centre of the room – a metal cross hung with flickering diamond lights. Amber could see the green baize surface of a snooker table beneath it, cues hung neatly on the wall alongside a chalk scoring board. Floor-to-ceiling windows ran down one side of the room, which presumably opened out onto the gardens. Kieran was standing by one of the windows, bent over a big wooden desk with sculpted feet and papers bursting out of every drawer. He was holding a torch and was systematically leafing through its contents, muttering to himself.

'What are you looking for?' Amber walked towards him, head held high.

'*Fuck.*' He jumped and turned around, twitchy as a hare in an open field.

'Kieran.' She could see the only male guest's mahogany tan now, his bright blue eyes, his dishevelled dark blond hair looking more wild than she suspected he might like.

'Oh. Hi.' His drawling voice made this sound like a five-syllable word. He smiled, clearly intending to charm. Amber narrowly refrained from rolling her eyes. Kieran had no idea who he was dealing with. Charm slid off Amber like butter off a hot slice of toast.

'What are you doing in here, Kieran?'

'Had to get away from that Melissa nightmare.' He folded his arms defensively. 'I can't believe the front of her, suggesting I might be a killer.'

'Can I ask why you chose this room, though?' Amber walked towards him, trying to see what was in the drawers of the desk. 'And why now?'

A muscle flickered in his cheek. 'And can I ask why you get to stick your nose into everyone else's business?'

Amber nodded. Aggression she could deal with. Decades on the force meant that she was used to being spat at, punched, called names and kicked. A few insults weren't going to bother her.

'Because the police asked me to, as I used to work for them. I've told you that. But you still haven't answered my question – why are you out here going through this desk? What are you looking for?'

'Nothing. I just like antiques.' His tone was staccato. Defensive. He scratched his neck and avoided her gaze in the manner of every amateur liar Amber had ever met.

'So, Kieran, you walked deliberately down here, putting yourself in danger – unless of course you are the killer, in which case you know you're safe – and you picked this room at random and came in to do a spot of antiquing?'

'Yes!' His eyes settled on the chandelier. 'And I didn't kill anyone.'

She watched him. 'Why this room, then?'

'What do you mean?' He couldn't stop looking around, his eyes drawn inexorably to the desk. What was he after?

Amber moved towards the desk, wondering if it was time to take a gamble. Hell, why not? She reached out and pulled open a drawer, seeing more paperclips than anyone could use in a lifetime. She slammed it shut and opened the next.

In a second, he was beside her, trying to edge her away. 'Don't look in there.'

'Why not? Just a random desk, according to you. Nothing special.' Amber rifled through the contents. She saw papers, some typed, some hand-written, mixed together with a mass of what looked like bills.

'It's private property, though.' Kieran's voice was rising. 'You can't just barge in here and go through it.'

'Didn't stop you, did it?' Amber moved on to a third drawer, which was full of legal documents – contracts and orders and a big cream envelope with *'Last Will and Testament'* on the front. Interesting. She folded it in half and pocketed it.

'You can't take that.'

She turned, folding her arms. 'This is Valerie's desk, isn't it? The one that she flew in from the States? The one Melissa said had been delivered to the wrong room?'

'Is it?' He shook his head, clearly doing his best to smile, his chin tipping up, his blue eyes glinting. 'I didn't realise.'

'Really?' Amber didn't trust him an inch.

'No.' Off went those eyes again, this time landing on the snooker cues.

Amber turned back to the desk, glancing over her shoulder to make sure he wasn't creeping any closer. 'It seems strange that you came straight here. It's almost like you're looking for something. Or like you know this castle pretty well already. Or you've been listening in to people somehow.' She leafed through some more papers. More bills. A lot of bills. No. He wouldn't have put it there. She had met journalists like Kieran before.

She pulled open the tiny cupboard door at the back of the desk. She checked one little shelf. Then the next. And then she found it. A tiny black device, which she slipped into her palm before turning round to face him.

She turned. 'So tell me, Kieran. How long have you been illegally recording Valerie?'

His eyes were on the move again. 'What?'

'How long?' Amber kept her voice cool.

'I'm not recording her.'

Amber arched an eyebrow. 'Yes, you are. I saw the way she looked at you – how shocked she was to see you and I want to know why. I'm guessing you invited yourself along to this weekend – trying to get more dirt on her, maybe? For that second article you're writing? And I think this...' She held out the small black recording device. 'That this might be how you found out whatever secrets you know about her. That's why you're in here – you're trying to get this device back, aren't you? So no one knows what you did?'

'I...' His skin was paling beneath his tan. 'I told you, I wasn't looking for anything.'

'Sure. You were just passing by. I know.' It felt so good to be back on familiar territory. Probing, interrogating, asking questions of others rather than playing bad memories on a loop. 'But I think that maybe I might listen to this, just to see what happened in this room – whether it might help us to understand who killed Valerie and why. I'm guessing you've been planting more devices since you got here, just like you probably did over at her place in the States. You're nothing but a tabloid hack, aren't you?'

Amber knew she was taking a dangerous step being alone with a man who might kill to keep his secrets. Anger flashed in his blue eyes. 'Hey. Give that back.'

She closed her hand around it. 'So it is yours, then?' In this mood she would fight anyone and win. In this world of no Wi-Fi and no forensics, she just had to follow her gut.

'Have you got any of these hidden anywhere else?' She narrowed her eyes.

'No. And it's not mine.'

'It's not yours? So why did you ask me to give it back?'

'I don't have to answer your questions.' The veins stood out on his neck and his fists were clenched.

She took a step towards him. 'Valerie didn't look happy to see you. Melissa hates you. So tell me, what do you know? What are you holding over Valerie?' Another thought occurred. 'Were you blackmailing her?'

'I...'

Amber stared at the man in front of her, her brain racing. She wondered whether Valerie's death might not prove to be the last killing tonight. This castle whispered with secrets, with resentments, with hatred.

'Kieran.' She spoke low. 'We all need to be really careful now. You knew something about Valerie and you might be in danger.' She turned towards the windows, watching the branches flailing in the wind. She thought about the envelope and what its contents might reveal. Together with the information on the recording device the clues might start to come together, to lead her to the killer. 'Someone might target you next.' She could see that she was upsetting him, but she felt wild, reckless, unleashed. 'You need to tell me everything you know – anything that might help us to work out who killed her.'

His hand reached out, surprising her, and his fingers closed around the recording device, snatching it away. She tried to hold on but he was too strong, pushing her down to the floor. Then he ran away towards the door.

She dragged herself to her feet.

'Kieran? You need to listen to me!'

But it was too late. Kieran was gone.

All she was left with was the sound of the door slamming behind him.

9
CLIO

In the Red Room, Clio's interview was not going well. Melissa had said she had to implement some emergency protocol and had disappeared towards the kitchen. Rather than answering Clio's questions, Jocelyn had spent ten minutes telling Clio why she loved Valerie so much. 'She was just such a talent – you know I ate in her Paris restaurant when she was first starting out – the most exquisite *amuse-bouche* in the world. She mixed...'

'Jocelyn.'

'Tuna tartare in a...'

'*Jocelyn.*'

'Yes?' Jocelyn blinked dreamily. 'It was the sweetest place, close to the Sacre Coeur, in Montmartre. It had...'

Clio cut her off, impatient now. 'Jocelyn, I know Valerie was a great chef. I know how sad you are that she is dead. But I think we should follow Melissa. I need to...' *See what she's up to*, was the phrase that sprang to mind. 'I need to keep track of everyone. Okay?' Clio backed the wheelchair up so she could steer it past the elegant chairs positioned at intervals along the table, where the canapés were now looking distinctly worse for wear.

Jocelyn glanced up. 'Of course. I got lost on memory lane there – I forgot that you and your friends were investigating. I'm so sorry.'

'No problem.' Clio pushed harder as one of the wheels stuck.

'It's terrible.' Jocelyn sighed as they moved along the hall. 'I still can't believe anyone could do such a thing. I'm so glad we have you three to help us.'

Clio flushed. 'Thank you. We'll do our best.'

'I know you will.' Jocelyn's huge bag was teetering dangerously on her lap and Clio grabbed it before it fell, catching a glimpse of a chaos inside that she could relate to: a bulky make-up bag, a bandage, a torch and a cluster of plasters.

Thunder rumbled outside and Clio wondered how Jeanie was faring. And where was Amber? She was taking ages.

She placed the bag back on Jocelyn's lap.

'Thank you, dear.' The old lady patted her hand. 'You look worried.'

Clio swallowed. 'I am. Jeanie's been outside a while now. I hope she's okay.'

Jocelyn was staring at her, sympathetic. 'She'll be back soon.'

'I hope so.' They were nearly at the kitchen now. 'She's like a sister to me.' Clio felt tears pricking her eyes, and forced her mind to change tack.

It was time to finally start interviewing Jocelyn. 'So, did you see anything?'

'What do you mean?'

'Anything that might be relevant to Valerie's murder. Anything that happened earlier...? I don't know, someone arguing, or lurking in a strange place?'

Jocelyn tapped her long fingers on her lap, thinking. 'No. I don't think so.'

'Shame.' Clio pushed open the door to the kitchen, which was four times larger than the static caravan that she fitted her whole world into. Her nostrils were hit by the smell of heaven – a glorious waft of beef, wine and herbs. Her stomach growled. And it would make sense to eat something – to refuel before the long night ahead. She looked around, seeing a sweeping space, with multiple hobs running down the middle and huge ovens up some low steps at the far end, next to an arched window. The air was steamy and warm and Clio felt herself start to come alive. She hadn't realised how cold she had been.

Jocelyn sniffed appreciatively. 'You know I find I'm rather hungry. And, being my age, I really need to do something about it, especially with my diabetes to think about. And food might help us both think, mightn't it?'

'Good idea.' Clio pushed her up to far side of the table and put on the brake.

'Boeuf bourguignon, how wonderful.' Jocelyn beamed as she saw a huge white casserole dish sitting in the middle of the table. 'I love this – it's one of Valerie's specialities, something she makes for her staff. I read that in a *Vogue* interview she did back in the nineties.' She spooned some into a white china bowl with a gold rim, and took one of the wrapped sets of knives, forks and spoons lying ready on the table.

Then her face fell. 'Oh dear, I suppose it isn't one of her specialities any more now, is it? Not now she's gone.' She stared at the plate, spoon still in her hand.

'No.' Clio shook her head. Where were the others? She thought Melissa had said she was heading to the kitchen but there was no sign of her now. Clio absently picked up a fork and tapped it against her hand. She knew she should eat, but she wanted to go and find her friends first. She needed them. This place was creepy. She put the fork down.

Jocelyn was eating now, devouring the food in her bowl. She saw Clio staring at her. 'Sorry. I always eat when I'm upset.'

'I totally get it.' Clio nodded. She grabbed a hunk of the sliced baguette that was lying next to the casserole dish. She pulled off a corner and popped it into her mouth. It was soft and sweet and tasted of Paris and romance. Corner cafes, hands held under tables, Clio smiling over at Gary.

Oh God. Gary. The man who had taken her money and her dignity and then got her arrested for his murder too. She rapidly put the bread down, all appetite gone.

Jocelyn was now using a hunk of it to mop up the sauce. 'Ooh, I do feel a bit better now. Let's see if I can think of anything to help you.'

'That would be great.' Clio waited.

Jocelyn mopped up the final drops of sauce. 'I did see Melissa earlier now I come to think about it. Arguing with someone. Something about Melissa not getting her fair share?'

'Really?' Clio slid into the seat opposite her, interest starting to prickle. 'Are you sure?'

'Oh yes.' Jocelyn nodded. 'They were having a right set-to. Obviously it was windy, but it sounded to me like whoever Melissa was arguing with wasn't paying her enough, that kind of thing. Melissa got quite heated.' She carried on chewing. 'Are you sure you don't want any of this delicious food?'

'Yes. I want to find my friends first.' Clio walked up the small steps that led to the area of the kitchen where the ovens were, and planted both hands on the windowsill, gazing out into the night. She took a deep breath, trying to work out how Melissa could have killed Valerie, whether she was capable of it. She leant forward and rested her head against the window. She tried to find comfort in the solid wood beneath her fingers, the cool of the window pane against her forehead.

'Maybe that conversation gave her a motive. Do you think so, Jocelyn?'

No answer. And something was registering in Clio's mind. Very slowly. Something she had glimpsed as she crossed from the steps towards the window. She looked at the floor to her right and saw a hand, outstretched. A hand with golden rings and a red sleeve above.

'Oh my God, Melissa!'

Melissa was lying flat on the floor of the storeroom that opened off the kitchen, behind the bank of ovens. There was blood. A lot of blood. Clio got down on her knees, checking Melissa's pulse. She stifled a sob. The killer couldn't have struck again already. Not so soon. Please.

Clio held her breath, her fingers around Melissa's wrist, waiting for that light drumbeat beneath her fingers.

And there it was.

Melissa groaned.

'Oh thank God.' Clio noticed the heavy stone mortar at Melissa's side. It was edged with red.

'Shit.' Melissa was blinking now, wincing in pain as she put a shaking hand to the wound. Blood was thick in her black hair. 'What the hell happened?'

'Jocelyn, can you help me?' Clio tried to grasp Melissa around her shoulders and help her up.

Silence.

Clio tried again. 'Jocelyn. I need your help.' She attempted to tug Melissa into an upright position, but there was too much blood. It was seeping over Clio's jumpsuit and hands and she couldn't hold on. Melissa was groaning now, and Clio was terrified that she was going to die. She needed to get to the landline in the snug, to see if an air ambulance could come, or whether a break in the storm meant that the police might somehow manage to make it over here.

'What happened?' Melissa blinked up at Clio.

'I don't know. But you're okay. I've got you.' Clio tried to smile.

'It hurts.' Melissa gritted her teeth. 'Must. Get. Up.' She tried to push herself up on her elbows, but collapsed back to the floor again.

'Jocelyn? I need some help here.' Clio was at her wits' end now. '*Jocelyn.*'

Still nothing. With difficulty, Clio managed to heave Melissa up and prop her against a cupboard in the corner, wedged against the wall so she couldn't slide down again.

Clio stood up, panting heavily, elbows against the marble counter, head down.

'Well, thanks a lot, Jocelyn.'

Silence.

She looked towards the table and froze. The woman she had been talking to only moments before was foaming at the mouth, eyes wide, her right hand clasping her throat. With her left she was pointing at the food, even as the breath inside her stopped. With a jerk she fell forwards onto the table, and was still.

Clio screamed.

She looked at Melissa and then back at Jocelyn and then screamed again. Because she was alone with blood and bodies and a mad murderer was on the loose. She knew only one thing. She had to find her friends now, before one of them became the next victim.

SATURDAY – 8 P.M

TEN HOURS UNTIL THE POLICE CAN COME

Two dead bodies

SATURDAY — 8 P.M.

TEN HOURS UNTIL THE POLICE CAN COME

10

JEANIE

In the shed, the hand over Jeanie's mouth smelt of cake, which was a bonus as Jeanie had only one plan – to sink her teeth into the fingers that were clamping her lips shut. She heard a squeal, and followed up by unleashing her elbow into the ribs of her assailant before spinning around, holding both her hands up, ready to fight.

'*Merde alors.*' A bulb flickered on above her head and she saw that it was Henri, the chef, his green eyes wide and staring. 'What did you do that for? Are you mad?'

'Because you grabbed me.' Jeanie wasn't about to apologise. 'What did you expect me to do?'

He gave a shrug. 'I was trying to save you from the killer.'

Jeanie's mettle was up. 'You might *be* the killer. You looked pretty angry earlier when you were throwing the canapé plates on the table.'

'Just because you're angry, doesn't mean you kill someone.' He lowered himself onto a rusting bucket, pushing his floppy hair impatiently out of his eyes. In the dim light of the shed she could see round white cake boxes stacked up high around him, tied with thick red ribbon.

'Why would I kill Valerie anyway?' He flung his arms wide. 'She was my boss. My – how do you call it?' He snapped his fingers, searching for the English word. 'My meal ticket?'

'Your meal ticket? Was she?'

He slumped forwards, staring at the ground. 'Now she is dead, I have no idea what will happen to me. I trained with her over in the States, you see. I have never worked for anyone else – I have no idea how to do things differently.' He puffed his cheeks out as he exhaled, resembling a little boy who had spent all his pocket money on football stickers and still hadn't got the one he wanted.

'You can get another job, surely?'

'Yes, but, starting again. You know? It's hard.' He sighed. 'At the bottom of the pile.'

Jeanie wondered if he was only telling her this to get her on side, to put her off the scent, as any good killer would do. 'Well, at least you've got a load of cakes to eat.' Jeanie reached for one of the boxes, balancing the white cardboard on her hand and opening it before he could stop her. Inside she saw a round cake, the edges smooth beneath cream icing, a tiny red rose in the centre.

'*Non*, don't touch that!' Henri leapt forward, trying to grab it but only succeeding in knocking it out of her hand. It fell to the floor, the box splaying open, the cake toppling downwards until it was skewered by an old fence post lying near the wall of the hut.

'Oh, sorry.' Jeanie ran over and knelt on the floor by the cake, trying to scrape it all up with her hands. Trust her to break it – there had been a reason she was always picked last for rounders in school. 'I'm sure we can make it look okay again. I mean, it's all about flavour, not style, isn't it? *Wabi-sabi*? Isn't that it?' She was babbling now, the events of the evening finally catching up with her. What was she doing in here, alone with countless lethal gardening tools and a potential killer? No walkie-talkie was worth this.

He was staring down at her, his face pale.

She filled the silence. 'I mean.' She picked up a chunk of cake, plonking it on top of another section to create a lopsided half-moon. 'Look. It's gorgeous! Whoever's buying it will never know what happened.' She accompanied this lie with some frantic attempts to smooth the icing down, succeeding only in making it look as uneven as the waves that had crashed against the rocky promontory as they approached the island.

Slowly, Jeanie realised that something was obscuring her view. She blinked and then gave an enormous sneeze. There was white powder flying all around her – landing on her arms, her face, her clothes. It reminded her of her last baking session with the twins, when Yumi had jumped on the icing sugar packet at the end and the entire kitchen had gone full snow globe.

But something told her this wasn't icing sugar. The expression on Henri's face said it all.

'Oh *merde*.' His mouth was a tight line, his eyes narrowed. 'What did you have to do that for?' He took a step towards her. She could see a vein throbbing in his temple and he was clenching his fists. Jeanie was in trouble. She stood up and grabbed the nearest thing she could find. She faced him, holding up a particularly pungent fishing net.

'Henri. Whatever this is, I promise I won't tell anyone.'

'Yes, you will.' He took another step, breathing heavily. 'You will tell those friends of yours – of course you will. Don't lie to me.'

Okay, this was bad. Jeanie took a breath. The fishing net was flimsy at best but she might get in a good swipe at his head if she was quick enough.

She tried to pacify him first. 'Look, Henri. I really won't tell anyone, okay?'

He took another step, before his face crumpled and – to her surprise – tears started rolling down his cheeks. He sank down onto the rusty bucket again. 'It doesn't matter if you do. I am dead anyway.'

'What do you mean?' She kept the fishing net raised. Just in case.

'Because she will kill me. The boss. Now the batch isn't complete. She said, when we set this up, that if the batch isn't complete, she will kill me.'

'Who? Valerie?'

'*Non, non*. Valerie only just found out about all this.' He gestured around the hut. 'That bastard, Ray, he find out what I am doing, that I have an extra – business on the side. I had to put them in his bloody shed when the builders working on the lodges ripped the other one down. And he pulled off the blankets and he found them!' Henri started wringing his hands. 'Inside these cakes, there are little packets – full of more than just sweet treats, yes? I am saving for my own restaurant, you see? I need to make a lot of money for that.' His chin rose defiantly as he tried to justify what he was doing. 'And the Boss, she approached me when I was in town getting supplies. We got chatting, she needed a new business partner – the old one had moved when Valerie bought the island. And here we are.'

'Yes. Here we are.' Jeanie looked at the white powder now settling onto the tools, the folded-up table in the corner, the leaf blower.

Henri's brows lowered. 'And of course Ray wanted me to give him some.'

Jeanie's head was whirling. 'He wanted you to give him some cocaine?'

'Yes.' Henri's eyes flashed. 'He is an addict, you see. So then he was in my face, every day, saying that if I don't give him some he will tell Valerie. And I say no, so...' He gave a shrug. 'So he tells her before she even came here. Text message? Zoom? I don't know. But she was still in the States so what could she do? She needed me to set up the kitchens for the launch.'

'And then what happened?'

'So, I thought Valerie knows and everything is okay, and I carry on. I work in the kitchens, and then in my spare time I package up the drugs inside the cakes, I take them to the mainland, I pass them on to my... business partner's people, I make a little extra money.' His mouth twisted bitterly. 'And then today Valerie arrives and she finds me in the kitchen and she tells me I am fired. After all these years together, working for her, cooking with her, doing every little thing she wants, setting up this new place, sourcing suppliers for her, getting the kitchen layout just right.' He was up and pacing now, spit flying as he hissed out his words. 'And the one time I have an idea, the one time I do something for me, she fires me. Poof. Just like that. Like us working together never meant anything at all.'

Jeanie watched him, listening, her heart thudding so loudly she was surprised it was still in her body.

'Did you fight with her?'

'What do you think?' He puffed air out from his cheeks. 'Of course! I argued and I yelled and she said I was ruining the reputation of the la Fontaine brand, but I said I was just trying to make my own little dream come true, just like she had done all those years before. She could never have got started without all the money she brought to the States with her.' He kicked a lawnmower in evident frustration and winced in pain. 'So then I was so angry, I said something I shouldn't have – about the rumours I have been hearing about her.'

'What rumours?' Jeanie slowly took a walkie-talkie from the rack on the wall beside her and clipped it over the belt of her dress. She needed to be ready to run – she sensed he might turn on her at any moment. Silently, she reached for another.

Henri stared at the ceiling. 'The rumours are that she isn't who she says she is. That she is a fake.' Jeanie thought of the snacks up in Valerie's snug. The Twirl and the Yorkshire tea. It fitted. She had the second walkie-talkie secure as Henri continued. 'I have heard the rumours before, for years now, but I never thought much of them. But when she confronted me about the cakes, I had to know that I had some – some power over her. So I asked her whether she was really called Valerie la Fontaine and she went crazy and stormed off. So I decided to pretend she hadn't fired me and carry on working, because I can't stop the cakes. My business partner would not be happy. She is far more terrifying than Valerie. You do not want to mess with the woman who is going to sell what is inside these cakes.'

Jeanie had a funny feeling she knew just who he was talking about.

'It's not Marg Redfearn, is it?'

His eyes widened. 'How do you know?' His hand went to his chest. 'Oh *non*, you don't work for her too, do you?' He got up as if to run.

'No. God, no. Never.' Jeanie shuddered. Marg was one of Amber's acquaintances from her days in the force, and she had become an unofficial ally of the Bad Girls Detective Agency in the past twelve months. She provided information – phone records, autopsy results – information the police would have but would never share with the agency who were their rivals. A spritely seventy-something, Marg dressed like she was about to go to church – all pearls and cashmere V-necks and crisp white blouses, but she was the queen of the Sunshine Sands drugs scene and you messed with her at your peril.

Henri was quaking at even the thought of Marg. Jeanie couldn't blame him. 'Now we are one bag down, she's going to come for me.'

'Not in this weather, she's not.'

'But tomorrow.' He sagged forwards, his head hanging.

'No. It'll be fine.' Jeanie wanted to comfort him. She saw a brush and picked it up. 'We can clean it all up and put it back inside the bag! Look!'

He was looking at her like she was mad. She started to brush, white powder flying around the hut.

'Stop.' He grabbed her arm.

'No, I...'

'Stop, please.' He shook his head. 'I can't get these to the boat, and I can't get them over to the mainland, so I might as well just give up. I'll work it out tomorrow.'

She picked up a third walkie-talkie. She thought of everything he had told her and knew that she needed to find the others. There was a lot to talk about. Henri must be a suspect now – Valerie had fired him and jeopardised his new business working for Marg. He had every reason to want her dead.

She edged to the door.

'I'm just going back to the castle. Do you want to come?'

'*Non.*' He shook his head. 'I will stay here until the storm ends.' He indicated the shattered cake. 'At least I won't get hungry.'

'But it might be dangerous. Out here. All alone.' She opened the door, staggering as the wind hit her.

'It is more dangerous in there.' He gestured in the direction of the castle. '*Au revoir.*'

Jeanie ran back to the castle, heart thumping in her chest at every crack or bang, at every rumble from the skies above her. She kept thinking she could hear footsteps behind her, feel a hand reaching for her, but all that actually pursued her to the side door was the hammering rain. She pulled it open and stood for a second back in the hall, dripping, wiping water out of her eyes. The door creaked shut and the castle whispered and groaned around her. She heard a rattle to her left and sprang around to face whatever or whoever it was, only to see nothing but darkness.

She had to find her friends. A light flickered dimly on one of the walls in the huge reception area, and she tried to get her bearings. Something was skittering along a corridor above Jeanie's head and she found that she was holding her breath.

But standing here wasn't going to achieve anything. She had to find Clio and Amber. The three of them had to start solving this, but more than that she wanted to see her friends, to feel their arms around her, to feel safe.

Frantically suppressing her fear, sensing danger all around her, Jeanie began to push open door after door. One room held a piano and two grandfather clocks. In the next she saw a sofa on sculpted feet, a circle of red velvet chairs and a gilt fireplace that belonged in *Bridgerton*. The next was empty except for a cardboard box by the door.

Where were Clio and Amber? Jeanie looked around frantically as she once again reached the Red Room. Champagne glasses had been left on the mantelpiece and on the windowsill. Plates had been abandoned on the long oak table. All those glorious canapés were now starting to slide and to slump, reduced to sodden puddles and sad smears, as if realising they were never going to be eaten. It was all getting a bit Miss Havisham in here.

Turning, Jeanie fled down another corridor, following the smell of food. She threw herself against the door, running through into a warm room where she bumped into Clio.

'Oh, thank God!' She hugged her friend, holding her tight. It took her a minute to realise that Clio was pushing her away. All Jeanie wanted was to hold on, to keep her close, to feel safe.

'Jeanie.' Clio finally managed to push her away.

Why wasn't she happy to see her? Why was she being so unfriendly? 'Clio?' Jeanie faltered, uncomprehending. 'What's wrong?'

'We have a problem.' Clio wiped her hand across her cheek and Jeanie saw a red stain appear. Red was also spattered across Clio's face and arms and blended into the red of her jumpsuit.

Blood.

'Oh God. Clio. Are you okay?' Jeanie took another step towards her, wanting to check, wanting to get out a plaster and make it all better, to patch it up as she did with the twins. 'Who did this to you?' She glanced around the room, taking in the body slumped on the table. She couldn't hold in a scream. This place. These bodies. This relentless killer.

'What happened?' She took a step towards Jocelyn's body.

Her mouth fell open. 'Has...?'

'She's been poisoned.' Clio's eyes had a manic gleam. 'And whoever did it has attacked Melissa too. Smashed her head in.' She pointed behind the cupboards that ran across the upper level of the kitchen. 'She's alive, but it's her blood on my hands.'

Jeanie put a hand to her head, unable to take it all in. 'So…?'

Her eyes met Clio's.

'Yes.' Clio nodded. 'We're in deep shit.'

Jeanie was reaching for a strength she didn't have. 'It's okay.' She had never sounded less convincing. 'We'll find them. We'll catch the killer.'

Clio nodded. 'Yes. We will.' She swallowed. 'Won't we?'

They both squealed as there was a thump on the kitchen door. Clio ran to the tower of kitchen knives by the hob, grabbing the biggest one she could see and raising it. Jeanie joined her and took one too, gasping as she looked down and saw Melissa propped up against the cupboards, her hair thick with blood, looking around her with half-closed eyes, clearly dazed.

Then the two of them crept over to the kitchen door, waiting either side, ready to trap whoever was about to come in and try to kill them.

11

AMBER

Amber had heard a scream as she was walking back to the Red Room, and she had run towards the sound. She was pretty sure it had come from behind the battered door in front of her and, after the frustrations of her conversations with Kieran, she was more than ready for a fight. She squared her shoulders, and threw herself at the door. It swung open, helped by two people on the other side and Amber found herself running headlong towards a table with what looked like a dead person on it.

Oh no. It really was a dead person.

'What the...?' She scrabbled to a stop, looking around wildly, trying to get in position to fight whoever had killed them. She turned back and saw two kitchen knives glinting.

'Oh no you don't!' She was about to fire herself towards them, but slowly her brain registered that it was her two best friends holding the knives.

'It's okay, Amber. It's just us.' Jeanie and Clio put the knives down on the table and held their arms wide. Breaking a lifetime tradition, Amber dived into them, feeling safe for the first time since she had found Valerie dead. Here they were. Her family. They could all go back to normal just as soon as... Her eyes fell on the corpse, sitting in a wheelchair, face-down on the table and she was jolted back into reality.

'What happened?' She drew Clio and Jeanie down onto a long brown settee that was tucked into the kitchen alcove, beneath a cork board covered in receipts and old shopping lists written in a scrawling hand. She looked at the body again. Grey hair flung across the table, a hand reaching. 'Is that Jocelyn?'

'Yes.' Clio's fingers were shaking in hers. 'I was in here – when it happened. She ate the food.' She pointed at the casserole dish on the table. 'And then I turned my back and when I turned towards her again, she was dying. The food was poisoned!' She put a hand to her belly. 'I had a tiny bit of the bread. Do you think I'll be okay?'

'Of course you will.'

'How do you know?' Clio's eyes were wide. 'I think I feel a bit queasy.'

'You'd feel a whole lot more than that if it was poisoned. How quickly did Jocelyn feel the effects?'

'A couple of minutes.' A tear rolled down Clio's cheek. 'It was horrible.' She swallowed, fighting back tears.

'I'm sorry, Clio.' Amber put a hand on her friend's arm.

'I'll be fine.' Clio flapped her hands in front of her face, as a tear rolled down her cheek. 'I'll get it together.' She took a long breath, clearly trying to regroup. 'Jocelyn did tell me something though. Just before – you know.' She glanced at the body and then away. 'She was eating and she was telling me that she'd seen Melissa arguing with someone, but she couldn't see who. Something about not getting her fair share?'

An American accent cut in. 'Well, that's a load of horseshit.'

Amber stiffened. 'Melissa?' She peered under the table but couldn't see her anywhere.

'Over here.' A hand waved above the counter top.

'Melissa was injured before we got to the kitchen.' Clio was shaking, words bubbling out of her. 'Someone hit her over the head. I found her while Jocelyn was eating so I was distracted, you know, checking on Melissa, getting her upright, doing what I could for her. She's still really woozy.'

'I'm doing a bit better now.' Melissa appeared above the cupboards, her attempt at a smile revealing a bloodstain on her front teeth. Her immaculate red suit was crumpled and there was blood all over her white shirt. Her dark hair was matted with it, and her eyes were glazed and unfocused. She looked like she had experienced a heavy night at a Halloween costume party. She was less smooth, less hard, less perfect now and Amber felt a flicker of concern as she watched her try to weave her way down the steps. Then Melissa saw Jocelyn and stopped, a hand flying to her chest.

'Oh *God*.' She staggered back, landing against a dresser and sending several plates flying as she tried to steady herself against it. She launched forwards once more, and Amber quickly walked over to take her by the arm and lead her to the safety of a kitchen chair.

'Thank you.' For a moment their eyes met and Amber felt a connection that surprised her. She looked rapidly away.

A shaking Jeanie was staring at Jocelyn lying dead at the table. 'Shouldn't we cover her or something?'

'Of course.' Clio was on her feet straight away. She grabbed an old grey rug from one of the chairs at the end of the table and threw it over Jocelyn, so that nothing was visible except her legs under the table, the cast still on. Clio washed her hands at the sink and sat down next to Jeanie again, putting an arm around her shoulders and hugging her tight.

Amber had so many questions. She looked at Melissa. 'What happened? Who hit you?'

Melissa's eyes were fixed on the floor.

'Melissa?' Amber needed answers now. 'There's a killer out there and we still have no idea why they attacked either Valerie or Jocelyn. Or you. And they might be heading this way, even now.' Jeanie let out a whimper. 'We don't have time to play games. You need to tell me what happened. Who hurt you?'

'That's the bummer. I don't know. I feel so dumb.' Melissa's eyes hadn't moved. 'I've been going over it, and I don't even remember hearing the door opening or anyone coming in. I was getting the food ready for everybody – I know it sounds weird, but I just thought I should try to do what Valerie would have done. She always said that in an emergency you need to keep people fed if you can.' She tucked a strand of hair behind her ear. 'Valerie always leaves food ready for the team, always has stuff in here, so people can keep their strength up. So I came in, heated everything up, chopped up the bread. To be honest, I didn't know what else to do with myself. I needed some thinking time.'

'Your boss has just been killed and you came in here to make supper for everybody?' Amber tried to keep the interrogatory note out of her voice, but it was a challenge. 'Really?'

'Yeah.' Melissa shrugged. 'I'm the manager. I have guests. I have to keep the show on the road, I guess.'

Amber continued. 'So you came in here and heated the food?'

'Yeah.' Melissa picked up on some kind of subtext. 'Why?'

'So you didn't hear what we were talking about just now? Even though you were right there?'

'My ears are buzzing from where my head was hit.' Melissa started nervously twisting one of her rings around her finger. 'I can't really hear that well. Why?'

'Because the food that you heated up was the food that killed Jocelyn.'

'Say what now?' Melissa looked like she was going to cry. 'You can't be serious.'

'She ate the food and then she died.' Amber put her head on one side. 'It's a pretty clear link.'

'And you think I did that? On purpose?' Melissa's voice was rising now. 'But all I did was heat it up. That is literally it. Nothing else. So how could that... poison someone?'

'Well, either the poison was already in there, meaning Valerie or anyone on the staff could have put it in, or someone added it after she'd finished cooking, or...' Amber stopped, realising where she was going.

'Or I poisoned her?' Melissa's face shut down. 'Seriously? Why would I poison a guest in the luxury retreat that I am the manager of? And did I kill Valerie too? Is that what you think? Because what do I get out of that?'

Amber played her trump card. She pulled out the envelope that she had found in the desk earlier when she was with Kieran. 'Well, Jocelyn did see you fighting with someone – it could have been Valerie. And I found out that you are going to get the whole estate now Valerie's dead. It's in her will.'

'What?' Melissa froze. 'What are you talking about?'

Amber held up the envelope. 'It says so, right here. You are the sole beneficiary.'

'What the hell are you doing with that?' Melissa grabbed for the envelope but Amber was too quick for her.

'No way, Melissa. I'm keeping this.'

Melissa put her hands on her hips. 'What right do you have?'

'Every right.' Amber swallowed. 'I have every right, given that this is valuable evidence and the police have asked me to take the lead here.' Speaking of the police, she had to get up to the snug to use the landline and report the second body soon. Just a few more minutes. 'Now, are you sure you can't remember anything?'

Clio spoke fast. 'Maybe someone came up behind you? You could have seen someone reflected in the window, maybe?'

'I told you. I saw no one.' Melissa sighed. 'One minute I was doing the food, the next I was waking up on the floor with Clio staring at me.' She took a deep breath. 'I'm sorry. I've got nothing.'

'Damn.' Amber felt a kick of frustration.

'Why do I get the feeling you don't believe me?' Melissa managed to get up onto her feet. She swayed a little, grasping Amber's shoulder for a brief second, then letting go. 'This has all gone so wrong. I should never have brought you here.' She walked towards the door.

Amber exchanged confused glances with Clio and Jeanie.

Clio's voice rose. 'Brought us here? What do you mean? We won a competition.'

'And who do you think made sure that you won it?' Melissa put her hands on her hips. 'Who put that competition leaflet through your door, Clio? Yours truly here, that's who.'

'Why would you do that?' Clio's mouth hung open. 'Why us?'

Melissa's eyes met Amber's. Her mouth hardened. 'Honestly? I'm not sure. But either way, I don't think I want to stick around here with people who think I might be lying to them.'

Jeanie spoke fast. 'Melissa. It's dangerous out there. You should stay in here.'

'No way. I see what you think of me – that I might have killed Valerie. My colleague. My friend. A woman I've worked with for a decade – starting in the US and now here. You think that I would kill her for an inheritance?' Melissa put a hand to her head. It came away bright with blood. She swayed for a minute but then straightened again. 'If only you knew.'

Jeanie put a hand on her arm. 'If there are things we don't know, then tell us, Melissa.'

Melissa shook her head. 'I'll save my breath. Think I'll go and round up the others instead.' Her fingers were on the door handle.

'Come on, Amber. At least try to persuade her.' Clio's elbow dug deep into Amber's ribs and she knew what her friend wanted her to do – to talk to Melissa, to persuade her back inside to safety.

Amber ignored her.

She couldn't do it.

The door shut behind Melissa and Amber told herself it was for the best.

12

CLIO

Clio felt a pulse of frustration.

'Melissa shouldn't be out there on her own, Amber.' Clio couldn't even look at the blanket covering Jocelyn's body now. 'Anything might happen to her.'

Amber sat down on the sofa again, her face setting into stone. 'She chose to leave. What can we do about it?'

Anger prickled inside Clio. 'You getting that will out didn't exactly help matters.'

'It's evidence, isn't it?' Amber gave an exasperated sigh. 'Come on, Clio. We have to work on the little that we've got here – and the will might be a factor in Valerie's death, mightn't it?'

Clio gave up. With Amber in gladiator mode there was no choice, especially with two corpses in the building. She had been the same at school – Clio could remember Amber almost visibly donning a shield and helmet as she faced the headteacher's censure for her latest misdemeanour. Back then, when Take That were the pin-ups *du jour* and 'Wash n'Go' had been all the rage, Amber had been a wild child, a rebel without a cause. She had been known for her one-word replies, her commitment to Marlboro Lights and for climbing every tall building in Sunshine Sands, every pylon, every tower. Then Jeanie's dad had intervened, gently pointing out that she had better options than going to prison at twenty.

Luckily, Amber had listened to him and her police career had been the result. But she certainly wasn't listening to Clio now.

'Right.' Amber sprung to her feet, looking around the kitchen. She walked over to a jam jar containing a variety of coloured chalks, before striding to the huge blackboard that was nailed to the wall by the kitchen door. It contained what looked like a shopping list – artichokes, herbs, bin bags. Amber wiped it clean before turning, tapping her chin with the chalk, a gesture Clio had seen before. She was about to summarise where they were with the case so far, to outline what they had worked out.

The chalk left a mark on Amber's chin, but Clio decided not to point this out.

Amber took a deep breath. 'Let's try and establish a timeline.' She started to write. 'At 5.30 p.m. we were all in the drawing room having drinks. Everyone was in there to say happy birthday to me, yes?'

Jeanie nodded obediently. 'Apart from Henri, who had disappeared towards the kitchen. Meaning he could have poisoned the food?'

'Got it.' Amber added this to the board.

Clio's gaze snagged on the blanket covering Jocelyn. It was freaking her out.

'Do you think we could – talk somewhere else? Jocelyn is giving me the creeps.'

'Let's just make it quick.' Amber indicated the board. 'We need to get some facts down and this is perfect.'

Clio felt a kick of frustration. Amber hadn't seen Jocelyn die, seen her eyes widening, seen her fighting for breath. She walked around and sat on the edge of the table, with the body behind her.

Amber turned back to the board, writing times on the left and events on the right. 'Then Valerie went up to her snug, I headed upstairs for about quarter of an hour – just finishing off some agency stuff, you know.' She coloured, putting a hand to her forehead. 'Jeanie followed me up and I found Valerie dead.'

'Yes.' Clio nodded.

Amber continued. 'So, within those fifteen minutes someone went to

Valerie and killed her by hitting her over the head, several times by the look of it.'

'Yes. Probably with that big vase we found.' Jeanie was on her feet now, twirling a curl between her fingers as Amber added this to the board. 'And the suspects were all over the place.'

'Yes.' Clio folded her arms. 'So how do we start narrowing down who did this?'

'We just have to go stage by stage. A pattern will emerge, I promise.' Clio hoped that Amber was as confident as she sounded. 'And there are a lot of questions to answer. Like, why was there a knife on the floor? Do you think she tried to defend herself? Same goes for the smashed wine bottle. And then how did the killer get back down again without meeting me coming up?' Amber was tapping the chalk against her chin again. The rainbow beard suited her. 'God this is hard without the internet. It would be really helpful to have some kind of background on the guests – to start working out the connections.'

Clio flung her arms wide, frustration and fear pulsing through her. 'How are we going to solve this? We haven't got enough information on anything. Or anyone.'

Amber frowned 'Well, we know about the will. And I found out that Kieran was bugging her – he had a recording device hidden in her desk. That second article he was talking about – I think it's an exposé.'

Jeanie's eyes widened. 'Henri did say there had been rumours about her.'

Amber's eyes narrowed. 'What kind of rumours?'

'That she isn't who she says she is.' Jeanie gasped, her hand flying to her mouth. 'Maybe he killed her because she was on to him? Or she tried to kill him to keep him quiet, but he lashed out first?'

'Or Melissa killed for the money.' Amber started scribbling on the blackboard again.

Clio wasn't convinced. 'Why are you so sure it's her? Why would Melissa make sure we won a competition to come here – three detectives, no less – if she was just planning to kill Valerie while we're staying at the castle? That makes no sense.'

Amber pulled a face. 'If she did ensure we got here, that is. We don't know that's true.'

Clio threw her hands up in frustration. 'Well, we don't know anything really, do we?' Amber ignored her, turning back to the board, adding two new columns, with names and possible motives on it.

Amber turned to Jeanie. 'Tell me more about Henri. What did you find out?'

'Oh yes!' Jeanie grimaced. 'Well, I was in the shed getting the walkie-talkies. And Henri was there, packing up a shipment of cocaine.' She watched them, eyebrows arched.

'What?' Even Amber looked surprised.

'You heard me.' Jeanie nodded. 'Turns out he works for your friend Marg, shipping her batches of cocaine inside freshly baked cakes. They set it up when he arrived here – he took over from someone else, apparently, who moved on when Valerie bought the castle.'

'No way.' Clio was starting to feel like she was letting the side down. All she had managed to find out was how long Jocelyn took in the loo.

Amber shook her head, an admiring expression in her eyes. 'So THAT'S how Marg is doing it at the moment. Bloody hell, she's smart. A stopping off point here, to avoid detection when she ships in from France.' She gave a low whistle. 'Did Valerie know about it?'

'Henri said she had just found out.' Jeanie shrugged. 'Ray sussed out what Henri was doing and told Valerie when Henri wouldn't give him any cocaine – he's an addict, apparently. Valerie fired Henri earlier today.'

'Wow.' Amber leant against the wall, thinking. 'Okay, so we've got several potential motives here. Henri killing Valerie to protect his drugs sideline and his job. Melissa killing to get the castle, Kieran lashing out when she found out about his dodgy recordings.' She paused. 'Or Ray killing her... not sure why. What would his motive be?'

'I don't know.' Clio shook her head. 'He's not the most friendly, but...'

Jeanie piped up. 'How about Angelo? Valerie expected him to sleep in a tent in the storm – maybe that tipped him over the edge?'

Amber pulled a face. 'Not sure. We'd need a lot more on the why, same for Ray.'

Clio cut in. 'But Jocelyn did say that Melissa had an argument with someone. About money. So maybe that? And she could have poisoned the food. So those are reasons for Melissa to do it, I suppose.'

Amber finished writing this all on the board. She turned to them, her face perplexed.

'That's a long list. Everyone alive is a suspect, apart from us.'

'Yes.'

Amber stretched her arms above her head, and Clio heard a distinct click. 'Could we maybe get somewhere on timings, then? Especially if it was a member of staff, why kill her now?'

'Maybe they wanted the storm as a cover for what they were doing. They would have known that the police wouldn't be able to come, and no police means they have time to hide what they've been up to.'

'True.' Jeanie came and perched next to Clio, leaning her head on her shoulder. 'But the fact remains they must have been incredibly fast. How did they get all the way down from the snug without anyone seeing them? And how did they leave it locked on the inside?'

'Valerie must have let them in.'

'But then how did they get out?' Jeanie sighed in frustration.

Clio thought fast. 'Could they have climbed down the tower from the snug?'

'Unlikely.' Amber scratched her head. 'It's at least thirty metres high and it's hard climbing. I had a look when we were up there.' She made a face as the other two stared at her. 'What? I'm a climber, okay? You know that!'

'Weirdo.' Clio rolled her eyes. 'All those ropes and clip-on thingies. Crampons. Weird.'

'Well, I don't like make-up and flouncing around doing jazz hands, but I don't judge you, do I?' Amber's eyes flashed.

Jeanie rolled her eyes. 'Stop it you two. I still wonder about what Henri said – that some people think Valerie is a fake – that she's not who she says she is. So that could be another motive – something to do with who she used to be. Some secret from her past?'

'Excellent work.' Amber finished writing. The board was now full and Clio felt like they were no closer to finding out who killed Valerie and Jocelyn.

Amber pressed her palms together, as if in prayer. 'Now we just need to work out how to narrow down our suspect list. And what the motive was for also killing Jocelyn. Did she see something? Did she overhear someone? Or witness the deed itself? I still have my suspicions about whether or not someone might have been in that huge crate in the corner at some point, lying in wait.'

'Or maybe they didn't just mean to kill Jocelyn?' Jeanie's face paled. 'Maybe they meant to kill...' Her voice became a squeak. 'All of us? Everyone? Including us – as detectives? We were obviously starving given the way we fell on the canapés – the killer would have seen that.'

'Oh God.' Amber swallowed, sinking down next to the two of them. 'You might be right.'

The three of them sat in silence for a moment.

'So what are we going to do now?'

Amber spoke first. 'Walkie-talkies.'

'Oh yes.' Jeanie handed them out, attaching hers to the thin belt around her dress. 'I'm guessing you press the button on top for comms, and say "over" when you're done and this looks like the "on" switch here.' She flicked it upwards and there was a rush of static. Jeanie glanced at Amber, who smiled encouragingly. Jeanie continued. 'I think we need to split up to see what we can find. We can check in with each other every half hour, okay? If one of us doesn't answer then the other two head straight to the Red Room for a rendezvous. How does that sound?'

'Good.' Clio glanced at her friend admiringly. Jeanie had come so far since last year, when she had been so afraid of the world that she had struggled even to take her twins to the park. Now she was leading them all, taking the initiative, brave enough to venture into a killer castle alone.

Clio needed to find her courage too. 'Who's going where?'

Amber exhaled. 'I need to go back to Valerie's snug. The landline phone works in there and I need to inform the police about the second murder.' She turned to them both, eyes serious. 'And why don't you two stick together for now? I think you need to round up all the others and keep them somewhere where there isn't a dead body. Talk to them, see what you can find out. OK?'

'OK.' Clio tried to smile, terror leaping inside her. 'I mean, not good, but it's a plan, isn't it?' She grabbed a piece of paper from the sideboard, and scribbled a note on top.

POISONED. DO NOT EAT.

She left it on the table so no one else would eat the food.

Jeanie's eyes were on the floor. 'I'm scared.'

'Me too.' Clio took her hand. 'But if I have to be trapped on an island in a storm with a killer, then I'm bloody glad I'm with you two.'

'Me too.' Jeanie gave a tremulous smile before reaching across and brushing the chalk dust off Amber's chin.

'Ready?'

'Ready.'

The three of them headed out into the whispering darkness of the castle. Just as the kitchen door swung shut behind them, a sound echoed down the hall.

It was a gunshot.

13

JEANIE

'What on earth...?'

They all turned and ran in the direction of the gunshot. Once upon a time Jeanie would have moved hell for leather in the opposite direction, but now she was different. Her husband, Tan, sometimes said how much she had changed since she had started working for the Bad Girls Detective Agency, but increasingly Jeanie felt as if she was just coming into her own. As she ran side by side with her friends, she felt the adrenaline pumping through her. She was scared, yes, but it was more important to do what she could to catch this killer, to save lives by stopping whoever it was from killing anyone else.

They were rounding the corner at the end of the long corridor now. Another one opened up, a long red carpet running down the middle, decorated with huge whirling blossoms in gold. The shot had come from the far end, Jeanie thought, where the light was so dim she could barely make out a distant figure there who appeared to be holding a rifle.

'*Stop right there.*' Amber sprinted straight for the shooter. Jeanie wanted to pull her back, to save her, but Amber was too fast.

'*I said stop.*' The figure at the end of the hall turned at the sound of Amber's voice. Jeanie saw dark hair. Wide, terrified eyes. White knuckles clenched around the long barrel of a rifle.

The shooter spoke. 'Don't come closer, I...'

Jeanie knew that voice. She launched herself at Amber, grabbing her by the leg and refusing to let go. Flailing, Amber fell forwards as a bullet pinged against a light above her. Clio dropped down beside them, breathing heavily.

'Jeanie. For God's sake. Let go! She's going to kill us all!' Amber swiped at Jeanie's hand but Jeanie clung on. She had stopped her twins from their regular attempts at starting World War III – keeping hold of Amber was easy.

Melissa spoke again, staring dully at the rifle in her hands. 'Oh my God, I'm so sorry. I thought I knew how this thing worked, and...' Her hair was dishevelled, the blood smearing her face. 'I didn't mean to do that. I just thought...' She lifted the barrel towards Jeanie.

'Melissa?' Jeanie's mouth was bone dry. 'Can you put the gun down please?'

'I'm trying.' Melissa appeared locked in position, her hands gripping the rifle. 'But it's got this – strap, thing, and...' She grimaced. 'Man, it's annoying. I think my hair is caught in it, or something.'

Amber got to her feet. 'Let me help you. I know— Woah.' She held her hands up as Melissa swung the rifle towards her.

'Can't. Get. My. Hair out.' Melissa was grappling with the strap, her face contorted.

'Why the hell have you picked up a gun?' Amber reached for it again. 'Let me help. You're going to strangle yourself at the rate you're going.'

Melissa was practically crying as she tried to free herself. 'I don't need your help.'

Amber put her hands on her hips. 'Yes, you do.'

Melissa gave a sob. 'Okay, okay.' She gave up on disentangling herself. 'Look, I'm sorry. I just thought I should come and get one of these to... to protect us all. You know?'

'Well, it's going well so far.' Amber couldn't keep the impatience from her voice.

'Well, maybe I'm not as good at this being stuck in a murder hell castle thing as you are.' Melissa swung the rifle towards Clio, who flinched away.

'Enough.' Amber held up a hand. 'Stay still, Melissa. You're going to kill someone.'

Melissa obeyed and Amber undid the strap, teasing it away from Melissa's hair. She then aimed it towards the ceiling while removing the cartridges, tucking them away in her pocket before propping the gun against the wall. Jeanie got up and tiptoed closer. It was an old hunting rifle by the look of things, like one that Jeanie had seen in an episode of *The Crown* last year.

Amber was now examining the cupboard behind Melissa. It was made of dark wood, and rose to head height, with five rifles on show through the open door.

She turned back. 'You didn't think it might be important to tell us about this gun store, Melissa?'

'No.' Melissa's voice shook. 'In fact, I wanted to keep it a secret, so the killer wouldn't know about it. Imagine what they could do with all these?'

'So you just came here by yourself instead?' Amber pinched her forehead with her thumb and forefinger, visibly fighting to restrain her irritation.

Melissa's expression was sullen. 'Yes.'

'You came here and *took out a rifle*? And then fired it?' Amber shook her head. 'Way to tell the killer that there are weapons in the house.'

'She didn't mean it, Amber.' Jeanie thought her friend was being a bit harsh, even by her standards. Anyone could see that Melissa was barely keeping it together.

Melissa muttered at the floor. 'Look, I didn't mean to fire it.'

'That's what you say.' Amber appealed to Jeanie and Clio. 'For all we know you were causing a distraction while someone else is killed.'

'What?' Melissa's eyes flashed. 'Are you kidding me? Like I said, I thought it could help protect us all while you guys figure out whatever the hell this is. Especially as you're hellbent on proving it was me.'

Amber's mouth twisted. 'Well, given what just happened you seem to be trying to prove it was you as well! You just shot at us!'

'I didn't think it had ammo in it. It's meant to be kept separate from the guns – I had no idea the rifle was loaded. It was an accident! I told you.' Melissa slumped down onto a chair.

Jeanie approached her. 'And are there any guns missing?'

Melissa wiped a tear from her cheek. 'No, thank God.'

'So there are how many, normally?'

'Six. Five in there plus that one against the wall.'

'So you say.' Amber glanced at Jeanie and raised an eyebrow.

Melissa's eyes flashed. 'I've had enough of you accusing me of being the killer.'

'I didn't. God, you're so sensitive.' Amber reached down and picked up the empty rifle. 'Listen, I have to get to the snug to call the police about the second murder. And yes, I have a firearms licence and yes, I am an excellent shot.' She hesitated. 'Lock the cupboard up so no one can see the guns. We don't want the wrong person getting their hands on them.'

She disappeared around the corner and Jeanie heard her footsteps echoing as she headed for the stairs.

'She really hates me, huh?' Melissa stood up to shut the cupboard door.

Jeanie wanted to make her feel better. 'She's like that with us quite a lot of the time.'

Melissa paused, padlock in hand. 'Why do you work for her then?'

Jeanie looked at Clio and they shared a smile. 'Because she's the best.'

Clio nodded. 'Crabby, but the best.'

Melissa bit her lip. 'Valerie was like that.' Tears glazed her eyes. 'Not perfect, but a damn good boss.'

Jeanie took her arm. 'Then I'm sorry she's gone.'

'Me too.' Melissa sniffed and Jeanie held out a tissue.

'Thanks.' Melissa wiped her eyes.

Jeanie spoke gently. 'Valerie must have been a fan of yours, leaving everything to you in her will.'

Melissa shrugged. 'Maybe. But given the financial situation at Chateau la Fontaine, it might prove a mixed blessing.'

'What do you mean?' Jeanie looked into those bright brown eyes. 'What situation?'

Melissa held the padlock with trembling fingers. She was just opening her mouth to say more when there was a loud crash from the room next door.

'What was that?' Clio reached for Jeanie's hand.

'I don't know.' Jeanie squeezed her fingers. 'But we need to find out.'

Amber was out of sight now and Jeanie felt a jolt of fear for her. Then she steadied herself. She had to believe that her friend would be okay. The three of them had their walkie-talkies. They had each other. They would survive this.

Melissa unhooked the padlock and grabbed another rifle. 'I don't care what Amber says, I'm taking this.' She swung the barrel in their direction and they both ducked.

Jeanie saw that something about Melissa had hardened. The set of her mouth reminded Jeanie of Amber on the days she did the company accounts.

Jeanie glanced at Clio before tentatively reaching for the rifle. 'Let me have it, Melissa. I can go in first. I have more experience of life and death situations than you do.'

Melissa's eyes narrowed. 'So you don't trust me either?'

'I didn't say that.' Jeanie blocked her path. 'But...'

Melissa shook her head. 'Look, Jeanie. You seem like a nice lady but get out of my way.'

Jeanie stood her ground, Clio beside her. 'Melissa...'

'I said, get out of my way.' Melissa's chin rose. 'I'm still the manager here and I need to go and see what caused that crash. And I'm taking the damn gun with me in case the killer is there waiting for me. Okay?'

'Okay, Melissa. Okay.' Jeanie and Clio held up their hands. It was hard to do anything else when having a conversation at gunpoint.

Melissa locked the cupboard and then stalked forwards, rifle held tight, her knuckles white around it. Her footsteps echoed as the wind outside temporarily stopped howling. A door creaked at the end of the hall and they all three froze. Then they walked forwards again, towards the door behind which they had heard the crash.

'The three musketeers, eh?' Jeanie whispered to Clio.

Her friend tried to smile. 'Well, two, anyway. She might still kill us all. She reminds me of Amber before she's had her morning coffee.'

The door was in front of them, with '*The Salon*' painted in gold across its battered black surface. Melissa held up a hand. 'If you could just stay behind me, I can cover us. That is, assuming you're going to insist on coming with me?'

Clio nodded. 'We are.'

'Thought so.' Melissa shook her head. 'Here goes.' She put her hand on the door handle, silently wrapping her fingers around it. The key rattled in the lock. 'Let's do this.' She rushed inside.

Melissa yelled, '*Who goes there?*' as she thundered into the room.

They ran in behind Melissa to find – no one there. A standard lamp lay on its side but the rest of the furnishings in the room were mostly covered in dust sheets. Jeanie saw high ceilings, a red cushion on a golden sofa, floor-to-ceiling shelves full of leather-bound books and a dusty chandelier dangling from a decaying ceiling. The room smelt musty and the floor was covered in dark blue carpet that was clearly popular with the local moth population. A nest of coffee tables had been knocked over by a big red armchair in the corner, lit by a single pendulum lamp.

Jeanie nudged Clio, her hand going to her mouth. 'Over there.'

'What?' Clio blinked around.

Jeanie felt a rush of frustration. 'Clio, will you please get your eyes tested if we're still alive tomorrow? *There.*'

'I've told you a thousand times...' Clio muttered. 'It's the fonts that are getting smaller!'

Jeanie walked over. '*Here.*'

'Oh God!' Finally, Clio saw the body lying with one foot beneath the sofa. Face-down. Arms splayed wide, as if begging for mercy.

'I don't believe this.' Melissa dropped the gun onto the sofa and ran towards him. She knelt down, hair falling around her face as she picked up his arm and felt for a pulse. 'It's Kieran. That crash must have been the killer getting away.' She held his wrist. 'No pulse.'

'That's three dead now.' Clio's voice was tiny as she turned away.

Jeanie stared down at the body. Kieran's blond hair was covering his face and blood pooled around his torso. A gleaming kitchen knife was embedded in his back.

She started to shake and reached for her friend. For a moment she and Clio clung to each other, eyes bright with tears. Then Jeanie found herself walking towards the sofa, searching for clues. She had to keep going, to keep thinking, to keep trying to catch the killer. Yes, this murder had probably happened when Melissa was with them, and no, she hadn't mowed them all down with her rifle, but still, for all Jeanie knew, Melissa could be about to kill them too. She could be in league with whoever had done this. She could be about to turn on them.

Jeanie saw that the rifle was lying on the sofa, where Melissa had left it. This was her chance. She paused, calculating timings, wanting to feel it in her hands, to have some kind of protection, or at least the illusion of it. She crept towards it, hoping she could snatch it before Melissa noticed. She was so close. One step. Then another. Melissa turned, seeing what she was up to, but then Jeanie's hands were on the rifle and she was holding it high. She felt stronger. More powerful. A woman to be reckoned with.

Melissa shook her head, her lip curling. 'You're just as bad as Amber, you know? You think I'm the killer too, don't you? Even though I was out there with you when this guy died, or when his killer left the room or whatever. Jeez.' She strode to the door. 'And none of you take the time to ask the right questions, you know? You are so keen to find your murderer, and make your agency great again, hey? So you don't ask me who I think might have done it. You don't get my views, even though I've worked for Valerie for a decade. And you don't ask me about how a killer might be able to get around this castle so damn fast, without anyone seeing them, do you?'

Clio stepped forwards. 'What do you mean?'

'Oh, now you're asking.' Melissa put her hands on her hips. '*Now* you want to listen to what I have to say. What a shame you didn't want to do that before now. Before this moment when I am so damn pissed with you both that I'm not going to tell you a goddamn thing. Bad move, ladies.' She wagged a finger. 'Bad move.'

She was nearly at the door now.

'I just can't deal with you two at the moment. I need some space.'

Jeanie moved towards her. 'But there's a killer out there.'

'In this mood, good luck to them if they run into me.' Melissa drew herself up tall. 'Now, I am going to have to lock you in here while I go and figure out what the hell to do. Maybe you can make yourselves useful guarding the body?'

She suddenly ran towards Jeanie and grabbed the gun out of her hands. She was back at the door before Jeanie could react.

'Don't leave us with the body!' Jeanie couldn't keep the pleading note out of her voice.

Clio took her hand, her voice defiant. 'It's okay. We'll just climb out of the window.'

'No, you won't.' Melissa was on the other side of the door. 'Trust me.' She slammed it shut and turned the key.

Clio and Jeanie looked at each other, breathing heavily. Then they ran to the window. Clio wrenched the heavy damask drapes open, only to find the windows were bricked up.

'Shit.' They sprinted to the fireplace, stepping on the twigs and scrunched up paper, gazing upwards. The chimney was bricked up too.

Clio made for the door and grabbed the handle, pulling frantically, all five foot one of her trying to wrench it open. Jeanie joined her and the two of them banged on it so hard her fists started to ache.

The door didn't move.

Jeanie put the gun down and pressed the comms button on her walkie-talkie. 'Amber. Come in. Over.' She blinked as she heard nothing but feedback in reply.

'Amber. Are you there? Over.'

Nothing.

It was Clio's turn. 'Amber – mayday, mayday. Over.'

Silence.

Clio tried again. 'Amber. *Code red.*'

'Clio, it's not code red, it's—'

'*Code red.*'

Clio slumped down, her back to the door and Jeanie stood there, trying desperately to work out what to do. She pressed her forehead with the heels of her hands, trying to stave off all the thoughts that were screaming in her mind. Maybe the killer had got Amber too. Maybe she and Clio were the only ones left. And here they were, trapped in a room with a dead man, and there was absolutely nothing they could do about it.

SATURDAY – 10 P.M

EIGHT HOURS UNTIL THE POLICE CAN COME

THREE DEAD BODIES

14

AMBER

The door to the snug was still bolted when Amber got there, but nonetheless she reloaded the rifle with the cartridges she had stashed in her pocket earlier, and aimed it into the room as she walked cautiously inside. The wind up here was as loud as the dysfunctional speaker at the Christmas panto Clio had been in last year. Even though the castle had been standing for decades, Amber could feel the building being slammed from the north, with trees dancing wildly at the windows and dense clouds scudding across the dark sky. This room was far from a snug now – the fire had long burnt down in the grate, leaving only a chill that was enhanced a hundred times by the dead body at her feet.

Amber only put the rifle down when she had established that she was alone and had shut the door behind her. She looked around, trying to establish if anything had been moved since she was last here. Her eyes scanned the sofa, the sideboard, the coffee table. Everything seemed the same. Valerie's body was still in its prone position, the wine chest was still locked shut and the windows were closed.

She checked her watch, returning to her original reason for being in here. She walked over to the corner and picked up the landline phone, ready to call the police as she had promised her friends she would. She needed to tell them about Jocelyn, and to ask them how to proceed. She held the heavy receiver to her ear, winding the long cord around her gloved hand, recalling a thousand teenage calls to Jeanie and Clio as she did so. Calls about homework, about dull part-time jobs with terrible bosses and about who was wearing what to the end-of-year disco.

It took her a second to realise that there was no dial tone.

'No way!' She put the receiver down and picked it up again, just to check, her heart rate rising as she still heard nothing. She pulled the phone cord towards her, to see if it had come out of the wall socket, only to see that it was still attached. Someone must have cut the central phone line, wherever the hell that was located.

Amber stood for a moment, feeling hope draining away. They now had absolutely no way of communicating with the outside world – no way of letting the police know that the killer had struck again, no way of calling for help. They were on their own.

Amber gripped the gun in both hands. At least she had a weapon. At least she could protect herself and her friends. She stiffened, feeling the hairs rise on the back of her neck. Was someone in here, even now? Were they watching her? She swivelled round fast, searching the room. Maybe someone was hiding behind the mannequin in the corner. Amber walked over to prod it in the chest, just in case it contained a human with murder on their mind. The mannequin toppled over, breaking in two against the wall on its way down, landing on the wine chest. Nobody in there, then. Amber exhaled, shaking her head. She was being ridiculous. Paranoid.

She had to seize control, somehow. She had her brain. And her friends. The three of them could conquer anything if they worked together. They had caught killers before, so they could do it again, even when the odds were stacked so high against them.

Amber sat down on one of the armchairs by the fire, drumming her fingers against the velvet, thinking quickly. She forced herself to stop, to breathe, to focus. All they had to do was follow the evidence, starting right now.

She knew what she had to do. She walked over to the table in the corner, pushing the useless phone aside, before starting to search through the folders stacked beside it. She would know what she was hunting for when she found it. She rifled through receipts and nail files, running through the suspects in her head. For now, Melissa and Kieran were definitely the most suspicious of the candidates. Kieran knew too much about Valerie, and she had clearly been extremely unhappy to discover him in her castle. Looking at this room, at the smashed glass and the knife, it seemed perfectly plausible that Kieran could have argued with Valerie and things had got out of hand. Maybe he had tried to blackmail her, she had refused, and then she had gone for him with a knife to protect whatever secrets he had discovered?

And then there was Melissa. Something about her verged on the unhinged, and again, she had a clear motive for killing Valerie: money. Yes, she had a head injury, but she could have inflicted that on herself somehow, perhaps to deflect attention. And the way she had got that gun out just now had reinforced Amber's impression that Melissa could be a killer.

Amber kept hunting through the folders as she thought. The second yielded very little – receipts from a Parisian boulangerie, a drinks bill from a hotel in London, some Post-its and an old Broadway theatre programme.

Amber opened the next. She found empty envelopes in all shapes and sizes, ancient biros, and a nail file. Underneath it, she discovered a half-eaten Galaxy bar, melted together with an open mascara wand and what looked like an antique ear plug. Clearly everything had just been dumped in here for Valerie to sort through at a later date, which now would never come. As she picked up another folder, Amber glanced over at the chest and saw that the mannequin had landed on the padlock. It had also cracked it open.

She leapt to her feet, grabbing the rifle and cocking it. She strode over to the chest, pulling it open, her gun half-raised ready to stop the killer from coming for her if somehow they were hiding inside. Logically, she knew they couldn't be in there – it was padlocked for goodness' sake – but these murders were starting to make her question what could be possible. But as she heaved the lid open Amber saw that it was empty. She stared at the empty wooden space, biting her lip. Maybe it could have been the killer's hiding place. But who would have known about it? Who set up Valerie's snug in advance of her arrival?

It had to be Melissa.

Amber knew what she had to do.

She stood up, slinging the gun over her shoulder again, and made for the door. She was so lost in thought that she jumped a mile when her walkie-talkie crackled into life.

'Amber. Come in. Over.'

Jeanie's voice.

'Amber?' Amber's heart clutched, hearing the panic beneath Jeanie's words. She fumbled for the comms button.

Jeanie again. 'Clio, she's still not answering.'

Clio's voice, some distance away by the sound of it. 'Try again. She probably hasn't switched the comms button on.'

Amber spoke. 'I heard that, Clio.'

'Well, good! At least that means you're not dead.'

Amber's heart was thudding. 'What's happening?'

Jeanie's voice rose higher still. 'We just found Kieran. There was a crash, we went in, and we found him. He's dead.'

'What?' Amber reached for the wall, seeking support. One of her prime suspects was dead? Why would anyone want to kill him?

Jeanie was accelerating. 'He was stone cold when we got to him, but we heard a crash in the room where he is just before we went in. It might have been the killer getting away. If we hadn't heard the sound, Kieran could have lain there for hours with no one knowing.'

'How was he killed?'

Clio now. 'You have to say "over," Amber.'

Amber gritted her teeth. 'For God's sake, Clio. Now is not the time.'

'You're the one who's always on about following the rules.'

Jeanie shushed her, and Amber could hear them tussling over the walkie-talkie, despite the fact they had one each. Jeanie won. 'He has been stabbed with a kitchen knife. There's so much blood.' She faded for a moment before another rush of words. 'And Melissa locked us into the room and we can't get out.'

'Melissa did what?' Amber was at the door of the snug now, about to run to them. 'It's okay, I'm coming.' She turned the handle but the door wouldn't budge.

'No.' She tried again. Nothing.

Amber unleashed a volley of swear words as she realised that someone had bolted her in too. Even as she started to fling herself against the wood, she knew it was pointless. She had seen how strong that deadbolt was. She knew that the killer had trapped her securely in the snug so that they could continue their killing spree below.

She tried to open the door again, really leaning into it.

Nothing.

She banged her palm against the wood, knowing there was no point, knowing that there was no way this door was going to let her out. She was well and truly trapped. And she knew that she didn't even have enough cartridges to shoot it down. What an amateur.

She tried to rally herself, to boost the friends she was now unable to reach. 'We need to start thinking laterally. The killer must know something we don't. There must be some secret passages or something leading around the castle – either that or at least two people are working together and have a serious masterplan going on. All we can do is try. Okay? So Jeanie, you stay with the body – make sure no one messes with it or tries to hide it. And...' She thought hard. 'Maybe there's some way out of that room that we don't know about. Because if Kieran was killed, and you didn't see anyone leave...'

Clio interrupted her. 'And the windows are bricked up, so they didn't leave that way.'

Amber's conviction was growing. 'So there must be another way out. Clio, you start pressing every wood panel, turning every handle, pulling every picture off the wall if you have to. Try and find a secret passageway or a trapdoor or something, okay?'

'We're on it, Amber.' Jeanie's voice sounded tiny. 'But what if the killer finds us?'

'They won't.'

'Are you sure?'

'Yes. They won't want to return to the scene of the crime. We're not their targets. We know bugger all.' Amber was, at least, sure of that.

'What will you be doing, Amber?'

Amber didn't want to confess that she was stuck inside the snug, which would hardly improve team morale. 'I'm following my own line of investigation. I won't be long.'

'Okay.' Jeanie sounded about as confident as a four-year-old getting ready for their first day of school.

Amber kicked herself. She should have stayed with them. Coming up here had achieved nothing. She was getting this whole case so wrong. She rested her head against the door, cursing herself. 'You can do this, girls. You've got this. Over.'

'Yes.' She could sense Jeanie gritting her teeth, could imagine her digging her nails into her palms. 'Yes, we have. Stay safe, okay? Over.'

Amber tucked the walkie-talkie back into her belt and stood surveying her prison. She had two urgent questions to answer: Who the hell had locked her in here and how on earth was she going to get out?

It was time to find out.

15

CLIO

Ten minutes later, things were not going well in the Salon. Clio sighed, running her hands over her face, exhaustion threatening to overwhelm her. 'I can't find anything – no passageways, no trapdoors, no nothing.'

'I know.' Jeanie was sitting on the sofa trying not to stare at the dead body on the floor. 'Maybe there aren't any. Maybe the killer slipped out when we weren't looking.'

'Maybe.' Wearily, Clio returned to her task, beginning her second turn around the huge room, tapping carefully against every panel, brick and window she could find. There was no other option – and at least it was a way of filling in the time until Amber got here. Clio had read somewhere online that the last owner had been an eccentric inventor, who had dramatically redesigned parts of the castle when he moved in. Maybe he had included secret tunnels, as Amber suspected? Clio just needed to find the way in. She whacked a particularly ugly gargoyle which was leering at her as he held up the fireplace with unfeasibly muscular arms, but nothing changed. Clio then hit his companion for good measure, but only got some dust in the eye for her trouble.

Of course, it might not be passageways. The killer might simply have hidden cameras all over the castle and might be monitoring them all and picking them off one by one, moving around when they could see that no one would detect them. Just in case that theory was true, Clio raised her middle finger at the ceiling and rotated slowly until it would most definitely have been spotted.

Jeanie was frowning at the bricked-up windows, her arms folded across her chest. 'This is a bit like that TV show, you know.'

'What TV show?'

Jeanie put her head on one side. 'Oh. You know...' She trailed off. Clio knew for a fact that Jeanie reliably fell asleep five minutes into any TV programme, however exciting, and had occasionally been known to snore before the opening credits had finished. Clio couldn't blame her. If Clio had to look after the twins, gorgeous though they were, she would be caffeinated to the eyeballs on a permanent basis.

Clio sighed, wiping her forehead with the back of her hand. She had never expected to be this starving hungry on a gourmet retreat. Thirsty, too. She sat down on an ugly green stool in front of the fireplace, that looked like it had been created long before the Norman Conquest. Her back ached, her mouth was dry and she couldn't find a damn passageway anywhere. She stuck her legs out, kicking a brick in frustration, and wondered what on earth was going to happen to them all.

As she was sinking her chin into her hand, a miracle happened. Slowly, hesitantly, the brick moved. Clio blinked. She had been tapping and knocking for so long that it wouldn't surprise her at all if she was hallucinating. She reached her foot out and kicked it again. This time it swung out, and then a door of about thirty bricks opened, releasing a gush of freezing cold air.

'*Yes.*' Clio punched the air. 'I've found it! I've found a passageway!' She peered inside the black opening but could see nothing. Her elation fizzed away as she realised what had to happen next.

'Oh no.'

'What?' Jeanie was now standing beside her.

Clio grimaced. 'Well, I have to get inside it now, don't I?'

'Oh.' Jeanie peered into the darkness. 'Yes, I suppose you do.'

Clio suppressed an urge to weep. She was scared of the dark. Ever since she had staggered up the cliff the morning after her forty-fifth birthday and found her ex-husband Gary dead by her caravan door, she had found it terrifying. She now had to sleep with a lamp on, much to her embarrassment. Every time she switched it off and told herself to be sensible, she lay imagining all the things that she couldn't see – men with guns or knives all heading in her direction, until she gave up and turned the lamp back on again.

And now here it was – darkness again. She stared dubiously into the tunnel. There was only one way to find out where it went – to work out if the killer could have used it to murder Kieran and Valerie and Jocelyn and escape without detection. Clio had to climb in and see where it led. She checked her phone, only to see that the battery was on 1 per cent. She wouldn't get much torchlight out of that. Jeanie used hers but it only had two.

'You can do it, Clio.' Jeanie squeezed her hand.

Clio inhaled deeply. In for four. Hold for five. Out for six. Repeat.

No. She still wanted to run away screaming.

She steeled herself. 'Right. I'm going in.' The entrance was narrow, to say the least. She cautiously inserted her face, smelling mildew and damp and ancient smoke.

She heard Jeanie behind her. 'Are you okay, Clio?'

No. She wasn't. But she wasn't going to tell Jeanie that. Clio was the smaller of the two of them, so she had to lead the way. Clio pushed and twisted her body, manoeuvring herself inside. She would do this. Her head and shoulders were inside now.

She waggled a foot. 'Push on my feet, Jeanie. Give me a boost to get in.'

'No!' Jeanie sounded horrified.

'Please?'

Jeanie swore. 'But what if the killer's still in there?'

'They won't be.' Clio hoped she sounded more confident than she felt. Her voice sounded weird in here – echoey and disjointed.

'And what do I do, Clio? While you're in there?'

'Look around. Check Kieran's phone for clues?'

'No.' She could hear the horror in Jeanie's voice.

Clio rushed to reassure her friend. 'Or you can just stay there. By the entrance of the passageway. Keeping watch.' Clio wished she could give her friend a hug but she was too busy trying to scrabble forwards. The ceiling of the passageway was low so she would have to stay on her belly for now. She called back over her shoulder. 'And Amber knows what's happening and she's on her way, remember?'

'Oh. Yes. I hope she gets here soon.' Jeanie sounded happier now and Clio could feel her feet being lifted up prior to being pushed. Something ran over her hand, and she bit down hard to stop herself screaming. Then she was pushed forward, hard and fast. Clio banged her head on the roof above her, but carried on, crawling, her eyes adjusting to the dim light. Her tummy pressed against the cold floor, and she followed the passageway forwards, metre by metre. Her groping hands felt the space ahead of her, blocking all thoughts of mice or rats shadowing her in the dark, of beady eyes and twitching whiskers. She had to keep going. She had to help to work this out before they all got killed.

She had no idea which direction she was heading in. Normally her unreliable sense of direction led people to bars that weren't there and that wasn't going to change when she was inside a dark tunnel in the middle of a killing zone. She stopped for a moment, breathing hard, to see if she could hear anything to help her identify where she was. She had joined the tunnel from the east wing, she thought, trying to remember the castle map that she had looked at while waiting for Jocelyn earlier.

There was a breeze coming from her left now – knowing her luck she had taken a wrong turn and was about to exit the tunnel and tumble down into the sea. She shifted her torso around, realising that the space was even tighter over here. Maybe it was just as well that she hadn't eaten much since getting here.

She gritted her teeth and started moving again. She just needed to find out where this led. She inched forwards, the tunnel so small now she felt like she was being inserted into a test tube.

Then she heard it.

Breathing, hard and fast.

Breathing that wasn't her own.

She froze, listening.

It was coming from in front of her.

Actually, not really breathing, more a sustained pant, as if the tunnel was running out of air.

Maybe it was? Clio forced herself to inhale then exhale again. She must think. If it was the killer in front of her, then Clio could handle it. This wasn't her first rodeo. She ignored the tiny negative voice in her head telling her that she was deluded, that she had got lucky in the past, that she was a fool for even being here. She wasn't going to listen to that. She was going to win.

She had two options. The first was to reverse the hell out of here, but this was unlikely to work, given the fact that she was currently wedged into the smallest space she had ever occupied. So it would have to be option two – heading forwards and trying to surprise them. She waited, trying to figure out what the killer was doing.

Because it had to be the killer in the passageway, didn't it? They had probably jumped into the tunnel after killing Kieran, and were biding their time until they could re-enter the castle proper. No one else would be making their way through a teeny secret passage on a stormy night in a castle that now boasted three dead bodies. Clio waited, listening. She had no weapon and could barely see. But she did have long nails and she wasn't afraid to use them.

Most of all, Clio had no choice. Hearing the breathing heading her way she got ready to pounce. Unfortunately her hand dislodged something in the ceiling of the tunnel above her, and whatever it was decided to detach itself and land on her head.

'What the hell?' She tried to flick it away.

Ooops. She realised she had said the words out loud.

Silence in front of her. She could sense the killer thinking. Hesitating.

There was nothing for it. She had to move first.

She launched herself towards them.

16

JEANIE

In the Salon, Jeanie felt a beat of pride as Clio disappeared into the tunnel. There was a scrabbling noise, some light swearing, and then her friend was gone. Jeanie shivered, suddenly feeling very, very alone. The room felt even bigger without her friend. The sparse furniture, the boarded-up windows, the long drapes and the body on the floor were in danger of overwhelming her. She wanted to lie down in the foetal position and wail until someone else made everything better, like the twins did when she forced them to give other kids a turn on the slide at the park.

But Clio was in the passage, doing her best to save them. Amber was in the snug doing the same. Jeanie had to do her part. Licking her dry lips, Jeanie forced herself to walk towards the body. She stared down at the man who only hours before had been eating canapés, drinking champagne and arguing with Melissa. She wondered if he would be pleased with how he had spent his final evening on earth, why he had come in here, whether he had been expecting the attack that came.

Now for the bit she really didn't want to face. His phone. She took a deep breath which completely failed to steady her, and knelt down beside the body. She put on the gloves that Amber had given her and started to go through his pockets. Any information would be helpful, she told herself, before accidentally delving too deep and kneading his left bum cheek by accident.

'Sorry.' She knew he couldn't hear her, but still had to say it. She pulled away, regrouping, well aware that she had to be quick. The killer could return at any moment, perhaps to rearrange the crime scene to ensure their guilt would never be uncovered.

Jeanie bit down hard on her bottom lip, as she started on pocket number two. Damn these bloody jeans he was wearing. They were as tight as her Spanx after a carbonara. She pushed harder, grimacing as she imagined Kieran's horror if for some reason he resurrected himself and found Jeanie with her hand this close to his underwear.

Her fingers encountered a set of keys and she gingerly pulled them out. Then she hit gold as his front left pocket yielded the phone he had been surgically attached to since arriving here. On the sofa it went. The next pocket contained a packet of Mentos, which was nearly empty. For a moment Jeanie was tempted. Her stomach was hollow now and she could do with a sugar boost. Then she laid them on the sofa as far away from her as possible. Not worth the risk.

Now for the small grey backpack that was still hooked over one of Kieran's shoulders. He had landed on top of it, the strap trapped beneath him. Carefully, she lifted his head, only surviving by pretending that she was starring in a late-night crime drama. She extracted the bag, and unzipped the main pocket with shaking fingers.

She saw a sheaf of papers and a laptop. She pulled them out, hoping against hope they would give the clues that the three of them so desperately needed. She prayed that the laptop would be unlocked, but of course it demanded a password as soon as she opened it. Her heart beating fast, Jeanie pressed Kieran's finger to the top right-hand button, but nothing changed. The prompt remained, irritatingly cheerful, demanding a password that Jeanie had no hope of guessing.

Instead, she turned her attention to the papers. There were five A4 sheets stapled together in the top right-hand corner. Jeanie read, her brow furrowing as she processed the title.

The real queen of cuisine? Who knows? Our reporter Kieran Anderson gets up close and personal with Valerie la Fontaine in this exclusive interview.

The margins were covered in handwritten notes, so it was clear the article hadn't gone to press yet. Maybe this was the exposé – the second article, in which Valerie's secrets were going to be revealed.

Jeanie sat back on her heels, reading the words he had written, her eyes racing over the pages. The title alone would raise suspicions, if you knew that Valerie's identity was in doubt.

She tried to make sense of it all. Phrases leapt out at her.

She likes telling extravagant tales about her poor Parisian childhood, yet strangely no family members were available to share their stories about her.

Or:

No records can be found of her ever being at this gourmet cookery school.

It was incendiary stuff, and there was no doubt that it would have blown Valerie's career apart if this ever came out – and Jeanie knew Kieran must have collected proof if this article was about to be published. Maybe Kieran had come here to get the final evidence he needed? Or to blackmail Valerie? And someone had stopped him?

Which pointed to – who? Melissa, maybe? Jeanie exhaled in frustration, putting the article down and throwing her head back. She bit her lip hard and pressed the comms button on her walkie-talkie.

'Amber? Clio? Over?'

Nothing.

She tried again. 'Amber? Clio? Over?'

Nothing again.

She sighed. Then she remembered Kieran's phone and picked it up, extending her arm as far as she could and holding it in front of him until the facial recognition kicked in and the screen glowed into life.

Somehow it didn't feel so bad scrolling through the messages of a potential blackmailer. She started to read. There was lots of chat about nights out, and he had exchanged at least forty messages with a woman called Samantha who clearly enjoyed taking highly personal photos. Jeanie shuddered and scrolled on.

Bingo. She punched the air, seeing exactly what she had been looking for: messages between Kieran and Valerie in which he was threatening to reveal who she really was. Messages in which she was denying what he had found out, then begging, then threatening, before finally agreeing to pay him a set sum per month to stay quiet. So confident was Kieran that he hadn't even bothered to delete the messages.

It was only then that Jeanie's rush of satisfaction started to ebb away. Because Valerie had not killed Kieran. Valerie had been dead hours before he was killed. Which meant... Jeanie sank back on her haunches again. Which meant... what?

She carried on reading the thread, seeing Kieran growing even more confident.

> **KIERAN**
> I know who you really are, SC. How are you going to stop me telling everybody?

SC. The same as Valerie's tattoo! Were these Valerie's real initials? Jeanie put a hand to her mouth. 'Oh my God.' She had done it. She had got the clue that could solve this whole thing. She...

A creak. Jeanie's head jerked up. The door to the Salon was opening. Amber was here at last.

Jeanie shoved the phone into her pocket and turned 'Amber. Hi. I...'

But it wasn't Amber.

Panicking, Jeanie leapt across to the entrance of the secret passageway and dived into it, fighting with all her might to get away, to hide, to stay alive, not to be the next victim on the killer's list.

17
AMBER

The door to the snug still would not budge. Amber indulged in some choice swear words, and then crouched down on her haunches, nursing her hands which were aching from repeatedly banging against the wood.

She looked around the room, trying to focus her mind, reviewing everything she knew about Valerie. If she was going to be stuck here then she might as well make good use of this enforced inactivity. She had a rifle so at least she could defend herself if the killer came to find her. So, seeing as she was stuck here she would focus on finding out more about Valerie. Time to get busy.

Henri had questioned Valerie's identity. Melissa was the sole beneficiary of her will. Angelo was sleeping in a tent on her orders. Kieran was about to expose her, but now he had been killed too. Amber sank down to the ground, seeing if she could think her way to an answer. She ran through their recent cases, seeing if she could find any parallels, but came up with nothing. She put her hands to her temples and closed her eyes, seeking answers that weren't there. The suspects' faces whirled around her head until she wanted to scream.

She got up and strode to the door, rattling the handle in frustration when it still refused to move. She reached down to her walkie-talkie, needing to tell her friends why she still hadn't appeared and saw a red light.

'Shit.' She flipped the switch and the light turned green. She pressed the comms button. 'Jeanie? Clio? Are you there? Over?'

Nothing.

Either her friends had switched theirs off too, or they were both unable to speak. Neither scenario made Amber feel any better. She needed to know what they had found out, whether there were any secret passages, whether they were okay. She threw her head back and shouted in frustration, before stomping over to the table again.

SC. She could focus on those initials on Valerie's wrist. *Come on, Amber.* She started going through the papers again, trying to find something that might explain the initials, becoming increasingly frantic as she found nothing.

With frustration smouldering inside her, Amber tried the door again. No bloody chance. Okay then. Amber put her hands on her hips, scanning the walls carefully, thinking about what she had told Clio to do downstairs. Could there be a secret passage that came in here too? She started to search methodically, starting at the desk and working around the room in a clockwise direction. No brick or painting was left untouched as she pressed every stone and flicked every switch. She moved the fire extinguisher, shifted every single candle out of place, and checked the bricks in the fireplace to see if there was a secret lever or panel lying behind them. After fifteen minutes she came to a halt, sitting on the chest, despair starting to choke her. Then, unwilling to give up, Amber scrambled onto a chair and started pressing the ceiling instead. There had to be a way out.

She pushed until her hands started to ache. And then the solution came to her – she was going to have to climb out of here. With her friends out of comms and no exit, she had no choice. She ran over to the casement window, the Gothic arched frame starting to splinter where the rain had got inside. The window pane was heavy, crossed with iron bars, held in place by a catch that looked like it hadn't been oiled since the late 1800s. She tried to move it, only for the rotten wood to split off in her hand.

'Damn it!' Amber stamped on the ground in frustration, waiting for a hopeful second to see if a secret tunnel would now finally open up beneath her.

Fat chance.

Sighing, she got her Swiss Army knife out and started to take apart the window bolt. She had been an expert at this back in her teens when she had climbed pretty much every building, pylon or crane in Sunshine Sands in her Adidas Gazelles, driving the police and every foster family she had ever had absolutely insane. She had never really known why she climbed – why she felt the need to do it when she rarely took anything from the high-rise flats or the grand houses that she scaled. Instead, she had enjoyed walking through other people's homes, looking at the lives that were not hers, lives with order and stability and a sure knowledge that the place you went to sleep would still be yours in the morning.

Even now, in her static caravan two along from Clio, with a neighbour who liked to play his guitar at 2 a.m. to no one in particular, Amber relished knowing that this was her home. No one could take it from her. She was the one in control now.

Frowning, she dug the screwdriver attachment in deep. The bolt was nearly undone. She looked around, conscious that the killer might join her at any minute. Amber could do a lot of damage with a screwdriver, but the more warning she had the better. She moved the rifle towards her, placing it on the floor at her feet. On her next try, the bolt finally came apart. Now Amber could open the window. She did so, only for the wind to blow so fiercely that it slammed back against her hand.

'Shit!' She put her fingers in her mouth, tasting blood.

Taking more care this time, she leant out into the storm. Her face was soaked in seconds and she jerked backwards as a tree branch did its best to scratch her eyes.

She pulled the window shut, holding it with all her strength as the wind tried to pull it away from her. This was going to be harder than she had thought. The world out there was all wind and rain and Amber could barely even stick her head out of the window without it being blown off.

But there was no choice. The killer had locked her in here and Amber wasn't going to put up with it. She was going to escape. And fast. She was a good climber. A great climber. She just had to trust herself.

Taking a deep breath, she opened the window again and, trembling, got both her feet onto the thick stone sill, holding on to the walls on either side of the window. She inhaled slowly. She just had to reach the turret two metres ahead and then hold on for dear life until she got to the bottom. It didn't matter that it was roughly thirty metres down this tower onto the gravel car park below. It didn't matter that the storm was so strong that it had stopped the entire UK rail and travel network. The police were powerless, but Amber knew she could do this. She was strong. She was capable. She remembered to take her magnesium supplements. She could overcome.

A voice came from the snug behind her, closely followed by the pressure of the barrel of a gun in her back.

'Oh no you don't. Get back down here.'

Amber was so shocked she nearly fell.

'Make one more move and I'll end you.'

Amber cursed silently, weighing up her options.

Then the gun prodding her back made her decision for her. Reluctantly, she turned and climbed back into the room.

She was a prisoner again.

18
CLIO

Clio knew that someone was facing her in the darkness of the tunnel. But Clio had momentum and Clio was going to win.

'Take that!' Still on her stomach, she flexed her fingers in front of her face, doing her best to scratch and slash, but her nails met only empty air. She strained her eyes to see, but it was so dark whoever was in front of her was a blur. Inhuman. A presence rather than a target.

She could still hear the breathing. Clio swallowed her terror, telling herself that she had got this far and no one was going to stop her now. And whoever was in front of her wasn't going to get past her to reach Jeanie. Not on Clio's watch. She swiped forwards again, this time successfully connecting with skin and bone. She heard a gasp of pain. That would show them. She reached forward, finding some hair and tugging it, hard. It felt thin and dry, and a clump came away in her hand.

'What the hell?' A male voice. Deep. Indignant.

Dangerous.

Clio tugged at the hair again, triumph building inside her. She was winning this. She was conquering her fear of the dark and she would overcome this man too. She was mighty. She was...

Wait up.

She knew that voice.

'Ray?'

'Who's asking?'

'Wouldn't you like to know?' She slashed forward again. She didn't care that he was one of the only people here who had no discernible motive to kill Valerie. He was here in the tunnel and that alone was reason to attack. She realised she was baring her teeth.

His words came fast. 'I would actually, so that I can sue you when I get out of here – for grievous bodily harm. Who are you?'

'Clio. And you should know all about GBH, Ray.'

'What's that supposed to mean?' She could hear him moving even closer. She wondered if his elbows were hurting as much as hers.

'I think you know what I'm talking about.' Clio had some grit in her mouth now. Or a mouse bone. Gross. It was all she could do to stop herself retching.

His voice deepened. 'What are you doing in here, anyway?'

'Exploring.' She clenched her hands into fists. In the dark she'd have just as much chance as him of landing a punch. 'I just thought I'd see where the passageway led.' She was starting to sweat. She was becoming genuinely worried she was about to run out of air, and her menopausal fires were beginning to burn. It was probably for the best that it was pitch black in here – she suspected her face was giving off angry postbox right now. She wondered if she should start reversing, if she should try to take him on back in the Salon. One more question first. 'Why are *you* in here, then, Ray?'

Ray coughed. Several seconds elapsed. 'I'm escaping. Someone was chasing me.'

'Who?'

'I don't know. I just saw them in the trees. When I was outside the castle.'

Clio frowned. 'You went outside? Why?'

'I was...' A pause, probably as he made up another lie. '...seeing if the protestors had really gone.'

Clio decided to humour him. 'Okay. And had they?'

'Um.' Seriously, this man didn't know how to think on his feet. 'Their tent was empty. But that doesn't mean anything does it? They might still be around on the island somewhere, waiting to kill the rest of us.'

Clio wondered if in fact Ray was the one planning to do that. Panic began to spiral inside her. She had to get back to Jeanie. She could work out where this tunnel led later.

Ray was talking again. 'Anyway, I heard a twig crack behind me and then someone was after me. So I ran inside as fast as I could, I jumped into the passageway in the Red Room, and here I am.'

Clio leapt on this information. 'So that's where this passageway goes? The Red Room?'

'Yes. It goes all the way from the east wing to the west.'

'And are there are more passageways?'

Silence. Clio could almost hear him thinking. Why was he being so secretive?

'Several.'

'Including one to the snug?'

A beat of silence.

'Ray. Killer on the loose. Tell me.'

'I don't know.'

Clio swore under her breath. She didn't believe him. She was now extremely sure that there was a direct route into the snug, and that the killer was both aware of it and had used it to make their getaway after killing Valerie.

She was about to ask him again, when she heard a sound behind her. A scrabbling. A clatter of stones.

She froze, speaking to Ray in a whisper.

'Ray. Is there another tunnel that connects with this one?'

'I think so.'

Her heart was thundering. 'That's bad news. Because I think there's someone behind me.'

'What?'

'Sssssshhhh. Keep quiet, okay?'

'But...'

'Sssssshhhh.' Ray fell silent as the sounds approached. Scratching, breathing and a lot of sweating by the sound of things. Whoever was behind her was close now, and Clio waited until she judged them to be only a metre away. Then she kicked. Hard. She felt her foot connect with a face.

She kicked a second time and heard a gasp, then silence.

'That showed you!' She turned back to where Ray was. 'Ray? There's definitely someone behind me. Can you reverse?'

Silence.

She crawled forwards, her pulse spiralling.

'Ray?'

Nothing. Blinking, she realised that she couldn't sense his presence any more.

'Ray?'

She heard a sound a few metres ahead of her, a body sliding over stones.

He had done what she asked. Now she could follow him. She could get to the Red Room, then run back to the Salon and find Jeanie and Amber.

But then a hand grabbed her ankle and held on, hard.

Clio froze, terrified. Then she started to struggle, needing to find her way back to her friends. Whoever the new arrival was, Clio was not going to let them stop her.

19
JEANIE

Jeanie hadn't had high hopes when she crawled into the passageway, but she supposed that being kicked in the face was preferable to being killed. She had heard Clio whispering to someone, and had been about to call her name when a foot had connected with her nose. Twice. She felt something spilling down her face, heard the crack as her nose gave way. She reached out and clung on to her friend's ankle, trying to stop her doing it again.

Clio spoke, her voice harsh and scared. 'Whoever you are, I'm going to kick you again if you don't let go.'

'Clio. No! It's me, Jeanie.' Jeanie's nose throbbed and she could feel her energy draining away as quickly as the blood rushing out of her nose. She tried to go into reverse, before remembering that, if she went back into the Salon, she would have to confront the person she had seen coming in, which was about as appealing as being kicked in the face again.

'You don't sound like Jeanie.' She sensed Clio hesitating in the darkness.

'That's because you just kicked me in the face!'

A pause. She braced herself for impact.

'Jeanie? Is it really you?'

Jeanie exhaled. 'Clio. Fancy meeting you here.' God, her nose hurt.

'I'm too bloody terrified for humour.' Clio's voice shook. 'What are you doing in here? You were meant to stay with the body.'

Jeanie found she was laughing, even though it hurt. 'Oh, I just thought I'd come in and get kicked in the face by one of my best friends.'

Still no laugh from Clio. Instead she sounded like she might be crying. 'Oh God, I'm so sorry!'

'It's okay.' Jeanie winced as some dust fell onto her face. She hoped it was dust, anyway.

Clio coughed. 'In my defence, I did think you might be about to kill me.'

'Never.' Jeanie gingerly touched the tip of her nose but it hurt too much. 'No one else will sing the *Titanic* theme tune with me.' She sighed. 'Well, my nose will never be the same again. The twins are going to have a field day when I get home.'

'I didn't know it was you, okay?' Clio's voice was rising higher. The last thing they needed was for her to reach full opera mode and for the whole tunnel to collapse. What a way to go. Dead inside a secret passageway with her best friend's boot print on her face.

Jeanie knew she was spiralling. Maybe she had concussion. Or a brain injury. She struggled for a coherence which had never felt further away. Perimenopause had nothing on this weekend for sheer unmitigated anxiety spirals.

She heard Clio mumbling and scrabbling in front of her. 'God, my elbows hurt. This is like that terrible exfoliating massage I had last month, where I got the trainee and I looked like I'd stuck my whole body in a deep fat fryer.'

Jeanie sighed. 'Well, I'm not exactly looking my best. Who were you talking to before you booted me in the face?'

'Ray.'

'Ray was in here? So he knows about the tunnels?'

'Yes. He told me there were more too. And I reckon there's one right up to the snug, and that the killer used it to get to Valerie and then to escape after killing her.'

Jeanie heard more scrabbling. It was impossible to move in here without dislodging debris. Clio spoke again. 'So that's probably what Melissa was hinting at earlier. When she was saying we should have asked her more questions.'

'I guess so.' Jeanie tried to find a more comfortable way of lying on her stomach. She failed. 'Though it's weird that she didn't just tell us about them.'

'Yeah.' Clio groaned. 'But she was really angry with us. I'm not sure what's going on there. All I know is I need to get out of here. I keep worrying that the killer will shut the doors at both ends and we'll be trapped in here for ever.'

'Oh God.' Jeanie was sure she could hear the skittering paws of a mouse behind her.

Jeanie wished she could see Clio's face, that furrow emerging between her immaculately arched eyebrows, her head tipping to one side as it always had during double science at school. Jeanie wanted to hug her so badly, to give some comfort and maybe receive some in return. A moment of feeling less alone. Of connection.

Clio coughed. 'I think I've just swallowed a piece of gravel. And a bat may have just flown past my head. I think this is officially the worst meet up we have ever had, including that time we went to the park in the rain and a tramp peed in my bag.' Jeanie snorted with laughter as Clio continued. 'And I'm so sorry for kicking you in the face, Jeanie.'

'It's okay.' Jeanie gingerly pressed her nose and regretted it. 'It's a bit less painful than when you hit me in the boob with a tennis racquet on that weird activity camp they sent us all on after GCSEs.'

'You are never going to let me forget that, are you?'

'Unlikely.'

Clio's voice softened. 'Why are you in here, anyway? Did you miss me?'

It was a relief to smile. 'I can't keep away from you, you know that. But I'm actually in here because someone came back into the Salon when I was looking through Kieran's stuff.'

'Shit. Was it Melissa?'

'No.'

'Did they see you?'

'Probably. I didn't stay to find out. I dived into the tunnel really fast. I couldn't think what else to do. They were holding up a weapon and I got spooked and got out of there.'

'What kind of weapon?'

Jeanie shuddered at the memory. 'A huge cudgel or something.'

'Bloody hell. How medieval.'

'Yeah.' Jeanie could still feel her stomach plunging at the thought. 'It was scary.'

Clio's voice rose a tone. 'So who was it? The person who came in?'

Jeanie's pulse rose again. 'It was Angelo.'

'The server guy?'

'Yeah.' Jeanie nodded. 'And he looked dangerous.'

'Wow. I wasn't expecting that.' She heard more scrabbling from Clio. 'God, it's impossible to get comfortable in here, isn't it? Not really designed for kicking back and having a chat, more of an A to B vibe.'

'Agreed.' Jeanie dropped her chin onto her hands.

'So...' Clio sounded business-like again. 'Let me just summarise. Behind us we have a possible killer.'

'Yes.'

'And ahead of us we have a possible killer.'

'Yes.' Jeanie nodded in the dark. 'And right here we have extreme discomfort and bleeding.'

'It's just as I've always said – Saturday nights are overrated.'

Jeanie tried to come up with a positive. 'At least we have each other.'

She sensed Clio's smile. 'True. Even if I owe you one until the end of time for breaking your nose.'

'Even if.' Jeanie nodded.

'Hang on.' Clio sounded like she was clicking her fingers. 'Ray said this tunnel splits in two. So we could take the other fork and escape both of them!'

'Which way?'

'I don't know.' Clio's voice wavered. 'But we need to find out. Because we can't stay here for ever, can we? There's Amber, for starters. She needs us, whether she knows it or not. And my Nina, she's at uni now, but she still needs her mum, whatever she thinks. And your Tan and the twins. We need to take control.' Clio's voice was gaining in strength. 'And we need to do it now, before anyone else dies.'

Jeanie knew her friend was right, but her stomach twisted at the thought of going into any more rooms, seeing any more dead bodies. But what choice was there? She had to find the strength to keep going. With Clio at her side.

She took a deep breath. 'You're right. Let's go. Love you, Clio.'

'Love you, Jeanie.'

Jeanie started to move, before she could question herself further, before her mind could throw up any more barriers. Sometimes it was so busy in her head that it was like a really bad party, with parts of her brain settling in to share their problems, their worries, all the things she was getting wrong. Well, she didn't have time to listen now. She only had room to think about survival.

She moved backwards faster and faster, her dress hiking up so that her bare legs scrabbled against the tiny stones that had settled at the bottom of the passageway. She held her breath as she hit a particularly narrow section. Maybe this was the split in the passageway. She hoped so. There was even more gravel here.

'Are you okay, Clio?'

'Hunky-dory, thanks.' She could hear how gritted her friend's teeth were as they veered left. Or had they? It was so hard to tell in the dark.

Clio gave a sardonic laugh. 'You know, one day I'll tell my grandchildren about this and we'll laugh about the day their gran went on a relaxing weekend away and everyone died.'

Jeanie felt a pang of concern. Clio didn't normally do sarcasm. 'You sound like Amber.'

At the thought of their friend, they both sped up, Clio's feet coming dangerously close to Jeanie's face. Scrambling backwards, Jeanie prayed they had successfully taken the other fork.

She swallowed, her throat dry. 'I don't know if we've found the other tunnel, Clio.'

'Just keep going.'

'Okay.' Jeanie swallowed her fear. They would have to arrive loud and fast and just run at Angelo if he was still there. They could take him. Couldn't they?

Jeanie breathed in and reversed through the opening at the end of the passageway, her legs dropping out onto solid ground. She turned instantly, wiping her hair out of her eyes, hands up to guard what was left of her battered face.

They had indeed failed to take the fork in the passageway. They were back in the Salon. Blue carpet. Golden sofa. Standard lamp knocked to the floor.

On the plus side, there was no Angelo wielding a cudgel. They were safe, for now.

The silence was eerie, until Clio landed too, her face grey with dust and cobwebs. She gave an enormous sneeze. Then she looked up at Jeanie and gave a scream.

'Oh my God, your nose!'

'How bad is it?'

'Um...' Clio came up close, eyes wide with concern.

'Yes?'

'Well...'

'Oh, for God's sake, Clio, just tell me.'

'Do you remember the time Martha Martin was run over by that tractor?'

'In Year 10? Yes.'

'Well, you don't look nearly as bad as that.'

'Great.' Martha had ended up having plastic surgery and a whole new nose. But frankly, right now Jeanie's face was coming second place in her worry list, after her primary concern, aka staying alive. Speaking of which...

She walked over to the sofa.

'Where is it?'

'What?' Clio pushed the entrance to the tunnel shut.

Jeanie pointed at the carpet. Kieran had been there when she left. Now all that she could see was a pool of blood at her feet and then a diminishing trail of red leading to the door. 'Um...'

'What?' Clio was trying to wipe the dust from the tunnel away from her face. She looked like a noughts and crosses board.

'He's not here.'

'Who's not here?'

'Kieran.'

'But...' Clio ran over. She looked around, searching under the sofa, behind the armchair, even flicking a glance towards the ceiling in case he had somehow levitated up to the chandelier. She flung her arms wide. 'How?'

Jeanie shrugged. 'Angelo must have taken him. But where? And why?'

She saw that one of the dust sheets had been pulled off a three-seater sofa, revealing its decaying green cushions. Presumably Angelo had used it to wrap up Kieran's body before dragging it away.

Clio was making for the door. 'We should check on Jocelyn's body.' Her eyes met Clio's. 'The killer might have moved that too.'

'Good idea. Let's just hope Angelo left the door unlocked.'

They ran across the room and Jeanie tried the handle. The door swung open and the two of them ran through it, before halting abruptly. Jeanie looked for a trail of blood but saw nothing – the sheet must have absorbed it all.

'Wait!' Clio held up a hand. She ran to the gun store, rattling the padlock. 'Shit! It's locked. We can't take a gun to defend ourselves.'

Privately, Jeanie wondered if this might be a blessing in disguise. Clio plus gun was an equation she didn't want to know the answer to. Clio ran back into the Salon and Jeanie heard wood splitting behind her. Clio emerged a minute later, brandishing part of the big standard lamp. Her teeth were set, her expression resolute.

'Let's go.'

And so off they went to the kitchen, holding hands and praying that the killer wasn't about to attack.

20

AMBER

Back in the snug, at gunpoint, Amber had no time to lunge for her own rifle. She had no time to do anything.

'Hands up!' Melissa walked over to Amber's rifle and picked it up.

Amber raised her hands, feigning an obedience that went against every fibre of her being. She eyeballed her assailant. 'You know, this really isn't a good look, Melissa. If you're trying to prove that you're not the killer then locking me in here and then aiming a rifle in my face isn't really going to help your case.'

Melissa rolled her eyes as she walked across and hurled Amber's weapon out of the window.

Amber watched her, mouth agape.

Melissa trained the barrel of her gun on Amber again, walking back to stand with her back to the door. 'You may not believe this, but I am actually trying to keep you safe.'

Amber held her stare, brown eyes on a level with her own, seething with fury. 'Why the hell would you do that? I don't need looking after, and especially not by you. I mean, I don't even know you. And pointing a gun at me isn't keeping me safe – it's threatening my life. And why did you lock me in here, anyway?'

'Because...' Melissa shook her once-smooth hair out of her eyes. The side where she had been hit was still tangled and bloody, her eye make-up was long gone and her suit looked as if it had just had a close encounter with an angry lawnmower.

'Yes?' Amber put her hands on her hips and took a step forward, only the length of the rifle separating them now. 'Because you want to shoot me? Because you want to stop me finding out who the killer is, because it's you? *Why*?'

She closed her eyes, expecting the shock of a gunshot at any second. She could smell Melissa's smoky perfume, feel the chill of the room on her skin. The window banged, still open behind her. Maybe she could run for it? Throw herself out?

She opened her eyes. Melissa hadn't moved. Even more strangely, she appeared to have tears in her eyes.

'I knew it would all go horribly wrong.' Melissa shook her head, lowering the rifle slowly.

Now what was going on?

Amber looked at the window again. She could probably make it in time. Melissa was clearly unhinged. Getting out of here was Amber's best bet.

Tears rolled down Melissa's cheeks. She was talking, as if to herself. 'Maybe it's just not meant to be. Maybe I should just give up on this.' Her voice was rising. 'We should never have come here. This was all my fault. If I hadn't brought her here, then...' She bent over, her shoulders shaking with sobs.

This was Amber's chance. She turned and sprinted for the window. She was up on the sill in seconds, her head out, one leg...

The gun nudged her in the back.

'I'm not that stupid.' Melissa's voice was more resigned than angry. 'Get back in here. You'll kill yourself out there.'

'I won't fall.' Amber stayed where she was, the wind shrieking through her hair. 'I'm amazing at climbing.'

'So am I. But it's crazy out there. Get the fuck down or believe me, I will shoot.' The trigger clicked into position.

Swearing, Amber climbed down again. She was sick of this room, sick of this castle, sick of this woman who kept getting in her way. She did her best to wipe the rain from her face and turned, wondering whether to simply run at Melissa and take her chances.

'God, this is so much harder than I thought it would be.' Melissa's eyes rested on Amber with that strange intensity again.

'What is? Murdering people?' Amber took a step towards her, arms held wide. 'Go on. Just pull the damn trigger and get it over with.'

Melissa's face contorted. 'If I wanted you dead, I would have let you climb out of the window, wouldn't I?'

Amber's chin rose. 'I told you, I would have been fine. I'm a great climber.'

'Oh yeah? What mountains have you climbed, then?'

Amber stopped, nonplussed. 'Mountains?'

'Yeah. Mountains.' Melissa was now the one advancing in Amber's direction. 'I've done Everest base camp.'

Amber had seen a documentary about Everest. Did that count? 'Well, I have a more – a more urban approach.' Inside, she was desperately trying to think of any mountains she had ever conquered. She came up with a grand total of zero but there was no way she was going to admit it. 'I've done the – the roof of the O2.'

Melissa's eyes narrowed. 'What's the O2?'

'It's huge.' Amber had no idea why she felt the need to compete like this. What did it matter who had climbed the highest? But somehow Melissa got under her skin. 'You'd be able to go to London and do it yourself now you've moved to the UK, if only you hadn't spent all afternoon killing people.'

'I told you.' Melissa hissed out the words. 'I am not the killer.'

Amber almost laughed. 'You have a gun. You locked my friends in a room downstairs. You have a motive. And you were... acting weird when we got here.'

Melissa rested the gun against the wall and folded her arms. 'I was acting weirdly?'

'Yes.' Amber remembered the way Melissa had kept appearing at her side. 'You kept... following me.'

Melissa huffed. 'That's hardly evidence, is it? I'm the manager here – it's my job to look after my guests!'

Amber kept her eyes on the gun. She just had to grab it. Or run at Melissa. Either approach had its risks, but if she did neither then she was highly likely to be shot through the head any second now.

Melissa folded her arms, and Amber could see she was shivering. It made her seem more human, more vulnerable somehow. 'Look, Amber, I need to tell you something.'

Amber was trying desperately to work out what to do. 'What? What do you want to talk about? What on earth do you want to tell me about before you shoot me?'

That was it. Melissa threw her head back, practically shouting now. 'I told you. I am not trying to kill you. How many times? *I am trying to keep you safe.*' She inhaled deeply before starting again. 'Look. You want me to prove I'm trying to help?' She marched across to the wine chest, sliding it aside with some difficulty, revealing a large trapdoor in the floor. 'Here is the secret passageway entrance that I reckon you've probably been looking for since I shut you in here. There are three passageways in the castle, okay? The Salon to the Red Room. The conservatory to a guest bedroom, and this one. From the USA, Valerie had Ray map them out ready for when she arrived, so he knows about them too. And frankly he is much more likely to kill people than I am.'

'Uh-huh.' Amber kept her voice cool but inside she was kicking herself. She couldn't believe she had missed that entrance. She would have words with herself later.

Melissa walked back to the rifle and Amber cursed herself again. Talk about missing a chance.

Melissa's voice was triumphant. 'So that passageway must be how the murderer got in and out. Why would I tell you that if I was trying to kill you?'

'Could be a double bluff.' Amber tucked the passageway information away, still focused on getting out of here. She took a step towards Melissa, testing the water, working out how reactive Melissa was. She barely seemed to register what Amber was doing.

Amber needed to keep her talking. 'And for your information, Melissa, I don't need anyone to keep me safe. *I* keep me safe.' Another step.

Melissa still hadn't seemed to notice Amber moving forwards. Her brown eyes were liquid now. 'Why do you keep thinking the worst of me, Amber?'

'It's not just you.' Another step. Amber was only a couple of metres from Melissa now. 'I think the worst of everybody. Especially when dead bodies start piling up.'

'But...'

Rage was starting to burn. 'No, Melissa, no buts. I don't know you and you don't know me. I don't know if you're the kind of person who would kill their boss or not. I don't know if you are about to finish me off too. I don't know anything about you except that you are the manager in this deathtrap of a castle, that you know where the guns and the secret passageways are and that you are going to inherit this place. And – if it turns out you're not a murderer and we do get out of here alive – then you'll find out that it takes me years to get to know new people. *Years.*'

Melissa arched an eyebrow. 'So that's why your two BFFs are from school? It took that long to break their way in, huh?'

Now Amber's anger really flared. 'They're my best friends because they are my people, okay? I didn't have a family, so...' She stopped, hating the tears that pricked her eyes. What the hell was happening to her? She was in the middle of a murder investigation. She didn't have time to cry.

'So, things were tough, huh?' Melissa's voice was softer now. Amber felt a strange urge to tell her everything – about the state the agency was in, her worries about her keeping her friends employed, how every childhood birthday had been spent wondering whether this was actually the day she was born. But the words stuck in her throat. Why would she tell Melissa anything? What was the woman to her? Time to get a grip.

Time to attack. She took a deep breath and charged.

Her shoulder met Melissa's torso, and she pushed through and shoved her aside. Melissa crashed to the floor and Amber was nearly at the door. Nearly free. But then Melissa grabbed her leg, holding on with grim tenacity even as Amber kicked and scratched to try to get free. 'Let me go!'

'No way!'

Amber had underestimated Melissa, who had somehow scrambled to her feet. But Amber was ready. In seconds she had rammed her knee into

Melissa's midriff and gripped her hand tight, bending the elbow up at what she knew was an agonising angle.

'Ow. Stop that.' Melissa was fighting to get away, her shirt escaping from her skirt, her hair wild. A rumble of thunder shook the turret.

'Just let me leave this room, Melissa!'

'*No.*'

'Why?' Amber twisted the elbow higher, hearing Melissa gasp in pain.

'Because...'

But Amber couldn't wait any more. She needed to get out, to find her friends, to get this woman out of her way. She let go of Melissa's hand and ducked round behind her, kicking her viciously in the back of the leg.

'Ow, Jesus! You're insane!' Melissa fell to the floor clutching her calf.

Amber stood over her ready to kick her in the face.

She was about to do it when Melissa put up her hands as if in prayer. 'Please. Don't.'

'Why the hell shouldn't I?'

'Because...'

'Yes?' Amber pulled her foot back, ready for the kick.

'Because... we're related.'

Amber paused, her foot half way towards Melissa's face.

Related? How was *that* possible? Amber had been left on a bus. How could any relatives have tracked her down?

Her mouth was so dry she struggled to speak. 'What?'

Melissa tried to smile. 'Surprise.' She attempted jazz hands. 'I'm your half-sister.' Her brown eyes stared up at Amber, pleading. And Amber knew why they had felt familiar earlier – because she saw them every time she looked in a mirror.

A half-sister. She had family? Blood family? Her mind couldn't compute it. It must be a lie. Or a get-out clause? Her head was pulsing, and she was starting to shake.

She heard a distant crackling. Then a familiar voice. 'Amber? Are you okay? Over.'

One beat. Two. Amber looked down at Melissa, fighting to assimilate her words.

What Melissa had told her was too hard. Too much. She turned away, pressing the comms button.

'Clio. Yes, I'm fine. Over.'

'Oh, thank God.' Clio's voice was high. Breathy. Scared.

Amber's heart plunged. 'What's happened?'

Melissa was on her feet now.

'It's the dead bodies...' Clio sounded like she was about to sob.

Amber stepped away from Melissa. She needed space. Distance. The woman had a whole castle at her disposal, why did she have to come and crowd Amber like this?

'What's happened, Clio? Over.'

Her friend's words jumbled together.

'They've gone, Amber. The bodies. Jocelyn and Kieran. They've both disappeared.'

21

CLIO

Clio and Jeanie waited for Amber in the kitchen, where Jocelyn's body very much wasn't any more. After a few minutes their friend stalked in, jaw clenched, chin lifted and made a show of roaming the room, opening cupboards and looking inside the ovens as if Jocelyn's body might somehow be stashed inside. Clio nudged Jeanie, and knew instantly that her friend had picked up on it too. Something was very, very wrong with their friend. A minute after Amber appeared, Melissa joined them, her expression equally flinty as she sat down at the table and laid her rifle across her knee.

Clio tried to catch Amber's eye so she could understand the subtext here, but Amber would not engage. Instead, she planted her hands on the table. 'Okay, so what could have happened here?'

'I don't know.' Jeanie lifted up the blanket that had covered the body, as if checking whether Jocelyn had really disappeared. There was nothing there.

Her brow furrowed. 'Do you think Angelo moved her too?'

Clio tried to ignore her rumbling stomach. 'That's what we've got to figure out. Amber, Jeanie saw Angelo in the Salon just before she jumped into the secret passageway I found, so we think it was him that moved Kieran's body.'

'But why?' Amber drummed her fingers on the table. 'What does he get out of it? And where did he take them?'

Clio considered this. 'Maybe he dragged them outside so he can put them in the sea. Hide the evidence?'

'Maybe.' Amber sank onto one of the chairs. 'Jeanie, did Angelo see you?' She looked at Jeanie properly for the first time. 'Oh my *God*, what happened to your nose?'

Jeanie shrugged. 'Um. Clio happened. In the tunnel. She thought I was about to attack her.'

Clio felt a renewed pang of guilt. 'I'm sorry. Chips at the Codfather for you for ever and ever.'

Jeanie gently touched her bloodied nose. 'And scampi?'

Clio nodded slowly. 'You drive a hard bargain, but okay.'

Amber drummed her fingers on the table. 'I just don't see Angelo as a killer.'

'Me neither.' Melissa shook her head. 'No way. Uh-uh. He's a good kid. Saving for a round the world trip and works really hard. If he was in the Salon, then it was not to move the body.' She stared at Amber, the air in the kitchen thickening somehow. 'I hope you believe me on this, at least.'

'What does that mean?' Amber's mouth tightened.

'It means that you seem to have trouble believing anything else I say.'

'Well, can you blame me? You're not a killer but you have a gun, and then you suddenly announce—' Amber stopped.

Was that a tear in her eye? Clio hadn't ever seen her cry before. She got to her feet. 'Announce what, Melissa?'

Melissa sighed, sagging forwards, folding herself over the rifle. 'I might as well tell you guys as well, just so you can think I'm faking it too.' She looked up. 'I'm Amber's half-sister. I just told her and she basically ran away.'

'Why would you say that?' Clio's fists clenched. She would always have Amber's back, even in the middle of a killing spree. 'We all know she has no family. She was...'

Melissa rolled her eyes. 'I know, I know. She was left as a baby on a bus in Sunshine Sands. I know that because I am her half-sister. Just like I know that she has no birth certificate, but that today is the day she thinks is her birthday. I know that she was brought up in the care system, I know that my mum is her mum, because...' Her eyes filled with tears.

Jeanie walked across, following the instinct that had seen her comfort strangers on trains, women crying in club toilets, colleagues trying and failing to meet deadlines. 'Because of what?'

Melissa covered her face with her hands. 'Because Mom told me when she...' She took a deep juddering breath. 'When she died. She told me about the beautiful baby girl she had been forced to abandon because she couldn't look after her. She told me about you, Amber. And...' She was fighting to get the words out. 'And you have her eyes.'

Instantly Clio moved towards Amber, whose face was ashen. She was leaning over, gripping the edges of the table in both hands.

Melissa continued, her voice a whisper. 'I was with Mom in the hospital. It was near the end, and I thought at first she was rambling. Then, she started talking about Sunshine Sands, so I looked it up, and found it was a real town. And then she used your name, Amber – she had found you online when you set up the agency – when there was some press about you all – and she figured out who you were. She told me about that line of moles you have on your left arm, just above your wrist.' Clio saw Amber looking at her wrist, as if to check. And there it was. A line of tiny moles.

Melissa carried on. 'You also have a birthmark on your lower back in the shape of a crescent moon, in case that helps convince you? Mom told me about that, too. And you look like her, to be honest. You look like our mom.'

Amber didn't even move. Not a flicker to show she was listening. But Clio knew that every fibre of her friend's being was focusing on Melissa's words.

'She told me how your dad left her, and her family kicked her out. She told me about how she had no money, and how she didn't think she could keep you alive on her love alone. So she left you on a bus, behind a nice-looking lady, someone she thought you would be safe with, someone who would help you. And she left you a letter too.'

Clio couldn't breathe. Melissa knew so much that her story must be true.

'A bus? Seriously? Anything could have happened to me.' Amber's voice was taut with anger.

'She did her best, I guess.'

No reply from Amber.

'And then she moved to the US, met Dad, had me.' Melissa was trying to connect with Amber, to catch her eye. But Amber was braced to resist. Tentatively, Clio put a hand on her shoulder. It was as rigid as the castle walls.

'It's not true.' Amber's voice was low.

Melissa stood up and approached her. 'Please, Amber? Please believe me. You're the reason I'm here. You're the reason the new Chateau la Fontaine is here, actually. I had to find you. To see if we could – build something. When Valerie had to leave the States, she put me in charge of finding a new location. And this place, so close to you, with secret tunnels so we could really create some magic for our guests – food mysteriously appearing in their rooms – impossible illusions – was perfect. We were working with a tech company to make it work – robot dumb waiters carrying the food. It was going to be great.' Her voice broke.

'And I knew *you* were here, Amber.' She held her hands wide, eyes burning in her bloodied face. 'And I was hoping that we...' She hesitated and Clio could see how fast she was breathing. 'That maybe you could... find room for me?'

Amber's head rose, eyes bright. One second. Two.

'No.' Amber stood tall. She was exactly the same height as Melissa. 'One, I don't know if you're lying. Two, I don't know if you're a murderer. And three, I don't need a half-sister or any kind of sister. I have all the family I need.' She indicated Clio and Jeanie. 'And then there's the fourth thing – we have a killer to catch.' She nodded briskly, as if this ended the matter. Only the way her fingers worried the edge of her top revealed that she was in any way struggling.

Clio wanted to argue with her, to make her see what a chance this was. It was pretty clear to her that Melissa was telling the truth about them being half-sisters. The shape of their chins, their thick, dark hair, their identical height and eyes. And the detail Melissa knew about Amber too.

The moles, the birthmark, the bus, the fact that no one had ever known the true day she was born.

But Amber was clapping her hands together as if bringing a meeting to order. 'Let's get back to the case, shall we? Enough of these distractions.' Clio noticed that she was resolutely refusing to look at Melissa. Was she still a suspect? Clio had no idea. She wished the three of them were alone, but given that she had a gun, it was unlikely that Melissa could be persuaded to leave them. For now, Amber's half-sister walked over and sank down into a chair, propping her chin on her hand. Clio felt sorry for her. This was hardly the Davina McCall reunion she had probably been hoping for. If only Melissa had approached Clio or Jeanie first – they would have shared how much Amber hated surprises.

Amber was speaking, words flooding out, presumably in a bid to block out Melissa. 'Okay, so let's see. Angelo probably moved Kieran's body. So it seems logical to assume he killed him. Clio? Any thoughts as to why?'

Melissa cut in. 'No way it was him. I told you. He's not the type.'

Amber ignored her. Clio jumped to attention. 'Um, let's see.' She narrowed her eyes at the chalkboard at the far end of the kitchen, as the words Amber had written earlier jumped and jumbled. Her eyesight was definitely getting worse.

She could think of zero reasons why Angelo would want to kill Valerie. 'Maybe he was doing it for someone else? In league or something?'

Melissa shook her head. 'No way. He's not a killer.'

'You've said that already.' Amber's voice dripped ice. 'But if he moved a body then he's hardly an innocent, is he?'

Melissa kept her voice low. 'What about Henri? He's not been seen for a while. Maybe he's doing all this?'

Clio nodded. 'He has motive. Valerie found out he's smuggling cocaine and fired him.'

Melissa's mouth fell open. 'He what now?'

Jeanie's eyes were fixed on the board. 'I saw him. Outside, in the hut? He's been smuggling cocaine for a local dealer.'

'Great.' Melissa slumped back in her seat. 'So not only was my boss a criminal, but her sous chef was too?'

'What?' Amber's head snapped round, her eyes narrowing. 'Valerie was a criminal?'

'Yeah.' Melissa rolled her eyes. 'She was kicked out of the US for being an illegal immigrant. Turns out she never got a green card, a fact she chose not to share with me. That's why she was keen to move out of the US. Valerie never did the immigration paperwork and now it's cost us – everything. We've managed to keep it out of the press so far, but – now she's dead... Well, I guess it doesn't matter now.' She took a moment to compose herself. 'I nearly killed her myself when she told me. But we were friends, you know? Really good friends – she helped me when I was starting out, taking me on, training me up. I wouldn't be anything without her. And her cooking! Just – sublime.' She was fighting back tears again. 'I still can't believe she won't be in that kitchen tomorrow adding something to something and creating gold.' She lost her battle and tears rolled down her cheeks. 'Man. This weekend sucks.'

Amber nodded. 'At least we can all agree on that.'

Clio saw Melissa's eyes rising hopefully towards Amber. They fell again when she saw the set expression on her face. Jeanie was there, again putting her arm around Melissa, giving her a tissue.

Melissa wiped her eyes, taking a shuddering breath. 'I suppose I should probably tell you the rest.'

'What do you mean?' Amber folded her arms, eyes narrowing.

Melissa sighed. 'The initials on her wrist. I asked her about them once and she told me they stood for Sacre Coeur – the church in Paris? She said it had meant a lot to her as a kid, that she had gone there with her parents, you know...'

Amber's eyes glinted. 'And?'

'Well, it always struck me as weird. I mean, who gets a church's initials tattooed on their wrist? Why not a picture of it?'

Good point.

'So I guess it just stuck in my head.' Melissa sat forwards, elbows on the kitchen table, hands together. 'And then one day I was in her office for some reason, and she hadn't shut her computer down, and there it was on her screen, a Google search for Samantha Cohen.'

Amber frowned. 'Who is Samantha Cohen?'

Melissa almost smiled. 'Just what I thought. So I looked her up. And it turns out she was a fraudster. An English fraudster called Samantha Cohen. She and a friend worked pensioners in residential homes twenty years ago, promising them the world in return for an investment up front. A Ponzi scheme, basically. They made an absolute fortune, and then Samantha vanished just as the police got wind of what they were up to. She ran off with all the money and was never seen again.'

'Oh my God.' Clio put a hand to her mouth. 'So Valerie is Samantha?'

'Exactly. She used the money to set up the first Chateau la Fontaine in Palm Springs. Man, I was so mad about that. What a sick thing to do. When I confronted her, she freaked out, denied it at first, said she wasn't Samantha.'

Clio could see the hurt on Melissa's face, but couldn't shake the feeling that the woman in front of her might be a lot more than hurt. She might be raging. Raging enough to kill.

'Did she confess eventually?'

'She did.' Melissa picked at a loose thread on her jacket. 'She told me everything. Said she hated lying to me, how she would trust me with this, with her biggest secret.'

Clio gave a low whistle. 'Wow. So she's not even French?'

'Not even.' Melissa shook her head. 'She was from Hastings.'

Jeanie sank into a chair next to Melissa, her mouth hanging open. 'And how did she disappear?'

Melissa sighed. 'She had a plan and she followed it. She changed her name, changed her image, had some serious surgery. She moved to Paris – her mum was French so she'd always spoken the language. She started cooking and worked her way up. The trail went cold and when she got famous, she just didn't look like Sam any more. She was a Michelin-starred chef with long dark hair, a husky French accent and cheekbones to die for, and they were looking for a blonde English woman with bad dress sense. It was the perfect disguise.'

Melissa ran her hands over her face, rubbing her eyes with the heels of her hands. 'And it was all okay, give or take a little financial moment or two, until that bloody publicity piece by Kieran. Everything went wrong after that.'

Jeanie spoke up. 'I found the next article by his body. The exposé? And I found out in his phone messages that he was blackmailing her.'

Melissa frowned. 'God knows how he found out. Valerie would never have said anything, and I certainly didn't.'

Amber cut in. 'I think I know. When he came to interview Valerie, I think he planted recording devices in her desk, and maybe in other places too. He was bugging her. Trying to get the big scoop.'

'What?' Melissa banged her hand on the table. 'The bastard.'

'Yeah. Well, it didn't get him very far, did it, seeing as he's dead now.' Amber's eyes snapped. 'Anything else?'

Melissa nodded slowly. 'Well, at least now I get why money started disappearing after she was interviewed. She would never tell me where it was going. We were trying to buy this place, and I was all in just trying to keep Palm Springs running while closing the deal here. It was all so hectic. But I just wonder if somehow the killer read the first article and came for her?'

A small frown puckered Jeanie's forehead. 'But if you knew what Valerie had done – taking all that money years before – why didn't you tell anyone? She was a thief.' She looked at Clio and she knew Jeanie was thinking of Gary taking all of Clio's money and her daughter's savings too. 'Why didn't you tell the police, Melissa?'

Melissa's face clouded. 'I feel so bad about that and I can't really defend it. I guess I'd seen how great she was, we were friends, I saw her hiring locals, sourcing sustainable food, doing good things to help those around her.'

Amber's eyes were cold. 'You didn't blackmail her then?'

Melissa gasped. 'What? No!'

'To get her to put you in her will?'

'Oh my God, no way.' Melissa pushed the chair back and rose. 'I can't believe you are even thinking that, let alone saying it.' She picked up the gun. 'Do you know what? I've had enough of you three. Screw this. And screw you.'

'I'm sorry?' Amber's eyes flashed.

'I said screw you. I'm not going to stay here and be insulted by you. I'm going to find this bastard killer and get the hell out of here.'

Amber's jaw clenched. 'Really? And how are you going to do that, Melissa? What's your plan?'

'My plan?' Melissa's voice was rising. 'What's my plan?'

'Yes.' A vein pulsed in Amber's neck. 'What's your plan once you leave this kitchen and head out there?'

'My plan is to look for him. And then to take this rifle and disable him.' Melissa brandished the gun.

'How are you so sure it's a him?'

'Well, I don't think you lot did it, and I know I didn't, so...' Melissa shrugged. 'There you go. Had to be a guy, didn't it? So, you ladies have fun in here, but I'm off. If I get him, I'll let you know.'

Clio swallowed. There was something so familiar about Melissa's bullheaded courage. She had seen it in Amber so many times – facing Clio's bullies; attacking a killer in a graveyard last year, just before he finished them both.

Amber crossed to the door, pushing against it with her hand. 'No, Melissa. I can't let you do that. You can't go outside.'

'Just try and stop me. Stand aside, please.'

The half-sisters stood facing each other, only inches apart. Jeanie and Clio watched them in silence, as gripped as a centre-court crowd at the Wimbledon final. Amber had met her match. Clio was glad she didn't have to bet on the outcome of this particular confrontation. For once she wasn't sure that Amber would win.

'I am not standing aside.' Amber's voice was low and urgent. 'And we're wasting time here.'

'You're the one wasting time. I'm just trying to save my ass.' Melissa's chin jutted forwards, mirroring Amber's.

'But you won't be saving your ass. You'll be making yourself vulnerable, like Jocelyn did or like Valerie did. Being alone is dangerous.' Was that a catch in Amber's voice?

'Why do you care if I'm in danger?' Both sisters tucked a strand of dark hair behind their ears in perfect unison. Melissa's voice was strong, but her eyes had softened, full of a new vulnerability.

Amber grimaced. 'I don't. I don't care.'

'Fine, then I'm going.' Melissa put her hand on the door handle and pulled it towards her.

'No!' Amber slammed it shut again.

'If you don't care whether I stay or go then I'm going. I need to look out for myself.' Melissa wrenched the door open again.

'Oh, for God's sake.' Amber pushed it shut.

'Same back at ya.' Melissa pulled it open.

'Oh God, you're so annoying.' Shut.

'Takes one to know one.' Open.

'You can bloody talk.' Shut.

Melissa exhaled in frustration. 'Oh, just let me leave. If you don't care about me, then just let me go!' Open.

'No, I won't.' Shut.

'Yes.' Open.

'No.' Close.

The poor kitchen door was having the biggest night of its life, but Clio knew this – both literally and metaphorically – wasn't getting them anywhere. It was time for Clio to take charge.

'You two. Stop it. Let's go in pairs and round everyone up, okay? We can search for clues at the same time.'

She was met with silence. Both Melissa and Amber looked mutinous.

Clio turned to Melissa. 'Look, I've known Amber for thirty years now. And she's not really comfortable with feelings. She's not a... sharer. But the fact that she's standing here, stopping you leaving – that means that she doesn't hate you and that she probably doesn't think you're the killer. And considering she's only known about you for about six hours, I'd take that. She's worth sticking with – she's one of the best.'

Melissa's mouth opened and closed. There was a beat of silence. Then she looked at Amber. 'Okay. I'll come with you. But I'm keeping the gun.'

Clio nodded. 'If you have to.'

'Can I just ask something?' Jeanie waved a hand in the air, as if awaiting her turn in class.

'Sure.' Amber turned to her.

'Do we think the killer actually wants us all dead? Or that they're just killing whoever hears something or gets in their way?'

Amber's face softened and Clio put an arm around their friend and squeezed hard. 'We won't know that until we catch them. Which we will. Won't we?'

'Hell, yes.' Clio felt Jeanie shaking beside her and pulled her close. Jeanie's voice was tiny. 'But I saw Angelo. And he must have seen me.' She gave a sob. 'So that means I'll be next, doesn't it?'

'No.' Amber took Jeanie's hands. 'No. Because we've got your back, Jeanie. Clio. Me. We've always got your back.'

'I know.' Jeanie's shoulders shook as she sobbed. 'But I'm scared.'

Clio squeezed her even tighter. 'I'll be right beside you. And they've just upped my HRT, so watch out world.'

Jeanie tried to laugh. 'Well, in that case...' She wiped her nose, wincing as she did so. 'Where do you want me and Clio to go, Amber?'

'The bedrooms and all the upstairs rooms, please. Melissa and I will search outside and downstairs. We'll meet back here once we've found everyone. Okay?'

'Okay.'

Amber hovered close for a second. 'Be careful and you'll be fine. This will all be over soon.'

'You too.' Clio took Jeanie's hand and held it tight as they edged into the corridor. All she could do was hope that Amber was right.

SUNDAY – 2 A.M

FOUR HOURS UNTIL THE POLICE CAN COME

THREE DEAD BODIES

22

JEANIE

The corridor was dark, even with the heavy pendulum lights that punctuated its ceiling. Red drapes hung limp on the walls and Jeanie had to look away as they passed a sinister portrait of a black and white whippet foaming at the mouth, its dark eyes seeming to follow them as they walked towards the staircase.

'God, I am never complaining about that hideous neon light in the laundry room at the caravan park ever again.' Clio's hand was tight around Jeanie's as she talked. Her words were so quickfire they almost ran into one another and Jeanie knew that her friend was trying to keep herself calm. 'I mean the neon makes me look like I belong in a morgue, but I'd take that over this...' Clio came to a halt, her eyes wide, 'Over this flickering light in the creaky hallway thing, wouldn't you?'

Jeanie squeezed her fingers. 'I would take pretty much anything over this.' Finally clearing out the loft? Bring it on. Arguing with her husband Tan about who had forgotten to take the bins out? Yes please.

Together, she and Clio crept towards the wide staircase that led up to the bedrooms on the first floor. Well, they tried to creep but frankly it was impossible given the state of the floor. The more Jeanie looked at the castle, the more crumbling it appeared to be. It was like her body since having kids – neglected, sagging, mouldering quietly away unnoticed, the bottom of the priority list.

Outside, the wind continued to rage and Jeanie could only hope that the noise would mask their own progress through the castle. She put a hand on the banister, hoping to steady herself, only for the rail to come off in her hand.

'Oh my God.' She managed not to scream in shock and put it down on the floor. Together, she and Clio started to climb the wide stairs, their feet sliding on the threadbare red carpet.

There was no light on the landing above them. Fear whispered in Jeanie's mind, threatening to overwhelm her. She and Clio could be walking into a trap, but what choice did they have? They had to search the rooms and round everyone up. They had to try to work this out and stay alive.

They were on the landing now. A door was in front of them and they approached it, checking whether anyone was nearby with every step. But all they saw was darkness and shadows. No eyes glinting. No hands waiting to strike.

Jeanie took the door handle. She inhaled. 'Ready?'

Clio nodded. 'As I'll ever be.'

A creak from the far end of this corridor made them both turn. Jeanie heard a skittering sound, then a sigh. She felt Clio stiffen beside her.

'What the hell was that?'

'I don't know.' Jeanie swallowed, her breath coming too fast. Her vision was starting to blur. 'But I really wish one of us had a gun.'

The door handle squeaked as she turned it.

'*Hi-ya*.' Clio barrelled in behind her, hands raised, ready to karate chop. She had never been the same since Amber had sent them both on a self-defence course last year. Clio narrowly avoided whacking Jeanie in the nose again as she suddenly whirled around, one arm disappearing behind her.

'What are you doing?'

Slowly, Jeanie realised that Clio hadn't moved of her own accord. Her arm had been grabbed by someone else.

'Let go of me!' Clio kicked out as Jeanie swung into action. She punched the grabber in the side, putting all her weight into it.

'*Not me. Him.*' Clio doubled over. 'Jeanie. Look before you punch.'

'I *was* bloody looking.' Jeanie straightened up, ready for more. All the tension of this endless night was fizzing through her. All the fear, all the unknowns, the bodies, the shouting, the storm, they were all just ready to burst out of her now in punches and kicks. She gasped as somebody's fist connected with her chin.

'Back off!' Jeanie could feel blood in her mouth. 'Whoever the hell you are, you have two pissed off and starving midlife women in here with you, so just give up now, okay?' She punched ahead of her, feeling a savage surge of pleasure as her hand met bone. Meanwhile, Clio had reverted to childhood and had grabbed their attacker's hair.

'Oh my God!' Whoever it was flailed in front of them. 'I'm just trying to, like, stay alive. I'm no killer, yeah?'

Jeanie paused, terror pulsating through her. 'Angelo?'

'Yeah. It's me.' She heard rasping breaths. 'You two are mad. Proper crazy.'

Clio's voice was sharp. 'You're the one who grabbed my arm.'

'Yeah. Because I thought you were going to murder me!'

Jeanie could see the whites of his eyes even in this darkness. She tried to find the light switch. Miraculously, there it was. Even more miraculously, it worked. The three of them blinked frantically at each other in the dazzling light.

Angelo had his hands up to shield himself. 'Please don't kill me. Please. I won't tell anyone I saw anything. I won't tell them that you killed him.'

Jeanie belatedly realised that he was looking at her.

'Me?' She swallowed. 'You think I killed Kieran?'

'Yeah.' He nodded. 'You were – with the...' His Adam's apple bobbed. He looked about twelve despite the fact he was a foot taller and wider than her. 'You were with the body. I saw you.' He put a hand to his mouth, the diamond stud in his ear catching the light. 'But I won't ever tell anyone. Legit. I promise. Never. Not a word.' He put a hand on his heart. 'I'll take it to the grave.'

'Angelo.' Clio put her hand on his arm, but he flinched away. 'Jeanie didn't kill anyone. We found the body in there, okay?'

'Sure. You just "found" it.' He nodded frenetically. 'Yeah. Like, for real. Yeah.'

'No, seriously.' Clio put her head on one side. 'We found him on the floor. Does Jeanie look like a killer to you?'

'I don't know.' Angelo held up his hands, as if to defend himself.

Clio, unhelpfully, was starting to laugh. Jeanie made furious eyes at her, but it only made her friend's shoulders shake harder.

'I'm sorry.' Tears were pouring down her cheeks, making white tracks amidst the blood and dust. 'It's just so funny. Jeanie. Of all of us. A killer! Ha.' She bent over, lost.

Well, at least she had diverted his attention. Angelo was watching Clio now, his eyes only marginally less full of fear than they had been earlier.

'What's funny about murder?' He started backing away, as if Clio had a balaclava and a sawn-off shotgun. 'What's wrong with you?'

Jeanie saw herself as she must have looked through his eyes when he came into the Salon. Standing over a body, going through the pockets. A woman with grey streaks in her hair and a frown on her face. A killer.

Clio had a point. It was funny. Jeanie felt a giggle bubbling up inside her and didn't want to stop it. She threw her head back and howled with laughter.

Clio doubled over again. 'Jeanie saves spiders. She once spent forty minutes getting an angry wasp into a tumbler and letting it out of the window so her sister didn't kill it. At her own birthday party!' She wiped her eyes. 'She is the least likely person to ever kill someone. She simply wouldn't know how.'

'So you say.' Angelo had stopped edging away from them now. 'But how do I know you're not lying?'

'Fair point.' Jeanie was overwhelmed by another gale of laughter. 'You don't. But the wasp stuff is true. And once I stepped on a bee and I held a funeral service for it. I made my whole family sit through it too.'

Clio snorted. 'Bet your sisters loved that.'

'You bet they did.'

Angelo was now backed into the corner, hands up as if to fend them off. 'You two are mad. There are – dead bodies – and you don't care. You just laugh. It's not funny.'

For some reason him saying this was very funny indeed.

'You see?' His eyes grew wider and rounder. 'You're crazy. I never should have come to work here. I should have just gone on the checkouts at Asda like my mum said. I just wanted to earn some money. It's not meant to be like this, is it? I only came into this room to hide. Can't you leave me alone?'

Jeanie looked down at him, knowing that he wasn't the killer. No way. He was barely old enough to order a pint and he looked terrified. Shaking. Eyes wild. Tears waiting to fall. She and Clio shared a glance and she knew that her friend was thinking the same thing.

Clio approached him and put an arm around him. He leapt away.

She tried again. This time he leant into her, starting to sob.

'I'm scared.'

'I know.' Jeanie moved to his other side. 'But we're here now. We're here with you. We'll get through this.' She had to stop him panicking.

'Look. Angelo. Maybe we do seem crazy. Maybe we *are* crazy. But we are also detectives. And best friends. And we have been in this kind of situation before. I promise. And we are still alive.'

He looked utterly unconvinced.

'So.' She tried again as Clio visibly got herself under control and started to search the room. 'We are in here because we are trying to round everyone up so we can all stay safe. I was in the Salon earlier because we heard a crash from inside and we ran to find out who was in there. When we got there we found Kieran's body. Clio went off to follow a lead and I was left in there and I was trying to find out everything I could by going through his pockets and his phone. You see?'

Silence, but at least he had stopped visibly shaking now.

'So. Now I have a question for you, Angelo.'

'What?'

'Did you move the body?'

He stiffened. 'No way.'

'Okay.' Jeanie believed him. 'Then did you see who did?'

'No. I was hiding.'

'Hiding where?'

'Under one of the sofas. I only just got underneath when they came in, and I just lay there, trying to be quiet. I didn't want to look. I just heard a dragging sound. I saw their feet going past. That's it. No speaking, just that dragging sound. And then I heard the door closing and I lay there for a bit, just in case they came back. Then I ran up the stairs and hid in here.'

'Got it.' Clio rose to her feet. 'So whose room is this?'

'I think it was his.' Angelo shuddered. 'The dead guy. I recognise his leather jacket on the bed. And earlier, just before you all arrived, I brought his bags up here.'

Clio went across and stood by the four-poster bed, her hand on one of the supports. 'Here's his suitcase. I'm going to look inside.'

'Good idea.'

Clio unzipped the small black case and dug around inside.

She gave a low whistle. 'You need to see this, Jeanie.'

Jeanie gave Angelo a reassuring smile before walking over to join her friend. 'What is it?'

Clio indicated the ground. 'These.'

It took Jeanie a second to see what they were.

Then her hand went to her mouth. 'So this *is* Kieran's room.'

'Yes.'

Before Clio could say more, the bedroom door handle began to turn. Jeanie ran over to Angelo, shoved him behind her and waited to see what would come next.

23

AMBER

Amber was struggling to focus as she walked outside and was hit by the full force of the storm. She couldn't believe what Melissa had told her in the kitchen. She couldn't believe that she might have an actual relation, blood family, something she had done her best never to want. And now that Melissa had spoken, Amber was besieged by memories. Hearing that she had a half-sister had stirred something in her – the little child looking for her mum on every street corner, in every supermarket queue. The girl who wasn't good enough to love, the memory of whom Amber had boxed away, covering the pain with black humour, work and denial.

She shook her head, furious with herself. She had lasted forty-six years without a family. She didn't need one now.

Melissa staggered as the wind hit them. 'Do you really think anyone will be out here?'

'Henri's probably still in the shed. We need to find him.' Another gust sent Amber staggering backwards, banging into Melissa and her rifle. She bent her head, trying to force her way forwards again. Her head was down, her body was braced, but this storm was taking no prisoners. There was no way she could push through it. There was no way of getting to the hut.

Amber swore in frustration.

'Come on!' Melissa's hand grabbed hers, pulling Amber sideways along a narrow pathway that ran between the trees. Amber had no choice but to follow, and they made progress despite the wind doing its best to stop them. Trees lashed over their heads, twigs flew, dust whirled around them. It was so ferocious that Amber wondered if they would find that the hut had been blown away, possibly with Henri still inside.

'Is it much further?' Amber wiped the rain out of her eyes.

'No. We can go this way.' Melissa indicated a dark trail running behind a huge greenhouse and then off into the forest. 'It's a shortcut.'

'Is it safe?'

Melissa shrugged. 'At this point it's hard to say that anything is safe, don't you think?'

'Fair point.' Amber nodded. 'Let's go.'

As they walked onto the pathway the darkness got even more oppressive.

'Christ, I'm spooked.' Melissa hunched her shoulders in a vain attempt to stop the rain from penetrating her suit even further. 'I never realised before how damn spooky the forest can be. But I guess you know all about that in your job.'

Amber stayed silent.

'Not a talker, huh?'

'Nope.' Amber slid on a patch of mud and nearly ended up face-down in a bush.

'You okay?' Melissa reached out to catch her.

'*I'm fine.*'

'Alright, alright.' Melissa gave a whistle. 'I'll just shut up, then.' She moved ahead, flinging words over her shoulder. 'You see? It's like we're sisters already.'

'I wouldn't know.' Amber marched on. She was trying to focus on the killings, on finding the murderer, but she was also trying to ignore another voice that whispered inside her. Melissa would know more about the woman who had been forced to leave Amber on the bus. She would know what made her laugh, whether she liked coffee as much as Amber did. Despite herself, she wanted to find out what she could, to take this unexpected chance. Even though her mum was dead, she wanted to know everything about her.

She stomped on. It felt as if part of her had become unpeeled, leaving her exposed. Unsteady. Vulnerable. But Amber didn't do vulnerable. Especially not now, when she had dead bodies to deal with, a killer to find, and friends to protect.

But one question was searing through her mind. She stopped. 'Why didn't she come and find me? When she saw the article about the agency?'

'Oh, hon.' Melissa reached out a hand and Amber stepped smartly backwards. Pity was an absolute no-no.

'Got it!' Melissa held her hands up. 'No sympathy. I get it. So here are the facts. Mom was too sick by the time she learnt where you were. And she thought you wouldn't want to see her anyways. She figured you'd be angry with her, that if you'd have wanted to find her, you'd have come looking.'

'How could I have done that? I didn't even have a birth certificate!'

'I don't know.' Melissa chewed her bottom lip. 'But I guess there are ways. It's too late now for all that, I guess.'

Amber felt regret flare inside her. She had always been too proud, too angry at her mum's rejection. In the letter she had left in Amber's basket she had just said that she loved her. Nothing more. No explanations, no name, no clues for Amber to follow. She had thought there was no point in meeting her mum in real life just to be rejected again.

Melissa nudged her. 'She was really proud of what she found out about you though.'

'She was?' Amber's whole body tingled with a need she had never known she had.

'She would have loved you.'

'You don't know that.' Amber walked on again.

'No, but she loved cacti so I think the two of you would have been a great fit.'

'Sounds like it.' Amber's mouth twisted up at the corner, grateful that her face was so wet from the rain that at least Melissa wouldn't see her tears. She walked forward as fast as she could. 'Come on. We have a killer to catch.'

'She told me she didn't want to give you up, Amber.'

'Then why didn't she keep me?' Amber flung the words out, a lifetime of rejection crystallising into six words.

Melissa's mouth was opening. Sympathy was softening those eyes, that mouth. She was reaching out her hand, and Amber knew she would explode if she connected. She scanned the forest frantically, seeking escape. And she saw something. A grey shape amongst the trees, in what looked like a clearing. She stepped towards it, peering through the darkness.

'What's that?'

Melissa frowned. 'It's the tent those damn protestors were in. They didn't want this place developed at all. It was totally crazy. It's literally private land. Ray kicked them off the island earlier this week and they didn't have time to take their things – they just got in the boat and disappeared.'

'They had a boat?'

'Yes. They moored round behind the castle where no one would see it – not in the main jetty where you guys arrived, but in a cove nearby. Ray said the old owner let them use it.'

'How does he know that?'

'Oh, Ray was the one who talked with them. They kept hidden otherwise but he bumped into them around the place, what with being the groundskeeper and all.'

Amber nodded. 'But they were here tonight – with that banner, weren't they?'

'Yeah. I guess.' Melissa sniffed. 'Ray said they'd all gone, but...' She stopped. 'Maybe one of them was the killer?'

'It's a possibility. And they would have a motive to kill Valerie, at least. I'm going to have a look.' Amber started sliding her way towards the tent, slipping on the muddy, rooty ground of the forest.

Melissa kept pace with her. 'But we're meant to be finding Henri.'

'We need to look at everything. No stone unturned.' Amber's blood was up now. This was perfect. No thinking about her mum, or her new half-sister. 'And there might be something in the tent that helps us to work out who the killer is.'

A thought occurred to her. 'How many protestors were there?'

Melissa thought. 'Ray said he met four different people, I think.'

Amber thought out loud. 'So maybe one stayed and decided to kill her, to claim the forest back?'

'Sounds a bit – random.' Melissa frowned. 'A bit – unlikely.'

'Well, we have to consider everything.' They had reached the tent. 'Let's just look inside.'

She unzipped the entrance, the canvas straining in the wind. The tent was divided into two sections, and was bigger than she had first thought, with an entrance that was tall enough to stand up in. It had clearly been well pegged down and she could see a camping kettle and a tin mug just in front of the canvas door that separated the entrance from the main sleeping area. A dirty plate stood ready to be washed and half a loaf of Hovis was slowly turning to mush by one of the guy ropes. Melissa was right – the protestors had left in a hurry.

Then Amber noticed something interesting. She turned to Melissa.

'How else did they protest, out of interest?'

'Broken windows. Signs. Graffiti. That kind of thing.'

'And you're sure there were four of them?'

'I'm sure Ray told me that there were four of them. But like I said I never saw them myself.'

Amber dropped to her knees, rooting through the sleeping bag in the corner, delving underneath the camping mat.

'Doesn't that strike you as odd? Given that they were protestors. They had one job. To make noise. Yet you never saw them?'

'No.' Melissa ran a hand through her soaking hair. 'I never thought that was odd.'

Amber swallowed, her mind racing. 'So, really, the protestors – they could be fake? Ray could have lied about them?'

'What?'

'Well...' Amber was widening her search area now. 'What if there were never any protestors? What if they were a lie made up by the man who interacted with them – by Ray?'

'Why would he do that?'

'As a cover story for what was actually going on.'

'Which was what?' Melissa crouched down next to Amber, shining the beam of her torch along the ground.

'I'm not sure yet.' Amber was still searching. She found an old hoodie, a pen, a waterproof notebook. One of everything. One. One. One. 'But if there were several of them, why is there so little stuff left here?'

'Because they grabbed some of their things when they left?'

'It's too uniform, though. One spoon. One pillow. One blanket. One...'

Amber stopped as she spotted something that made her pulse spiral. 'No way.' She picked it up.

'What?' Melissa looked at her, eyes wide. 'What is it?'

Amber felt a pulse of triumph as she tucked it away in her pocket. She felt the rush as a theory, a version of events, started to write itself in her head. She felt the facts starting to organise themselves – Ray, Henri and his cakes, Valerie and her past as Samantha Cohen.

'What are you doing?' Melissa's voice was rising. 'What aren't you telling me? Is Ray the killer?'

Amber crawled to the entrance of the tent. 'Melissa, I need you to go back to the castle. Find Ray.'

'What?'

Amber rushed on. 'Keep him with you. Use the gun if you have to. Okay?'

'Oh my God. Is he the killer?'

Amber laid a hand on her arm. 'Just find him. Now. We can't let him get away. Can I trust you with this?'

'One hundred per cent.' They both reversed out of the tent and stood for a moment, the trees shaking around them.

'You can do this, Melissa.'

'Can I?' All Melissa's bravado seemed to have disappeared.

'Yes. You can.' Amber looked her dead in the eyes. 'Now. Put your torch out and run.'

'What will you be doing?'

Amber still didn't know if she could trust Melissa, but she had no choice. 'I'll be putting the final pieces together, but I'll be with you as soon as I can. Stay safe.'

'You too.'

And then Melissa was gone, leaving Amber alone with the storm and the evidence she had just gathered and a hell of a lot of work to do to prove that her theory was right.

24

AMBER

Amber wasn't alone for very long.

She heard footsteps behind her and spun round.

The person she saw somehow didn't surprise her. As soon as she had heard about the cocaine, she had been expecting her.

'Marg.'

'Oh. It's you.' As ever, Marg Redfearn was dressed for a WI meeting. Whoever her current bodyguard/boyfriend was – the last one had lasted a mere matter of days – he was holding a black umbrella above her head while a second man was lighting her way with a torch so bright that it wouldn't have been out of place in an MI5 interrogation. He shone it into Amber's eyes and she flinched, shielding her eyes as well as she could from the glare.

Marg examined Amber in the torchlight. 'Well, you look like shit.'

'Thanks. I'm on a relaxing weekend away.'

'Well, don't do it again. It doesn't suit you.' Marg looked around. 'Have you seen Henri?'

'Your errand boy?'

Marg fingered the string of pearls at her neck. 'My business partner.'

'No. I haven't. But I was just about to look for him.'

'Then I suppose you can come with me.' Marg stalked across to the main path. Even the storm seemed to respect her, and the rain now appeared to be receding in her honour. 'If you must.'

Amber raced to catch up with her. 'How did you get here, Marg? Even the police can't make it across in this weather.'

Marg waved a hand dismissively, gliding forwards as the two men frantically tried to keep pace with her shiny black loafers. 'They know nothing. Fools.'

Amber smiled, impressed despite herself. It wouldn't surprise her if Marg had a submarine at her disposal.

Amber was thinking about the piece of evidence she had found in the tent as they approached a hut at the edge of the trees. Having Marg here could be useful, if only Amber could persuade her to be helpful. She knew that the south coast's leading drugs baron must be seriously worried if she was here in person. Normally Marg left her many subordinates to do what needed to be done. So what was it about this part of the supply chain that had got her so worried?

The way that Marg was striding ahead it was clear that she had been on the island before. Again, this was unusual. When Amber had been in the police force, she had frequently tried to catch Marg out – to prove that she was the queen of the Sunshine Sands drug smuggling scene. But whenever she had busted a lorry load of cocaine, Marg had been conveniently far away, surfing or kayaking or going to a show in the West End, divorced from the action by burner phones and subordinates running the county lines on her behalf.

A phone rang as they reached the door of the hut and Marg pulled a mobile out of her pocket. Amber watched open-mouthed as she looked at the screen.

'How do you have reception?'

'Sat phone.' Marg flicked a hand dismissively and diverted the call. Her bodyguard pulled the door of the hut open and Marg swept inside. 'What happened here?' She surveyed the interior, tucking the phone back into her pocket.

Amber went after her, brain whirring. Could Marg's presence here be linked to the murders? Amber followed the torch's beam around the hut and gasped.

Henri wasn't there any more. However, wherever he was, it seemed he must be wounded. Blood was splashed all over the tottering pile of cakes in the corner. The white cardboard cases were covered in crimson spatters, and most of the boxes were part-opened, white powder clouding the air as it fell onto the woodpile in the corner and the toolbox that was splayed open on the floor.

Marg reacted fast. Of course she did. You didn't stay on top for as long as she had without some seriously quick thinking. She clicked her fingers at the two men. 'Clean this up, take whatever product you can.' She pulled her phone out again, then walked across to Amber.

Marg asked the question that Amber wanted to know the answer to herself. 'Do you know who did this?'

Honesty was always the best policy with Marg.

Amber met her eye. 'No. But I do know that there have been three murders tonight, and it's pretty likely they're all linked.'

'Three?' Marg considered this. 'You've been digging into it, I suppose?'

'Yes.' Amber considered her options. 'And if you tell me why you're here in person, I'll tell you what I know.'

Marg's eyes narrowed. 'Product has been vanishing. I'm here to find out why. The storm is the perfect cover as the police are so useless at coping with weather.' She tutted impatiently. 'Now. What do you know?'

Amber considered for a moment, 'Well...'

'What else do you want?' Marg peered at Amber over her the narrow black frames of her glasses. Behind her, the men were on their knees, closing boxes, stacking them neatly together. Marg glanced their way. 'Hurry up, you two.'

Not a word of protest from the men. Sensible. A year ago, the Bad Girls Detective Agency had discovered that one of Marg's bodyguards-with-benefits was seeing another woman as well as Marg. Amber hadn't seen him since sharing this information with his boss.

Marg's eyes were sharp. She was so close Amber could smell her violet perfume. 'What else do you want, Amber?'

Amber tried not to look too eager. Eager and Marg did not go well together.

'I want ten minutes with your phone.'

Marg weighed it up. Amber held her breath. 'You can have it for five.' She held it out. Amber reached for it. 'But...' Marg pulled it away from Amber's fingers.

'Yes?'

'You tell me what you know first.'

So Amber did. She told Marg about who was dead, about how, about the fact that Valerie was really Samantha Cohen from Hastings. Marg did not look surprised by that, so obviously she knew already. Maybe Henri had worked it out and told her, or maybe Marg's unbeatable information network had given her a heads up. Knowing Marg, she had done her research – getting the lowdown on Valerie so she could use her secrets to dissuade her from asking difficult questions about what Henri was up to. She told Marg about the secret passageways, about Melissa and Ray and about the other two guests, Jocelyn and Kieran, being murdered. She skipped over Melissa's relationship to herself, both because she didn't want to think about it and because Marg would have zero interest in the emotional tapestry of Amber's life.

Amber also didn't share who she thought the culprit was.

When she had finished, Marg thought for a moment. 'Do you have a plan?'

Amber nodded. 'I do.'

'But you're not going to share it?'

'No.' Amber folded her arms across her chest. For a moment she considered asking for Marg's help in catching the killer, but she knew how pointless that would be. Marg just wanted her product. She wasn't going to hang around here to help Amber.

Amber took a deep breath, squaring her shoulders. 'Now, can I have the phone please Marg?'

Marg put it into her hand. 'I don't need it, so you can keep it.'

'But it's a satellite phone.' Amber knew how expensive these were.

'So?' Marg waved a hand dismissively. 'You can go away now.'

Amber did so.

Outside the hut she stood thinking, the phone in her hand, before opening up the search engine and starting to type. Three things. Three things which could prove her theory right.

The screen loaded agonisingly slowly.

Amber looked at the search results, scrolling through one then another then another, right down to the bottom of the page.

Then she saw it. An old photo. One that tallied with what she had found in the tent. Only here, there were names.

She had found what she was looking for.

And now she knew for sure that her friends were in danger.

She had to get back to the castle. Now.

25

CLIO

In Kieran's room, fresh from finding three recording devices in his luggage, Clio was ready for the man who had just burst through the door. She tripped him up and he landed face-first on the rug. She pressed her boot into his back and frowned down at him. 'What are you doing in here?'

'Get off me.'

'Not until you tell us why you're in here.'

Ray wriggled and groaned, trying to push up onto his hands, but Clio kept him pinned. He looked different to when she had last seen him. His hair was wild, his face was pale and his eyes glittered dangerously. Clio hadn't been able to see Ray when they had met in the secret passageway, but now his overalls were covered in dust. She looked around for something to secure his hands with but could see nothing.

'Let me go!' He turned his head and his eyes roamed the room, unfocused, searching for something. Or someone. She noticed that his heavy boots were covered in fresh mud. Still face-down, Ray stuck a hand deep into his top pocket and a puff of white powder coloured the air as he tried to pull out a clear plastic bag. Clio met Jeanie's eyes. Cocaine. It seemed that Henri had been correct about his addiction. Ray had clearly been back to the hut and helped himself to Henri's supplies.

Ray took advantage of Clio's distraction and rolled sideways, levering himself onto his feet. He took a step towards Clio and she could smell the bitter tang of his sweat. 'Who do you think you are, getting in my way?' His words flew out of his mouth, machine-gun fast, flecks of spit landing on her cheek. Revolted, she wiped them away.

Fists clenched, he turned to Angelo. 'And why are you in here?'

Jeanie barred his path. 'He's trying to stay alive. Just like the rest of us. We're rounding everyone up so we can all stop the killer striking again.'

'Not this crap again. Like you could protect anyone.' Ray sniffed loudly, rubbing his hand across his nose.

'I don't care what you think – we're doing what we have to in order to protect us all.' Clio looked him up and down. 'And frankly, now you're clearly high as a kite, I suggest that you stick with us.'

'High?' Ray scowled, sniffing loudly. 'I am not high.'

'No?' Clio indicated the plastic bag in his pocket. 'You could have fooled me.'

Ray swore at her, focusing again on Angelo. The teenager appeared to be trying to hide behind the curtains. Ray beckoned him over but he stayed still. 'I don't know why you're listening to these two. You should come with me.'

Angelo stared resolutely at the floor. 'No thanks. I'm good here.'

'Come on.' Ray bypassed Jeanie and grabbed Angelo's elbow.

Angelo's chin was up now. He unfurled himself to his full height, squaring up to his colleague. 'I said, I'm good here. I'm not as dumb as you think I am, Ray. I know your secret.'

Clio listened, alert for clues.

'I don't have secrets.' Ray's hand hovered around the packet in his pocket, as if desperate to get inside it.

'Oh no?' Angelo seemed to be growing taller by the second. 'That's weird. Because I followed you out into the woods last week when you were —' he held up his hands to make inverted commas '—"Dealing with the protestors." And it's weird, yeah? Because I couldn't see any protestors at all.'

Red spots appeared on Ray's cheeks. 'You take that back, you liar.'

Angelo held up his hands. 'Not a lie, Ray. And you know it. There was no one there. Just a tent. I had a look inside, didn't I? Just to check. And nope. No one there. Not one person.'

Ray spoke fast, his eyes narrowing. 'They were probably elsewhere on the island, setting up their next banner or spraying their graffiti somewhere.'

Angelo shook his head. 'Nah. I never saw anyone.'

'Whatever.' Ray reached into his pocket and pulled out the packet. White powder went everywhere but he didn't seem to care. 'That doesn't prove anything.'

Clio eyed him warily. He had lied about the protestors, and he had been in the passageway.

He was her prime suspect.

'Screw you all.' Ray clumsily tipped some powder onto the bedside table, chopping it into a chunky line with a battered credit card from the pocket of his jeans. He took out a rolled-up castle map and sniffed the powder up hungrily, raising his head with a roar as it disappeared. 'I'll do what I like.' He reached into another pocket and pulled out a hip flask, unscrewing the top and downing the contents. '*Yes.*'

He stumbled and Clio reached out to keep him upright.

'Get off me, you cow.' He batted her away.

'Fine.' Clio rolled her eyes. She had met too many men like Ray – perfectly pleasant until things got difficult, when their true colours came out. 'I was just trying to help, Ray.'

'I don't need your help.' He staggered towards the fireplace and started tapping the golden plaques that were attached to the walls above it, commemorating the various guests who had stayed in the room. 'Here.' He waited. 'No.' He swayed like a sapling in a breeze before trying the next one. 'It must be this one.' Another tap. 'No.' He looked around, eyes bloodshot now. 'Where the hell is it?'

Sighing, Clio turned her attention back to Angelo. 'So you're saying there were never any protestors?'

Angelo shrugged. 'Never saw them if there were.'

'That's a load of rubbish.' Ray's face was now a mottled red. 'There were protestors. I saw them. I chased them off the island.'

Clio threw a look at Jeanie. Ray was talking quicker and quicker, a man on fast forward. He was still tapping the fireplace, as persistent as a squirrel searching for a buried nut.

Reading Clio's mind, Jeanie untied her belt and grabbed Ray's left wrist, tugging it behind him. Then she seized the other one before he could protest, tying them together tight. 'You...' She gave him a shove in the chest and he reeled backwards before landing against the wall. It was fortunate he was so wasted – it made Jeanie's job easier. 'You stay there.'

'You bitch!' He jerked his wrists apart, only to find that he couldn't. Jeanie was good at knots. She had been a sailor once upon a time.

'I hate you.'

'Very original. And well done, Jeanie.' Clio turned back to Angelo. She felt almost maternal towards him now. He must be about the same age as Nina, her daughter, who was currently off at university studying to be a doctor, while this poor boy was here, dealing with murders and madmen. Clio wondered where his mum was – what she would say to make Angelo feel better. What his favourite food was. If his mum cooked it with extra butter or her own special mix of spices.

Clio looked at Jeanie. 'What do you think?'

Jeanie exhaled. 'I think Angelo is probably right – there were never any protestors.'

Clio sat down beside her friend. 'But someone must have put the tent up. Ray?'

'*No!*' Ray roared, before keeling over sideways.

Clio ignored him. 'Maybe he's been cooking up this plan for a while. Long enough to invent protestors, to pretend to be them, maybe while learning as much as he could about how the castle runs, waiting for an opportunity?'

Jeanie frowned. 'But why?' She ran a hand through her increasingly wild curls.

'I don't know.' Clio stared at her friend, her mind racing. 'But either way, I think we need to listen to Kieran's recordings.'

Jeanie nodded, her face grave.

Clio squeezed her friend's hand, knowing she needed encouragement. 'It feels like we're really close now. Fake protestors, perhaps as a cover for the killer. Kieran identifying the killer's motive. Maybe he tried to blackmail them too, as well as Valerie, and they killed him to keep him quiet? And then they poisoned the food to kill the rest of us but Jocelyn was the only unlucky one.'

'Could be.' Jeanie's voice was tiny. 'But doesn't that mean they still want to kill us?'

'Probably.' Clio nodded. 'And I'm as scared as you. But if we listen to these recordings then maybe we'll get more of an idea about who did it. Bluetooth should still work, shouldn't it? We can listen on my phone.'

Jeanie tried to smile. 'Okay.' She sighed. 'Let's do it. But first, can you get in touch with Amber? Tell her what's happening?'

'Sure.' As Clio raised the walkie-talkie to her mouth, Clio prayed that Kieran had recorded something that would show them the way out of this nightmare. Something that would save them from whoever the killer was. Something that would get them all safely home.

26

AMBER

Amber walked back along the path towards the castle, thinking about what she had learnt online. It was all starting to make sense. She just had to get back to the others and put her plan into action.

A bullet whistled past her head. She turned and dived into the trees, knowing only that she must keep moving, praying she could outpace whoever was behind her. As she sprinted through branches and over bumpy tree roots, her sodden trainers weren't even pretending to grip the rough path beneath her feet. She caught a flash of movement to her left, before tripping on a root and falling forwards. Rain poured down her face as she flew through the air, arms flailing in a desperate bid to avoid crash-landing into a tree.

Too late. Her face slammed against the rough bark and she fell down, winded. For a second, she lay, rain or possibly blood blurring her vision, her hamstring screaming at her for landing so hard. Then she heard footsteps behind her, closer now. She pushed herself up, ignoring the buzzing in her head. She had to get moving. She had to get back to the castle.

She looked down the slope at the edge of the forest, seeing the dark grey shape of the castle walls below her. She had to get inside before it was too late. She pushed her wet hair from her face as trees lashed above her, the storm raging. Her heart was pounding but she was close now. She could do this. Speed. And silence. That was all she needed. She had to be as silent as the grave.

'Clio to Amber, over.' The walkie-talkie on her belt crackled into life.

Amber jumped, hearing the boots behind her changing direction, starting to veer her way now. She reached for the off-switch on her walkie-talkie, but couldn't find it, her cold fingers scrabbling over the plastic.

'Clio to Amber, over!'

Amber ducked behind a tree before cutting down to the right. She was running the wrong way now, but at least she might have put the killer off the scent. She tried to detach the walkie-talkie from her belt, but her fingers were too cold. She bent over awkwardly, pressing the comms button, speaking in a whisper. 'Clio, shut up.'

'We've found something. Over.'

Amber's head hit a branch and she reeled, struggling for balance.

'Amber? We've found something. Over!'

Amber permitted herself a silent swear as she once again tried to remove the damn thing from her belt. No luck. She gritted her teeth, whispering again. 'Clio, stop talking. Now.' Amber saw a movement to her right and raised her fists. Fat lot of use they would be against a gun, but they were all she had.

'Oh, thank God you're alive. I was so worried. Over.'

Swearing, Amber bent down, pressing the comms button again. 'I won't be for much longer, if you keep talking, Clio. Over.'

At last, the penny dropped. 'Shit. Got it. Over.'

Where was the killer? Amber stared frantically around her, before darting left, cutting down a steep slope towards the castle. Just a few more metres. Just a few more...

The walkie-talkie squealed, feedback cutting through the air.

'Clio!'

'Sorry. Dropped it. Over.' More feedback.

Amber started to sprint. The killer must be about to catch her now. Any second, she expected to feel hands around her throat or a gun jabbing her spine. Her only option was to keep moving. The castle loomed above her, turrets steadfast, immune to the storm. If Amber took enough twists and turns, maybe she could still make it.

She turned as she came out onto the gravel drive, her trainers skidding as they hit the sharp stones. But she didn't break her stride, determined to get inside, to get to the rifle store, to get her hands on a weapon that could protect her. She was nearly there. Just a few more metres.

But then, just as Amber was reaching for the heavy metal door handle, somebody grabbed her. Now she was being wrenched off her feet, falling backwards, powerless. She crashed against the gravel, all the breath knocked from her body. She looked up, eyes blurring, knowing that this was the end. She did the only thing she could do. She pressed the comms button on her walkie-talkie.

Amber closed her eyes. It was official. Relaxing weekends away were not her thing.

27

JEANIE

In Kieran's room, Clio frowned at her walkie-talkie. 'That sounded bad.'

Jeanie nodded, her stomach dropping. 'I know. But we have to have faith in her. Okay?' Her own heart was beating so hard she might burst. 'We have to carry on. And this recording device isn't working. I can't hear a thing, and it was the same with the first one.'

Clio pressed a hand to her forehead. 'I know.'

'What else can we try?' Jeanie tried to come up with another line of enquiry, doing her best to ignore the pit of doom in her stomach. She felt something pressing against her thigh as she sat down on the edge of the bed and felt the compact form of a phone.

Kieran's phone. She had forgotten that she had taken it from the Salon. She pulled it out. 'We can look on here, Clio. It's Kieran's phone. Maybe there'll be more evidence on it that I didn't find last time.' She tapped the screen, only to remember that she needed a passcode. One that she very much didn't know.

'Oh God. We can't get into it.'

Clio launched into a frenzy of swearing that was so loud that neither of them heard Angelo speak. Jeanie peered at him, saw that his mouth was moving.

'Clio, be quiet. Angelo's trying to tell us something. What is it?'

Angelo swallowed uneasily. 'It's just that when I brought his bags up I saw him tapping the code into his phone.'

'Oh my God, I could kiss you.' Clio made a run for him and his face stiffened in terror.

Clio stopped. 'Don't panic. I'll restrain myself. What was it? The code?'

'1307.' Angelo gave a shy smile. 'I only remembered it because it's my birthday.'

'You are an absolutely bloody marvel.' Clio ran back to Jeanie. 'Tap it in. Go on.'

Jeanie grinned as the phone unlocked.

'What shall I look for?'

Clio leant over the screen. 'I don't know. Payments?'

As Jeanie scrolled through apps, Ray was still slumped down in the corner, muttering, nose tipping down towards the precious plastic packet in his top pocket. Angelo started pacing up and down the length of the room, unable to settle, looking as if he feared there might be a murderer around every corner.

Poor kid.

Clio tapped the screen. 'Is there a banking app on there?'

'Yes, but there's no Wi-Fi, remember, so we can't check it.'

'*Shit.*' Jeanie could see that Clio was now not only hangry but exhausted too.

Inspiration struck. 'Maybe we can find something in his photos. He could have screenshotted something useful – a transaction or something. Couldn't he?'

'Good thinking.' Clio nodded and Jeanie tapped on the photos icon.

'Ewwwwwww.' Clio closed her eyes as Jeanie scrolled through a particularly personal trio of pictures. 'Well, there's an image I'll never be able to forget.'

Jeanie hastily swiped on. Seeing a dead man's bits was yet another reason to forget this weekend as soon as she got home.

'Okay. This looks better.' She swiped on, finding a shot of a banking receipt for five thousand pounds from a Lloyds Bank account belonging to L. R. Green. 'Who is this?'

'Beats me.' Clio still looked a little nauseous. 'Could be anyone.'

'Why would they be paying him five thousand pounds?'

'Presumably for doing something dodgy for them.' Clio sighed. 'But of course we can't check anything. It just feels like we're clutching at straws. Without the internet we can't link anything. I bet the killer switched off everything just for that reason. So they could bloody well hide in the storm and the passageways and we're just – powerless to catch them. Or at least to prove it was them. You know?'

'I know.' Jeanie felt defeat swirling around them. 'It's so frustrating.'

Clio tapped the walkie-talkie against her leg. 'And it's so hard not to check in on Amber again, Jeanie.'

'I know.' Jeanie was still searching the photos. 'But she asked us not to. She needs us to stay quiet and keep investigating. She's Amber. She'll be fine.'

Jeanie only hoped she was right.

'I can't just stand here waiting.' Clio stood up. 'Let's go and switch the Wi-Fi back on.'

'What?' Jeanie looked at Clio askance. 'Clio, you can barely switch your kettle on and you blew up your oven the other week. How would you know how to find the router, let alone switch it back on?'

Clio puffed air out of her cheeks. 'Oh, ye of little faith.'

Jeanie eyed her friend suspiciously. 'Seriously, Clio…? The phone line's been cut off. The internet isn't going to work, is it?'

'Ah, but Jeanie.' Clio grinned and Jeanie realised how much she had missed her friend's smile in this hideous place. 'We have help, don't we?' She indicated Ray and Angelo. 'They might know how to do it.'

Jeanie smiled. 'Oh yes.'

'What?' The groundskeeper seemed to have run out of his customary resistance. 'Can't you lot just leave me alone?'

'Not yet.' Clio shook her head. 'Not until you tell me where the Wi-Fi router is.'

'Why should I tell you?'

Clio shrugged. 'Because if you don't, I'll flush your special packet down the loo.' She grabbed it from his pocket, ignoring his howl of protest. She put her head on one side. 'And if that doesn't work, I'll hit you over the head with the poker until you say yes.' She gave another smile. 'It's your choice.' She dangled the packet in front of his nose. 'What's it going to be?'

'It's in the north tower, in the basement.' Ray spoke quickly, eyes darting around the room. 'Now give it back.'

'Not yet. Can you fix the phone line?'

He shook his head. 'I'm the groundskeeper, not a telecoms expert.'

Angelo coughed. 'I'm good at technology. Got a 9 in my GCSE. I can give it a go.'

'Great.' Clio arched an eyebrow at Jeanie. 'Then let's all go and try to fix the phone line and get the internet back, then we can start linking the clues together. We don't have databases or forensics or the Police National Computer. We just have us.' She grabbed Ray by his arm and pulled him to his feet. 'I'll go first.' Clio moved towards the door. 'I've done a self-defence course.'

'Oh, la-di-da.' Ray rolled his eyes.

Clio sighed. 'Positive thinking, Ray. Have you heard of it?'

'You're keeping me prisoner. Am I meant to be happy about that?' Ray sniffed, righteously indignant. Behind his back, his fingers wove in and out of each other. He was wired. Restless. Dangerous.

Clio shoved him into his place behind her. 'Let's go. It's time to get whoever did this.'

There was a crackle from Clio's walkie-talkie. A slamming sound. Then nothing.

'Amber?' Jeanie's pulse spiralled as she distorted feedback pierced her ears. She grabbed her own walkie-talkie and held it to her lips. 'Amber?'

Static and silence.

'*Amber?*' She screamed the name into the silence.

Jeanie threw her head back and screamed again. '*Amber!*'

The silence went on and on, with no Amber to fill it.

Their best friend was gone.

28

AMBER

Lying on the gravel, Amber thought she must be dead.

One minute she had been about to enter the castle, then she had been pulled backwards and her head had slammed onto the gravel. She lay still, eyes closed. She wasn't ready to see what the afterlife looked like yet. But she was still freezing cold, so if she was now dead, then clearly whatever awaited her was just as depressing as Earth. Typical. She sighed, scratching one hand with the other as she did so. Was she just meant to lie here until she was summoned through to whatever came next?

Hang on. She scratched harder.

She could feel her nails against her hand.

Maybe she wasn't dead.

Summoning all her courage, she opened her eyes. She could see trees. The sky. A light flickering overhead, high on the castle walls. A string of fairy lights clanging against one of the windows.

Groggy, she pulled herself up on her elbows, groaning as her head began to throb, summoning what little strength she had.

'*Merde alors.*' A figure appeared above her, gun in hand. 'You are okay?'

'Henri?' Amber blinked. What was he doing out here with her?

She pushed herself up into a sitting position, every bit of her aching now. 'What – what happened?' She put a hand to the back of her head.

'I saw you heading into the castle and I ran after you.'

'Why?'

'Because it's safer to be together, yes? You told us that.'

So it hadn't been the killer chasing her? Or was Henri lying?

'Why did you pull me backwards?'

'I did not pull you.' His face was the picture of indignation. 'I just give you a little tap on the shoulder and you fell down.'

Indignation flared inside her. 'But you shot at me. And you chased me.'

'I did not shoot at you. I just accidentally fired the gun in your direction. Thank God I am a terrible shot. And I was chasing you because I was trying to catch up with you.'

'Henri, you have a rifle. Where did you get it?'

'I found it! I just found it, I promise.' His voice rose indignantly. 'I found it in the bushes.'

'Why were you in the bushes?'

'Ray put me there, the bastard.' His face darkened. 'He was in the hut earlier, wanting cocaine. I say no, he hit me many times and then he drags me into the forest. And then I find this gun.'

Amber remembered Melissa throwing one of the rifles out of the window of the snug. Henri's story could be true.

'That doesn't mean you needed to shoot me.'

'I told you. It was an accident.' He put a hand on her arm but she jerked it away. 'I have no idea how a gun works. I just picked it up and – boom.'

Amber frowned. Was this the truth? Could he be the killer? Henri was a drug smuggler, yes. Very scared of Marg, yes. But she didn't see him as a murderer. Plus, if he was the killer he would have ended her by now, surely?

In the flickering light above the door, Amber noticed spatters of red on his soaking chef's whites. 'So Ray beat you up?'

Henri scowled. 'He took me by surprise. It wasn't a fair fight.' He let off a volley of French swear words, spit flying like confetti at a wedding. 'That man is a nightmare. He is the killer, no doubt. He took some of my – my product, and then he drags me into the forest and dumps me there. Marg will kill me when she finds how much is missing.'

Amber thought this highly likely. She tried to get to her feet, but the gravel was too slippery for her shaking legs. She tried again, knowing that the two of them couldn't stay out here. Once again she fell. She looked around. They were too exposed. She had to get back inside to share what she now knew. And the theory she was working on seemed so unlikely – so audacious – that Amber could hardly believe it herself. She was desperate to talk it through with her two best friends, but to do that she needed to stay alive.

'Where were you going? When you saw me?'

'To the castle. To find Ray and tell him to leave me alone. To tell him a little bit about my boss and how he does not want to get on the wrong side of her.'

'Marg? I just saw her. She was on the island.'

Henri visibly paled. 'She was here? Oh, *non*.'

Amber couldn't help but agree. Marg didn't have a high tolerance for failure.

'I need to get inside before she sees me.' Henri glanced fearfully over his shoulder.

'It's okay. She'll be gone by now.' Amber got unsteadily to her feet. 'Let's go in.'

'Good idea.' A muscle flickered in Henri's cheek. 'You are sure she's gone?'

Amber saw the terror in his eyes. 'Yes. And don't worry too much. Ray is the one who Marg will go after, if he stole from her.'

'Well, at least I now have a gun, if she does come for me!' He raised it to the sky. A loud explosion followed and his body ricocheted backwards.

'*Merde*.' He sank to the ground. 'Sorry.'

Amber shook her head slowly. 'Don't worry about it, Henri. It's hardly the worst thing to happen today, is it? Just give it to me.'

He did as he was told. Holding the rifle under her arm, Amber turned the door handle, and soon they were inside the cavernous hallway, water flowing off their clothes and onto the floor. Amber slammed the door shut, trying the comms button of the walkie-talkie as she did so. 'Hello? Amber? Jeanie? Over?'

She turned to Henri, trying not to sound despairing. 'No answer.' Fear started to thrum through her. 'God, I hope they're alright.'

Then she heard footsteps. She gestured to Henri. 'We should hide. Just in case. This way.'

He nodded. The two of them crouched down behind a sideboard, barely breathing, as the footsteps came towards them.

29

CLIO

One minute Clio had been leading Jeanie, Angelo and Ray down the halls to try to reconnect the castle to the outside world, and the next she had got separated from everyone else. It must have been when she had swapped with Jeanie and placed herself at the back of the group. In one particularly dark corner she had paused, thinking she heard someone behind her, only to realise the others had gone when she started moving again.

Now, she was walking alone through the castle, feeling with every step that she was being observed by someone who did not mean her well. Every footstep seemed to land on a creaky floorboard and this corridor was full of drafts that could – if you were feeling paranoid – feel like human breath on your cheek.

Clio didn't believe in ghosts, but if she didn't know better, she would have sworn that the stuffed stag head in the corner was staring at her. When she had been an extra in a BBC movie of *Macbeth* she had been forced to spend hours on set next to one just like it. She hadn't really taken much notice of it until the pushy young director had claimed that it was acting better than Clio herself, leading to a dramatic walk-out that had felt triumphal until she had realised she was outside the studio with absolutely nobody trying to bring her back.

Something groaned to her left and she halted, terror starting to pulse.

There was definitely someone close by. It felt like the walls not only had ears, but also potential murderers waiting to burst out and destroy her. She started to whimper. Amber might be dead. Clio was alone. Everyone was dying and she had no idea where to go to even begin to feel safe.

She sank down to the floor, rolling onto her side, and folding herself into the smallest possible space. She dimly remembered doing the same when she hadn't got the recurring role in *Hollyoaks* that would have set her career on fire according to her then agent, Nigel. That evening Amber and Jeanie had come to find her, had fed her martinis and dragged her to the pier for fish and chips and arcade games. They had brought a fiver's worth of two pence pieces with them to play the slot machines with, and by the end of the evening Clio was herself again, having won a bright pink fluffy pencil and eaten her own bodyweight in candyfloss.

She closed her eyes, stiffening as she heard breathing. She had to fight, and yet had never felt more like giving up. She had to stand up for herself, and yet she didn't know how. The knife would plunge between her shoulders. The poison would drip into her veins. Nina would be motherless and would leave her medical degree to devote her life to becoming a failure and all because Clio had chosen to enter a competition to take her friends away for a relaxing weekend when a leaflet had been pushed through her letterbox.

Thinking of Nina was the spur she needed. Clio opened her eyes. She was always telling Nina to fight. It was about time she did the same herself.

She had been right. Someone was here. She saw feet next to a sideboard in front of her, a figure crouched, waiting. She felt determination rise within her. She would do whatever she could. Starting now. She was about to spring upwards, fists raised, when she looked again at the feet. Knackered old trainers with very skinny jeans above them.

She tipped her chin upwards, not quite believing she was right. 'Amber?'

'Clio.' Amber turned, putting a finger to her lips.

'I thought you were dead!' Clio threw her arms around Amber, not caring that her friend had never been a hugger. 'When you just cut off on the walkie-talkie like that.' Tears of relief overcame her. 'Oh, thank God.' She hugged Amber even tighter.

'Can't. Breathe.' Clio reluctantly released her. Amber arched her eyebrows. 'Me? Dead? Never. We're going to start a commune and live for ever, remember?' Her voice shook.

Clio did her best to smile. 'Well, wherever you've been, you look terrible.'

'Takes one to know one.' Amber pulled Clio across the shadowy hallway towards Henri. He appeared to have been stabbed, blood spattered all over his chef's whites.

'Are you OK?' Clio eyed him nervously. 'What happened?'

'Ray.' Amber crouched down next to him.

'Ray?' Clio struggled to follow. 'But we tied him up. Just now. Jeanie used her belt.'

'That's my girl.' Amber nodded admiringly.

'So he's the killer, then?' Clio's knee clicked as she dropped to the floor behind the sideboard, which had a purple diary and a tall white vase full of flowers on top of it.

'It's a long story.'

'So why were you waiting here?'

'We heard you coming and wanted to check who you were. The killer could be anywhere.'

'Adrenaline and danger. It's like our old Saturday nights at that dodgy club in Southampton.' Clio could joke now that she was with Amber.

Amber nudged her, speaking in a whisper. 'Where's Jeanie?'

Clio's spirits plunged again. 'With Angelo and Ray.'

'On her own? Shit.' Amber gasped. 'Why aren't you with her?'

'We got separated.' Even as she spoke, Clio felt guilt start to churn. 'One minute we were together, and then the next I was the only one there – somehow the other three got away from me. I don't know how. I feel awful. And I'm bloody worried about Jeanie.'

'Me too.' Amber looked at Henri. 'Do you know where they're headed? Where the main phone line is?'

'The north tower.'

'Where's that, Henri?' Clio glanced across at him.

'That way.' He pointed to the opposite end of the hallway.

Clio got to her feet. 'We need to find Jeanie.'

'Agreed.'

Clio opened her mouth to speak, before closing it again as she heard footsteps at the far end of the corridor.

Clio put her palms together in prayer. 'Please be Jeanie, please be Jeanie.'

They heard a loud whisper. 'Ray, are you sure it's this way? Because I think we've been here before, and we've lost Clio, and I'd like to go back and find her.'

'*Jeanie.*' Clio rushed across the hallway, enveloping her in a hug.

'What happened to being quiet, Clio?' Amber followed more slowly. 'Way to tell the killer where we are.'

'I told you, he's tied up!' Clio frowned indignantly. 'See?' She pointed at Ray.

Jeanie detached herself from Clio and leapt at her friend. 'Amber! You're alive!' Amber narrowly avoided being knocked over by the full force of her friend's adoration.

She disentangled herself and scanned the hall. 'Where's Melissa?' She took the two of them aside, eyeing up the three men who were standing awkwardly by the door, staring in opposite directions, for all the world as if they were in a queue for the loos.

'I don't know.' Clio felt a rush of confusion. 'What's going on, Amber?'

'I need to find her.' Amber frowned. 'I sent her back in here a while ago – after I saw Marg.'

'You saw Marg? Here?' Clio felt a flash of fear. She never wanted to actually meet Marg. She was one of those mythical figures, like Medusa or the financial ombudsman. Unpleasant, but you never actually had to deal with them.

'Marg has gone now, I expect.' Amber shook her head dismissively. She seemed worried about Melissa. Maybe the two of them had bonded during their time together. Clio hoped so.

'Are you sure you haven't seen her?' Amber's brows lowered. 'I sent her to find Ray.'

Clio licked her dry lips. Not another corpse. Please. 'Could she have misunderstood?'

Amber considered this. 'Unlikely. You know me, I say what I think.'

'Then where is she?'

The side door creaked open and Melissa came in, dripping wet and looking very sorry for herself, the rifle still in her hands. She strode straight over to Amber, who took the gun before Melissa could work out what she was doing. Melissa sounded breathless, as if she had been running. 'I couldn't find him. I couldn't find Ray. I looked inside and then went outside again. Nothing. I'm soaked through.'

'Don't worry about that. We found him.' Amber stared at her, her face impassive. 'And you and I need to talk.'

Melissa bristled. 'What is it this time?' She planted her hands on her hips. 'Are you going to accuse me of being a terrorist now? Because that's really the only place you have left to go.'

Amber didn't answer. She looked at Clio and Jeanie. 'Keep an eye on the rest of them.' She narrowed her eyes at Ray. 'Especially him. Don't let him get away.'

'You can count on us. Ray won't be going anywhere.' Clio sounded more confident than she felt. Internally, she was wondering why Amber was going outside and leaving them. What did she need to tell Melissa that she couldn't share with Clio and Jeanie?

Amber handed Clio a gun. Clio had never used one before and she didn't want to start now. But she forced herself to take it in her trembling hands. Amber herself kept hold of the second rifle.

Ray's eyes widened as Amber pulled Melissa towards the door. He tried to stand but fell backwards again. 'You can't keep me prisoner. This is illegal.'

'You keep telling yourself that.' Amber grabbed Melissa by the arm. 'Come with me.'

Melissa looked at her, shocked. 'Why? Amber, I thought – after everything we said out there...' Her jaw jutted out. 'I thought you trusted me.'

Amber laughed dismissively, the harsh sound completely at odds with the concern Clio had seen on her face earlier. 'I was just playing along with you, Melissa. That's what I do. I work out how to make people tell me what really happened. And you were an easy nut to crack.'

'I didn't need to be cracked because I haven't done anything!'

'Yes, you have, Melissa. Now get outside.' Amber pulled the front door open and shoved Melissa hard.

'You're crazy.' Melissa appealed to Jeanie and Clio. Clio looked away. She had no idea what Amber was doing, but there was no way she was going to show it. Past experience had taught her to trust her friend no matter what.

Melissa was still protesting as Amber led her outside. The door shut behind them. The silence was suddenly very loud indeed.

Jeanie's eyes were full of questions, but they had a job to do and Clio was ready.

'Right, you lot.' Clio put on her finest threatening expression. 'No messing about, okay?' She waved the rifle in the direction of the three men by the wall. 'We've got a gun and we're not afraid to use it.'

'Yeah.' Jeanie's voice shook.

Clio was unwavering. 'Don't move a muscle or I'll shoot.'

Jeanie nodded. 'Yeah.'

'Really?' Ray had somehow managed to get to his feet and had freed his hands. 'You'll shoot?' He swayed from side to side, while Henri and Angelo cowered against the wall, their hands over their faces.

Clio stared at Ray and started to shake. Yes, she was pointing the gun at him but she knew that she could never pull the trigger. Ray started to laugh. 'Thought so.' He charged towards her. Before Clio could react, he pushed her rifle aside and charged up the stairs.

'Jeanie! Get him!'

Jeanie started to sprint, but Ray's cocaine consumption gave him wings. He was nearly at the landing by the time Jeanie had got up speed.

'Sorry, Clio, he's getting away!'

And so it proved.

By the time Clio managed to point the rifle in the right direction, Ray had disappeared.

SUNDAY – 4 A.M

TWO HOURS UNTIL THE POLICE CAN COME

Three dead bodies

30

AMBER

Outside, Melissa was proving determined in her resistance despite the fact that Amber was holding a rifle. Amber almost admired her for it, but the majority of her mind was occupied by the murders. She hadn't wanted to leave the others alone, but there had been no choice. She hoped that the rifle she had given to Clio would deter the killer from attacking them in her absence.

Melissa came to a sudden halt. 'Amber, what the heck are you doing?'

Amber strode on, dragging her onwards. 'I need to check something without people finding out. And you, Melissa, are my cover story.'

'What does that mean?' Melissa stumbled, and nearly went face-first into the gravel.

'It means that I need everyone to think that I'm out here because I want to talk to you – that I brought you out here to interrogate you. Instead, we're out here because I want you to show me where the cove is. The one you mentioned earlier? Where Ray said the protestors kept their boat?'

'Why should I?'

'Because it holds the key to solving this thing.'

Melissa eyed her suspiciously before reluctantly trudging on through the lessening rain. 'Okay, then.' She sighed deeply. 'But I hope you won't be doing any more weird mind games from now on.'

'I'll try not to.' Amber shrugged. 'But I can't promise anything.'

They marched on in silence until they reached the jetty.

Melissa ran a shaking hand through her dripping hair. 'You know, after this, I think I'm going to stay indoors for the rest of my life.' She held on to the rickety wooden platform, staring out at the roiling sea. She pointed towards a thick copse of trees. 'It's over there. The cove.'

'Thanks.' Amber felt a kick of excitement. She was so close now. 'I need to get down there.'

'Sure.' Melissa seemed to have moved to a place beyond surprise. She gazed balefully at the sky. 'Actually, forget staying indoors. I'm emigrating to the Maldives as soon as this is all over.'

Amber tried to imagine herself with the sun on her back, a cocktail in her hand. Nope. She couldn't do it. Too damn cold. 'I'd take Bournemouth right now.'

'I'd take kidney stones over this.' Melissa frowned. 'Why do you need to get down to the cove?'

'Insurance policy.' Amber shouted over the wind before twisting Melissa's left arm behind her and snapping on the handcuffs she always carried with her.

Understandably, Melissa wasn't delighted by this development. 'What the hell...?' She was even less impressed when Amber pushed her down until she was sitting on the jetty with her back to the wall. Amber efficiently closed the other bracelet around a heavy steel ring used for mooring boats.

She pulled out the satellite phone.

Melissa stopped swearing for a second. 'Hang on. Is that... a sat phone?'

'Sure is.' The corner of Amber's mouth curved upwards.

'Does it work?' Melissa reached for it with her right hand but Amber snatched it away.

'It does.'

'How did you get it?' Melissa sank down again.

'Marg gave it to me.'

'Who's Marg?' Melissa frowned.

'Doesn't matter.' Amber started to walk away. 'Back in a minute.'

She ran down the steps at the back of the jetty and raced through the trees. Even though she was pretty sure the killer was otherwise engaged, she didn't want to leave Melissa alone for long. The cove was deserted, except for a pile of heavy branches high up in a sheltered area of the rocky beach. Amber ran towards it, lifting one up to see what lay beneath.

Five minutes later she was unlocking the cuffs. Melissa looked furious and did her best to swing her fist towards Amber's face. Amber caught it, and the two women were so close to each other that Amber could smell Melissa's sweat.

'Look, Melissa. I get that you think I'm a nutter. I get that you have no idea what I'm playing at. But I promise you, we will get out of this alive if you do what I say.'

'You mean you want me to trust you.'

'Yes.' Amber started walking, tucking the handcuffs into her back pocket. Melissa fell into step beside her. 'That's exactly what I mean. I have a plan and I need your help.'

'Does it involve tying me to a stake?'

Amber smiled. 'No. But I can't do it without you. I'll tell you all about it as we head back.'

Melissa folded her arms and stopped walking. 'And what if I don't want to help? What if I'd rather stay out here and take my chances on my own?'

Amber shrugged. 'Well, then, I'd have to make you go inside, wouldn't I?'

'And how are you going to make me?'

Amber walked towards Melissa, until their noses were inches apart. She wondered if Melissa's back hurt in the mornings too, if her fingers were so thin that she had to get rings resized as Amber did. She had so many questions. But for now, none of that mattered. For now, all that was important was getting back to the castle.

Amber indicated the rifle in her hands. 'Well, I do have this…'

'So you do.' Melissa arched an eyebrow in acknowledgement.

Amber carried on. 'But I won't use it. All I'm asking is for you to have a little faith in me. I know I've handcuffed you and accused you of murder, but please believe me, Melissa. I need you to help me catch the killer. Do you want to hear how?'

She waited for several seconds. Then Melissa raised an eyebrow.

'Okay then, you crazy lady. But only if you give me some proof.'

Amber nodded eagerly. 'The phone was the key. It helped me to correlate Valerie's real name with the photo I found in the protestors' tent. Because someone at the castle *was* involved in Valerie's scam back then. And Kieran's article is how they found her again, after all those years.'

Melissa glanced sideways. 'Who was it?'

'You'll find out very soon, if my theory is true.'

'You're not going to tell me?' Melissa scowled at Amber. 'Trust my bloody luck. Finding my long-lost half-sister and then learning that she is a closed book.' She sighed dramatically. 'I just wanted to find my only remaining family. Maybe have a hug or two, see each other at Christmas, send each other dog memes when we're bored, that kind of thing.'

'Don't ever send me dog memes.'

'Well, I'm hardly going to send them to you once I'm dead, am I?' Melissa was practically growling now.

They were nearly at the castle.

Amber turned to the woman at her side. 'You're not going to die, Melissa.'

'Well pardon me for not trusting you, when you just put me in handcuffs for no apparent reason.'

'I told you. I did that in case anyone was following us. It had to look legit, didn't it?'

'Why?'

'I have a plan. If you'd just listen...'

Melissa held up a hand. 'I don't want any part of it.'

Now panic was rising inside Amber. 'But you have to do what I say.'

'Oh no I don't.'

'Oh yes you do.'

'Oh no I don't.'

'Oh yes...' Amber stopped. 'Look, we're not in a bloody panto here.'

'What the hell's a panto?' Melissa folded her arms, her expression stony. 'Tell me why I should trust you? Why should I listen to you?'

Amber took a deep breath.

'Well?' Melissa was exuding all the patience of a police siren.

'Because I want to keep you alive, Melissa. I want to keep you alive so I

...rds so much harder than chasing killers or

... 'So I can get to know you better.'
...ped a hand behind her ear, stepping forwards.

...erated. '*So I can get to know you better, okay?*'
...rved upwards. 'Oh, well, now you've told me you

...say that.'

Melissa's eyes glinted. 'Sure. You're a shy one. I get it.'

Amber realised she was clenching her fists. 'I am not...'

Melissa held up a finger. 'No, I know, but it was so much fun seeing your face. So...' She was moving fast towards the castle now. 'What's the plan?'

Swallowing down her discomfort, Amber told her.

Now she just had to hope everything would come together as she had planned.

31

AMBER

Angelo ran to greet them, his chest heaving.

'Ray's gone crazy.'

Clio and Jeanie appeared, sprinting down the stairs together.

'I'm so sorry, Amber.' Jeanie skidded to a halt, her face flushed. 'He got away.'

Amber shook her head, trying to keep her panic down. 'My bad. I shouldn't have left you with him.'

Clio was on her other side, breathing fast. 'No, it's our fault. I…'

Amber held up her hand. 'It's okay, Clio. But we haven't got much time. Melissa, can you do what we talked about?'

Melissa nodded. 'Okay.'

There was a loud crash from upstairs. Whatever Ray was doing, he was giving it his all.

'I told you.' Henri was pacing up and down. 'Ray is crazy. All he wants is cocaine. More cocaine.' He let off a string of words that made Amber wonder how swearing sounded so much better in French, before marching off towards the kitchen, flinging his hands around.

'Don't eat the food in there!' Jeanie yelled after him.

Angelo looked worried. 'Why shouldn't he?'

Amber explained. 'The food in the kitchen is poisoned – the beef bourguignon in the casserole dish, anyway. Clio and Jeanie left a sign on it, saying not to touch it.' Even as she spoke, she wondered if it had still been there when they had discovered that Jocelyn's body was gone. Maybe the sign had fallen off. Maybe the killer had removed it.

'But...' Angelo put a hand to his mouth.

'But what?'

'But I ate some of that.' His hand went to his stomach. 'I didn't see a sign, so I just – tucked in. I was hungry.'

'When did you eat it?' Jeanie was at his side now, eyes wide with concern.

'I ate it...' He looked at his watch. 'At least an hour ago?'

Clio put her head on one side. 'That's weird.'

'Why?'

'Because you should be dead by now.'

'I should?' He was breathing fast now, sweat breaking out on his brow, a panic attack in the making. Amber didn't have time for that.

'Angelo, there's no way you've been poisoned. You'd already be dead if you had.'

He pressed his hands to his stomach. 'Oh my God. Dead?' He collapsed down to the floor, head in hands. 'I hate this place. I just want to get out of here.'

Amber grabbed him by the hand, pulling him to his feet.

'Let's go into the Red Room.' She marched down the long corridor, past ancestors staring at her with a disdain that was now entirely merited based on the total and utter state of them all. In the distance she could hear banging and smashing. It sounded like Ray was getting stuck into some serious destruction.

Jeanie appeared at her side. 'Are you okay, Amber?'

'Of course.' Amber felt guilt flaring inside her. She hated covering up her real intentions to her friends like this, but it was too risky to talk. As she had stood outside earlier, the phone screen glowing in front of her, the threads of the case finally weaving together in her mind, she had known that there was only one chance to get this right and bring the killer out into the light.

'Are you sure, Amber?' Clio's face was serious. 'You just seem a bit...'

'I'm fine.' Amber knew she sounded abrupt, but she really couldn't tell them yet. Soon. Very soon, just as long as her plan played out the way she wanted it to. 'I'm just trying to keep us all alive until the police get here, okay?'

'Okay, boss. Pardon me for caring.' Clio held up her hands.

Amber shook her head. 'I hate it when you call me that.'

'I know.' Clio nudged Amber with her elbow. 'That's why I do it.'

Amber frowned.

'No sense of humour either, I see.' Clio tutted. 'Oh well. A girl's got to try.'

'Ssssshhhhh.' Jeanie was leading Angelo, who shuffled along as enthusiastically as a prisoner going to the gallows. 'You'll upset him.'

Seeing the trembling teenager, Amber felt a renewed surge of panic. The shreds of evidence had been tricky to mesh into anything resembling the truth. But finding the photo had been a pivotal moment, with the phantom protestors suddenly dissolving to reveal a killer with every reason to hate, with every reason to chase a long-cherished revenge. Amber could see their thinking, could understand how they had used the secret passageways to navigate their way around the castle.

Now, Amber had to prove it by catching them out. She stalked into the Red Room to see Melissa chucking logs on the fire, ignoring the sparks flying up into her face. Smoke was being blown back down the chimney by the storm outside, and the smell of charred wood made Amber's eyes water.

The fire was lit. Step one.

Melissa bustled past, heading for the kitchen. A second later, the fire alarms began to shriek throughout the castle – a high-pitched wail that was so piercing that Amber covered her ears. Step two.

Then Amber heard more crashing from the staircase that led to the snug. She walked back out into the hall to investigate further. She walked forwards, sniffing. Smoke was coming from the staircase that led to the snug.

She stopped. There wasn't meant to be an actual fire. That wasn't part of the plan.

Clio's eyes were wide. 'The crime scene – he'll burn all the evidence!'

'*No!*' Amber started running for the stairs, keen to get to the snug before too much damage was done. She wondered what was going on inside Ray's drug-addled brain. Maybe he was trying to destroy evidence, or maybe he had totally lost it now. Either way, he was dangerous. She ran up the stone steps two at a time, praying that Ray was too wasted to have really set anything on fire. But that hope died as thick smoke billowed down the staircase, threatening to overwhelm her. She put her hand over her mouth, trying to keep breathing.

'Ray.'

Nobody replied.

'Ray!'

The snug door was unbolted, and she ran inside. The once chilly room was thick with smoke, flames licking the curtains, the sofa alight. All the candles had been pushed onto their sides, setting fire to whatever they touched.

On the floor she saw a man next to Valerie's body.

'Ray.'

He didn't move.

'Oh, for God's sake.' Her eyes streaming now, Amber grabbed his arm and pulled. He was unconscious and appeared to be made of lead. She tried again, bracing her feet against the floor and pulling hard. He started to slide along the floor, away from Valerie's body.

His eyes were shut. Lord knew what state he'd be in when he woke up. He had fallen off the wagon so hard he probably had concussion.

Amber was gasping now, the strain of pulling his dead weight along almost more than she could handle. Somehow, she got him out to the landing and turned her attention to the snug. She ran in and grabbed the fire extinguisher that she had spotted earlier under the window and unleashed it on the sofa and curtains. For a minute she wondered if she was winning, but slowly, the flames grew smaller and went out. Valerie lay untouched amidst the charred and blackened furniture and curtains around her.

Amber took one look around, checking that the fire was really over, before closing the door and running back out to Ray. She had nothing to secure him with, but he didn't look like he would be going anywhere in the near future. He was asleep against a pillar, his head lolling to one side.

It was time to get downstairs to see if her plan would work.

She was just reaching the first-floor landing when her friends appeared.

'Amber!' Jeanie put a hand to her heart. 'Thank God. Will you stop running off like that? I can't take it any more!'

'I will.' Amber tried to get her breathing under control. 'Look, there isn't much time. So can I ask you to do what I say and to trust me?'

Jeanie looked at Clio. Clio looked at Jeanie.

'Always,' they said in unison.

Amber exhaled, handed Jeanie the rifle that she had taken from Henri, and told them what she wanted them to do.

'You're sure we can do this?' Clio swallowed, gripping her own gun.

'Yes.' Amber looked her straight in the eyes. 'The killer won't know what hit them.'

'Um. If you say so.' Clio was pale. 'And I just wanted to say – to say how sorry I am for bringing us all here. This whole nightmare is my fault.'

'You didn't know what was going to happen.' Amber squeezed her shoulder.

Clio bit her lip. 'But...'

'No buts.' Amber shook her head. 'You're the bravest and the best. Both of you. Now, let's do this.'

Jeanie was already on the move, heading as directed towards the Salon. Her head was high, but Amber could see that she was shaking, her fists clenched, her nails digging into her palms.

Amber took a deep, steadying breath. There was such courage in both her friends. They would get through this.

'Go on, Clio. You know what you have to do.'

'I'm on my way.' Clio's eyes glistened with tears, but her mouth was set firm. Amber knew that she could rely on her, just as she could rely on Jeanie. They would always be her people. Nothing could ever change that.

Clio was walking away too, heading for her designated position, clutching her gun.

Amber headed in the opposite direction. She didn't have a gun but she would have the element of surprise.

Now all they had to do was wait.

32

JEANIE

Jeanie shivered as she waited in darkness of the Salon, clutching the rifle. With the lights out, she felt even more jumpy. Amber had told her to switch them off as soon as she entered the room. As she waited, she wondered if she would ever be able to shoot someone, however evil they were. How did anyone ever do that? She couldn't imagine the anger you must feel to end someone else's life.

In all her previous encounters with killers, she had been weapon-free, acting on impulse – to defend a friend or to prove herself and reveal the truth. Now, the gun felt wrong in her hand. Everything felt wrong, even the sodden dress that had been glamorous once upon a very long ago, back when she was sipping champagne, back when gourmet food and giggles were the only things on the weekend menu.

Jeanie sighed, her hand pressed against the fireplace, the entrance to the secret passage next to her. What if Amber was wrong? Jeanie might be waiting here only for someone to spring through the door behind her to take her down. Or what if they appeared from a different direction? What if Jeanie was looking the wrong way? Nothing would surprise her. Once upon a time this weekend was about comfortable beds and fine dining. Instead, her main memories would be hunger, dead bodies and distrust.

Jeanie told herself to hold her nerve. She could feel herself spiralling –

her mind running to all the bad places, the jagged places, the ones where she didn't make it back to the mainland alive. She took a deep breath, telling herself that she could do this. She could wait alone in a castle for someone to emerge from the shadows. She had done harder things. Giving birth to twins in a lay-by had been pretty special. She was strong. She was a mum, a friend, a wife, a detective. She was ready.

The grandfather clock in the hall ticked on, its long gold hands inching slowly towards 5 a.m. A floorboard creaked. More thunder rumbled outside the boarded-up windows. Despite herself, Jeanie felt sleep overcoming her.

And that was when she heard it. A scrabbling in the wall.

She bit down hard on her lip, trying to stop herself from crying out with fear. She pressed her ear to the cold hard stone of the fireplace, listening with every fibre of her being to what was coming her way. Slowly, the scrabbling moved along inside the wall, as if a very large rat was making its way towards a source of food.

Jeanie felt her stomach lurch. She wanted her friends here with her. She wanted to feel less alone.

She wanted to run.

But she knew what she had to do. Amber had explained out in the hall that a suspect was going to appear downstairs, either via the passageway exit in the Salon or via the exit in the conservatory, flushed out of the tunnels by the threat of fire. When they did, she, Clio or Jeanie would be waiting, and all they had to do was overpower the killer and call for help. It was a simple task, really – just as easy as her usual jobs of carrying out online surveillance on a fraudster or tracking a husband to an illicit hotel stay. Surprise would be on her side. The killer wouldn't know that she was waiting.

She took a deep breath as the noise became louder. Soon, the person approaching would be sticking their head out, looking around, only to feel Jeanie's gun pressing into their neck. She would not let them go. She would be as strong as Amber believed her to be. She gripped the rifle tightly, breathing as quietly as she could, ensuring that the killer wouldn't realise she was there and disappear again down the tunnel. She pressed herself against the wall as the sounds approached. There was a scraping noise and then a rush of cold air as the passageway door opened, and two trainered feet popped out.

Jeanie was ready, gun raised.

Except the Salon door burst open behind her and Henri appeared. He ran towards Jeanie, his mouth open in what sounded like a war cry. 'I will save you!'

'What the...?' Jeanie looked towards him, giving the new arrival the perfect opportunity to smash the gun barrel into her face.

'Oh *God*.' Jeanie dropped the rifle, accidentally kicking it behind her. She saw that her assailant, hooded and wearing a balaclava, was already moving away, punching Henri deftly in the groin as they went. He fell to the ground, moaning.

'Henri...?' Jeanie staggered to her feet. The figure had already vanished through the door.

'I thought I could save you.' Henri's eyes were watering with pain. Or he was crying. Jeanie couldn't tell. As she moved towards him the smell of brandy was so thick you could set fire to it.

Irritation flickered inside her. 'Well instead you've saved the killer, you idiot.'

Jeanie scrabbled for her walkie-talkie. This bloody castle was so big that her friends wouldn't hear her if she simply shouted for them. '*Amber!*' Jeanie yelled. '*Clio. Amber. The suspect is on the loose.*'

No answer.

She gave up and ran as fast as she could, her chest burning, her breath coming in gulps. '*We have to stop them.*'

She was in the hall now, the killer sprinting towards the front door, nearly out, nearly free.

'Oh God, *no*.' Jeanie surged forwards, powered by an overwhelming sense of fury. She was tired of people like this, people who believed that they had the right to decide who should live and who should die. Rage made her quicker and she powered down the hall, head down, fists pumping.

She was catching up with them now. She was so close. They weren't as speedy as they had first seemed, and they were now only two or three metres ahead of Jeanie. She could hear wheezing and the stumble of a foot tripping over carpet.

Jeanie gritted her teeth, ignoring the screaming pain in her face, ignoring the fact that her heart was about to explode out of her chest. Nothing mattered but catching whoever this was.

She reached out and one hand grasped the soft fabric of the suspect's top. She yanked it backwards, throwing them off balance, and bringing them crashing to the floor. Jeanie leant down and jerked the black balaclava off their head, wanting to see who could have done all this, who could have ruined a weekend and ended three lives.

The face she saw made her gasp.

No. It couldn't be.

Jeanie began to scream.

33

CLIO

Clio ran towards the front door as if her life depended on it. Which, in a way, it did as Jeanie looked like she was about to be flipped backwards by the figure in black writhing on the floor, and a life without Jeanie was unthinkable. As Clio ran, the suspect plunged two fingers deep into Jeanie's eyes.

'Oh God.' Jeanie's hand went to her face and for a moment Clio was sure it was all over for her friend. '*Shit*. That hurt.' But then Jeanie went back in, fighting with renewed vigour.

'Use the gun!' God, this corridor was long. Clio felt like she would never reach Jeanie. 'Jeanie, the gun!'

Jeanie's voice was high. 'I dropped it!' Clio was nearly with Jeanie now, and could see that her friend was wrestling with her assailant. Clio raised her own, before realising that she might well hit Jeanie, so she put it aside and took the only available option, flying through the air, landing on the person's legs.

'I'm here.'

'Thank God.' Jeanie's curls were flying around her face as she fought to suppress the person on the ground.

'You okay?' Clio put all her weight into stopping the suspect from kicking her in the face.

'Yes.' Jeanie's voice was thick with effort. 'Could do with a margarita, but apart from that I'm tickety-bloody-boo.' She punched the suspect in the face, kneeling over them, panting, as Clio pushed their arms down.

Clio looked down at the face on the floor beneath them.

'Oh my God, it's you!'

She felt a rush of shock. The suspect was a woman. One who now had short red hair instead of her previous long grey locks, whose ankle cast had gone, who seemed to have lost the port wine stain that had once dominated her left cheek and whose teeth were now entirely straight.

Clio gripped the woman's wrists tighter. 'You seem to have made a bit of a miracle recovery, Jocelyn. How's that ankle of yours?'

'Piss off.' Jocelyn spat. To think Clio had wasted time feeling sorry for this woman. 'This is assault.'

'Not really. It's a citizen's arrest.' Amber was now with them, Melissa at her side. 'Hi, Jocelyn. Or should I say hi, Lynda.' She turned to Clio and Jeanie. 'She and Samantha used to know each other, back in the day. They met when they both worked for a cafe in Hastings called Espresso Yourself. Meet Lynda Green.'

'L. R. Green!' Clio clicked her fingers. 'She paid Kieran £5k!'

Amber gave a low whistle. 'Did she now? That figures.'

Jeanie held her hand out for the cuffs and forced them on with a triumphant click.

'My name is Jocelyn Robbins.' The woman adopted a pleading expression. 'I told you. Clio, dear, you know I couldn't have been the murderer. You were with me when Valerie was killed.'

Clio eyed her doubtfully. 'I was also with you when *you* were killed. Except here you are, alive and kicking. And looking like a very different person.'

Lynda bared her teeth. 'This is an outrage.'

'No.' Amber shook her head, her face hardening. 'What you have done is an outrage.' She pulled Lynda to her feet, swerving to avoid the gobbet of spit that her captive fired in her direction. 'I thought the fire alarm would get you out of those tunnels, though. I knew you'd head for the ground floor to get away from the flames. You see, I had to stop you hiding in the passageways, waiting until we all disappeared so you could make your escape as your real self. Nice of Ray to lend a little extra fire to proceedings too.'

Lynda's mouth set into a thin line. 'I don't know about any passageways.'

'That's strange, seeing as you've been hiding in them for quite a while now. And seeing as you've just exited one into the Salon.' Amber shrugged. 'You were terrified of going down in the fire – so you took the risk of running out and making your escape. It's just what I would have done in your shoes.'

Lynda stared at the ground, mute.

Clio looked at her friend admiringly. 'So you were laying a trap?'

Amber nodded. 'I was.' She gave a sheepish smile. 'Sorry I couldn't share before – but I was worried that Lynda would somehow overhear me. I knew that's where she was hiding, just as I knew she was just going to wait until the police came, stick on a disguise to make her blend in with them – maybe a SOCO suit or even a police uniform – and then she was just going to sail away in the boat she had stashed in the cove, ready for a new life.'

Melissa smiled. 'That's what you were checking out there?'

'Yes. I was seeing if the boat was there. But I was also finding out whether Kieran's body was in it. Which it was.'

Lynda threw up her hands. 'That's nothing to do with me.'

'Sure, it isn't.' Amber raised an eyebrow. 'Even though you are the only one amongst us who would have had long enough to put his body there. Because once we left you in the kitchen you went to work, didn't you? You must have had a right old laugh as we hunted around for the killer. You crept down to the Salon, listened outside until you were sure it was empty – you were wrong, but never mind – and then you wrapped Kieran up in a drape and took him to the boat somehow. What were you going to do – put to sea and then drop him over the side? That way both dead bodies would have vanished, and you would be home free. No one would look for you. Very clever, really.'

Lynda's eyes swirled with hatred. 'You're making all this up.'

'I wish I was.' Amber took a deep breath. 'But just in case you try to run now, I should tell you that I disabled the motor while I was outside, so that you couldn't get off the island even if you wanted to. And I've already told the police who killed Valerie and Kieran using the satellite phone Marg gave me. They're looking forward to meeting you, Lynda.'

Amber took a breath, surveying her captive. 'Now, let's take her to the Red Room.' She marched an unwilling Lynda into the vast room, pushing her down onto the sofa.

Melissa sank down onto one of the armchairs, closing her eyes for a minute. 'My brain's shot to hell. This kind of drama takes it out of a girl, you know.' She exhaled. 'I really do need a coffee. Can we make one now?'

Amber grinned. 'In a minute.'

Clio sat down too, feeling as if she would never move again. 'Start at the beginning. So Jocelyn/Lynda/whoever she is, she was Valerie's accomplice in the Ponzi scheme? Is that what you're saying?'

Amber nodded as Henri and Angelo came in with Jeanie and sank onto a long red chaise longue. Jeanie touched her nose and winced and Clio hoped that the police would bring a paramedic with them when they came.

'Back in the nineties, Lynda and Samantha worked together to set up the scheme, but Samantha, soon to be Valerie, ran off with all the money, leaving Lynda here with nothing. She got all the flak and a lengthy prison sentence too. When she got out, Lynda searched for years, decades even, to find Samantha, but of course she was long gone and Valerie la Fontaine was unrecognisable. That kept her safe from Lynda here.' She indicated their captive, who was staring mutinously at the ground.

'How did you work it out?'

Amber pulled a photo from her pocket. 'I found this in the tent that supposedly belonged to the protestors. I recognised Jocelyn straight away, despite the fact she's way younger, minus the false teeth and the wig and the cast, and then I saw Valerie next to her – look, the eyes are the same, despite all the surgery. Same colour and shape. Look...' She tapped the satellite phone. 'You can see the similarity in the picture that accompanied Kieran's first article, too. You'd have to be looking for it, but it's there – and the title of the article, "Who is the real Valerie la Fontaine?", makes you wonder who Valerie really is, doesn't it?'

Amber looked around the group.

'Then I found Lynda's name in a piece about the pair in an online archive of their town newspaper. I Googled the scandal – the Ponzi scheme

– and found coverage of Lynda's trial and a picture of her with Samantha at the cafe, so I guessed that Lynda had seen Kieran's article and came hunting. And it makes sense that she paid Kieran for more information on her old accomplice. Just to make sure she'd found her target.'

Melissa gave a low whistle. 'So Kieran's article – and the picture – kicked this whole thing off?'

'Exactly.' Amber grinned. 'It finally gave Lynda the information she needed to go and get what she was owed. She even got one of the staff to make sure she won the competition to come here.'

Clio's heart beat faster. 'Not Melissa?'

'Hell, no.' Melissa shook her head 'That one's not on me.'

'So who…?'

But Amber was talking again.

'But before the launch weekend she stayed on the island in her tent, pretending to be a group of protestors, using wigs, outfits, props to disguise herself. Valerie hadn't arrived yet, so there was no risk of anyone knowing who she was. And she made her plan, scoping the castle, and set up her escape. She was never coming out of here as Jocelyn Robbins. She was going to become someone totally new. Taking a leaf out of Valerie's book, I guess.'

Lynda snarled. 'You have no proof.'

'I do have proof, actually. I have the photo.' Amber held her gaze. 'And in those tunnels the police will find everything else they need to convict you of her murder, while in the boat they'll find Kieran's body with your DNA on the drape covering it, unless you were the kind of careful that means you can carry or drag somebody a long way without transferring any DNA.'

Clio frowned. 'But I was with Lynda – who we knew as Jocelyn then – when it happened. When Valerie was killed, I mean. So how could she have done it?'

'Were you with her, Clio?' Amber held her hands wide. 'Or were you outside the loo, while she was inside it?'

Jeanie's mouth dropped open. 'Oh my God. Do you mean there's another secret passage from that disabled loo? One that goes all the way to the snug?'

'I do.' Amber nodded. 'And that's where I was waiting while you and Clio were in the Salon and the Red Room exits.'

Clio's mind whirled. She looked at Lynda. 'But you were – singing. You were bloody singing!'

Amber walked quietly to Lynda's side. 'A recording on her phone, I suspect.' She reached into Lynda's pocket and pulled out a mobile. 'I'm sure this will show that she has quite a few recordings lined up. Creaking floorboards. Whispering voices. Shouting protestors. The lot. She was very well prepared for this murder. The only thing she hadn't planned for was the storm.'

Lynda kept silent, her gaze on the floor.

Amber folded her arms. 'So that's how she did it. The only thing I don't know is whether you meant to kill Valerie, Lynda. Maybe you told yourself you wanted to go up there to get what you were owed. To get a big fat cheque and then run. And maybe Valerie wouldn't play ball. Maybe she argued with you – said she didn't have the money? Or said you didn't have proof of anything you were saying? And it was then that you discovered you'd lost the photo that was your evidence? Or maybe she went for you with the knife as soon as you spoke?' Amber shrugged. 'I don't know. But all those years of hating her just came out and you hit her over the head more than once, and then ran back down the tunnel, leaving her to die.'

'This is ridiculous.' Lynda's eyes darted around the room. 'You don't know any of this – you're making it up.'

'Do you know what?' Amber held up a finger. 'I think you might have got away with it – in fact, I think you came pretty close to doing just that.' She sighed. 'It's just such a shame that your accomplice isn't as good at all this as you are.'

Lynda's head shot up. 'I don't have an accomplice, because none of this is true! Why won't you listen to me?'

A voice rang out from the doorway. 'Hands up!'

Ray stood in the doorway, a rifle in his hands.

It must be Clio's rifle. The one she had left in the hall. Clio groaned as Ray lifted the barrel and pointed it straight at Amber's heart.

34

AMBER

Amber had been waiting for him. 'Ray?'

His eyes were wild, his hair flying in all directions. 'You don't get to talk.' He jabbed a finger in her face. 'You just do what I say.' He had deep hollows beneath his eyes and he was tapping his foot, a flickering, restless presence, his knuckles white around the rifle.

She opened her mouth, but he got there first. 'Shut it.'

'But...'

'I said shut it.'

Amber held up her hands, moving deliberately in front of everyone else. She sensed Clio and Jeanie to her left, poised to spring, but she held up a hand in a clear signal to stop them. She had this handled, she tried to tell them telepathically. Everything would be okay.

She returned her attention to the gun and the man holding it, her mind racing to work out how to get the result she wanted.

'Ray, you can't help her now. Put the gun down.'

'What do you mean? I don't even know her.' He pointed the barrel at Lynda on the sofa before training it on Amber again. 'I thought she'd broken her ankle?' His brow creased. 'Actually, I thought she was dead. What the fuck?'

'Nice try, Ray.' Amber took a step forwards. 'But I know you're her son.'

'You're crazy.' He held the gun higher, pointing it at her head. 'And step back. I'm not afraid to use this. Nice of you to leave this out in the hall for me.'

Amber heard Clio swearing beneath her breath. She wanted to tell her that it was okay, that she didn't blame her, but there would be time for that once all this was over.

For now, she must concentrate on him. She held up her hands. 'Look, Ray. I know that you did this together. You and Lynda.'

He shook his head, trying to laugh. 'What?'

Amber sighed. 'Ray, you even look like Lynda – the same eyes, the same chin. And it's my guess that if we do a DNA test, we will find that you are her son.'

He put his finger on the trigger. 'Then it's best you don't do one, isn't it?'

Amber felt a jolt of fear. He was high. He was desperate. There was every chance he might actually kill her. 'Don't drag yourself down with her, Ray.' She needed to offer him a way out. 'You didn't know she was going to kill Valerie, did you?' She softened her voice. 'You thought she was going to get a load of money from her, maybe make her sell the castle, give you a cut? Was that it?'

Ray held his ground. 'I don't know what you're talking about. You're making all this up.'

'I wish I was.' Amber kept her eyes on him, her voice low and insistent. 'But the truth is she always screws things up for you, doesn't she? A whole childhood with a mum in prison. Can't have been easy, can it?'

'I told you. I don't know what you're on about.' Ray's voice shook.

'You see, Ray, I think she dragged you down with her. It's my guess that she talked to you after the murder somehow, and said the plan had gone wrong. She said that Valerie had refused to hand over Lynda's half of the money, or something along those lines. Maybe she told you that Valerie had got violent instead, and I bet Lynda said that she had no choice but to kill her. Self-defence, maybe?' She saw a gleam of recognition in Ray's eyes. 'And since then I think you've been stuck in the biggest nightmare of your life. I think you've both been scrabbling to cover up what your mum did. I think she ordered you to find Kieran and kill him, because he had worked out who Lynda was, and her connection to Valerie, and made the mistake of telling her so after the first murder. Maybe he had even recorded what happened. God knows, he was doing dodgy recordings around the castle – who knew what he had captured?'

Ray shook his head. 'You've got no proof.'

'You're right, Ray. But it's all there in the tunnels, isn't it? And in the boat. Your prints on his body. Because you were disturbed after you killed Kieran – you heard a gunshot in the hall and then voices. Melissa, me, Clio and Jeanie were outside. So you got a bit stressed, moved too quickly, knocked something over as you were trying to escape into the secret passageway.'

'And you wouldn't even have had to kill Kieran if it wasn't for your mum. Because of her, everything went up in smoke – the money, the dreams you had. The two of you had planned a quick getaway in the boat after Valerie handed over Lynda's share of the Ponzi scheme money, and you did your bit like the good son you are. When you came in to light the fire last night, that was your mum's signal that Valerie was coming down, wasn't it? When you dropped that log on the hearth? That was when she asked to be taken to the loo, yes?'

He stayed silent.

'You must have thought you'd be out of here soon after. Heading back to the mainland with all your lovely money. You must be fuming. You'd been planted here for two months, uprooting yourself to work setting up the chateau, having to be a groundskeeper, mapping out the secret passageways, doing all the heavy lifting. You even had to pretend to see non-existent protestors, for God's sake.'

'No.' His fists were white where he held the gun. 'That's not what happened.'

'And you had to attack Melissa too.'

Melissa sat up, eyes glinting dangerously. 'That was him?'

'It must have been.' Amber nodded. 'His mum was far more prepared than he realised. She had always had a contingency plan in place. Because she knew that if she did kill Valerie then she couldn't just hide in the tunnels – she had to take herself off the suspects list too. She had to die, alongside her real victims. She had everything ready in her bag to fake it, but asked you to check that the kitchen was clear first. Then she could pretend to die, hide out in the tunnels and leave when everything died down.'

Ray still said nothing, but Amber sensed she was close now. Just one more push.

'So you crept in and hit Melissa, because Lynda needed the food to stage her own death, didn't she, so she could pretend she had been poisoned? Then you went on for Kieran. It must have been a bit stressful, attacking Melissa before Lynda went to the kitchen with Clio.'

'This is all lies.' His head was down.

'It was a great back-up plan. She would fake her own death to avoid suspicion for Valerie's murder. You would kill Kieran, and then you would both escape using the boat and dump his body when the coast was clear and the storm had died down. There was just one problem...'

Silence from Ray.

'The problem was that you had found Henri's cocaine, hadn't you? And you couldn't resist helping yourself, could you? The pressure got too much, and it was an easy fix.'

Ray swung his whole body round so the gun was pointing at Henri. 'You bastard. You told everyone.'

Amber grabbed the barrel and rotated the gun back to herself. 'Ray, you were high. Henri didn't need to tell anyone.'

Clio chimed in. 'You had a packet of the stuff in your pocket. We all saw you.'

'No, I...'

'You stupid bastard!' Lynda leapt to her feet, her face a snarl. She leapt at her son. 'You did *what*? How many times have you been to rehab?' She hit Ray squarely across the face and kept shouting. 'Ten years of NA and it goes up in smoke when you face a little bit of pressure. You've always been bloody useless. I've given you so many chances and you just mess them all up.'

'Mum.' Ray's voice was husky with emotion. 'You're the one who bloody killed her, not me. "We'll go to the Caribbean with all the cash," you said. "We'll live like kings," you said. Instead, you lost your temper again and killed her. We're not going to get to the Caribbean without her money, are we Mum?'

Lynda was off now, ready to give Amber the confession she had been hoping for. 'Well it's not my fault Valerie said no, is it? I mean I should have known that bitch would pretend that she didn't know me, but I really thought she would at least give me some cash to stay quiet. But instead she lied that she had no idea who I was and then I stepped towards her and she just went for me with a bloody knife! I mean...' Lynda looked around the room. 'What's a girl to do? Self-defence, wasn't it?'

Amber grimaced. 'Not the second blow, no. I imagine she was down by then. And it looked like there were more.'

'She deserved it.' Lynda's face was dark with hatred. 'Stealing all my money, disappearing, leaving me in a cell. That bitch deserved everything she got.'

'Did you get that, Melissa?'

'Sure did!' Melissa held up her phone.

'It seems you've confessed, Lynda. Ray, do you want to join in?'

'You bitch!' Lynda launched herself at Amber. Jeanie and Clio pulled her back again, but Amber already had bigger problems.

Ray was aiming the rifle at her chest again.

She took a step forwards. 'Come on, Ray. Why would you protect her now? What has she ever done for you except drag you into her mess?'

'She's...' His mouth was working. Amber was nearly there.

'Ray, she has let you down over and over again. You don't need to protect her now.'

His voice was a croak. 'Please stop.'

Amber had no choice but to do the opposite. 'You know, you think she loves you but the opposite is true. She was just using you, all along.'

'You're lying.' His face darkened. His voice sounded different now. Rough-edged. Breathy.

She couldn't stop now. He was about to crack.

'She was just using you to get to Valerie. She made you come here, do a job you didn't want to do, and she was probably going to stay in those passageways for as long as it took for you to be convicted. She was quite happy with you being in the frame. Your own mum.'

'Stop saying that.' She could see him shaking. 'I'll shoot you.'

She held his gaze as he pointed the gun at her heart.

'I warned you. Again and again.' He looked around the ragged group. 'You all heard me, right?'

No one answered, but he didn't care.

Amber spoke once more. 'You...'

And then he pulled the trigger and the world went black.

35

AMBER

Amber opened her eyes to see Clio and Jeanie looking down at her.

'What happened?'

'Um...' Clio bit her lip.

'You fainted, Amber.'

'Oh no.' Amber closed her eyes. She had fainted. How embarrassing. Twenty years on the force and this was the time she had chosen to pass out cold. It was mortifying.

'Where's Ray?'

'Here.' Jeanie pointed to her left and Amber saw Ray, who was standing over her, his face contorted in confusion.

'What the...?'

'I think it went over my head, Ray.' Amber ran a hand over her face as she pushed herself up into a sitting position. She felt wobbly, like she had run a marathon with no water or done a twenty-four-hour shift with no food.

'Bloody hell, Amber, you had me worried there.' Clio knelt down and threw her arms around Amber, and Amber let her. For once she wasn't enduring the proximity for Clio's sake – it was for her own. Ever since being told that Melissa was her half-sister, Amber felt as if she had been unravelling. Her outer layers – normally as strong as elephant hide – were being peeled away, leaving her long-lost soft underbelly exposed.

She looked at Lynda, writhing on the sofa, her face a scream. And she looked at Ray, staring at the gun which was now in Melissa's hands, clearly furious that it hadn't blown Amber apart.

It had worked. She had pushed them into confessing their guilt. Because of the lack of DNA evidence or CCTV, she had known it was the only way to catch them.

Supported by Clio and Jeanie, Amber dragged herself to her feet. 'Wow, I feel bad.' She swallowed. 'Fainting sucks.'

'Well done for only finding that out at the age of forty-six.' Clio patted her on the back. 'I was on the case aged five, when a man stole my Mr Whippy and I fainted in shock. It had a Flake and everything.'

'A tragic story.' Amber felt herself sway, but Jeanie caught her, her arms warm and welcoming. Maybe hugging wasn't so bad after all. Amber leant into her friend.

'It was all good in the end.' Clio smiled happily as Henri wrestled Ray's arms behind his back. 'The ice cream van gave me an extra one with three Flakes in it.'

'I'm happy for you.' Amber pulled away from her friends and approached Ray, who was still staring at the gun. She removed her belt and tied his hands behind him. Even she didn't travel with two pairs of cuffs.

'What the hell?' His head whipped round, as she pulled the belt tight around his wrists.

She avoided his foot as he kicked out at her. 'Well, you did just try to kill me.'

'I told you I would.'

'I'm not sure that's a defence that will stand up in court.' Amber sat him on the sofa next to his mum.

Jeanie appeared at her side. 'Happy families, eh?'

Amber hugged her. It felt good, choosing to be close to someone, rather than holding back in case they rejected you. She wasn't a little girl any more, with doors being slammed in her face. She knew she was loved. It felt like power. It felt like hope.

Clio nudged her. 'How did you figure it all out?'

'Yes. Go on. Tell us.' Jeanie placed her chin on her hands, her tired blue eyes shining.

'Well...' Amber walked to the fireplace. 'As well as the photo, there were the passageways. Once we knew about them, it all got a lot easier. And then I thought back and I realised that no one had taken Lynda's pulse when she died, meaning that she might in fact have faked her death and still be alive. There was so much going on all night – so much panicking and searching and fear. We all missed it. And it sounds like she gave a very convincing death performance, which, of course, she had practised before she did it, as it was one of her many potential escape routes. She must have had all the stuff she needed in that massive handbag – just in case. And then she managed to lie there for such a long time while we talked about who the killer might be. She was listening to all of that. You have to hand it to her – it's pretty impressive, really.'

'It was.' Clio's cheeks burned. 'Anyone would have been fooled by it.'

Jeanie patted her hand. 'I know I would. I mean, I was, wasn't I?'

'Me too.' Amber nodded. 'And then the photo, the phone and voila!'

'You bitch.' Lynda's face contorted. 'I was so close. I could kill you.'

'I don't think so.' Amber put her head on one side. 'The police will be here any minute now so I think this is the end of your killing spree.'

'You have no right to imprison us like this.'

'Well, you had no right to kill two people, did you? But you did it anyway. So guess what?' Amber smiled. 'We're going to do exactly what we want with you until the police can arrest you and take you back to the mainland to interrogate you.'

'Mum.' Ray looked like he might cry. 'I'm scared.'

'Oh, grow a pair.' Lynda stood up. 'You're such a whiner. You've always been the same. "*Mum, you're in prison and everyone's nasty to me.*"' She put on a high-pitched mocking voice. '"*Mum, no one will go out with me because they're all scared of you.*"' She sighed. 'Pathetic.'

Ray turned, spitting his words into her face. 'That's so unfair. Of course I moan at you because you ruined my life. I mean, look at me now.' He groaned. 'I didn't even want to come here, I was quite happy back at home, and now I'm going to bloody prison and it's all your fault. You and your bloody temper. Can't you just put a sock in it for once?'

Amber glanced at Clio and Jeanie.

'Melissa.' Amber turned to her half-sister. 'Is there anywhere you could put Ray in a room that definitely has no secret passages, so we don't have to listen to them arguing for the next hour? And can we move Lynda somewhere else?'

'Absolutely. It would be my pleasure to separate them.' Melissa's bunch of keys rattled as she stood up. 'Let's go, big guy.'

She led Ray away. As she reached the door Amber felt an impulse growing inside her, a feeling that she needed to do something to reach out to this woman who had moved across the globe to find her. She followed it, before she could think too hard, before she could retreat as she usually did. She took a breath and followed her heart.

She would spend a lot of time with her punchbag later to make up for it, of course.

But for now, she crossed the room towards her half-sister. She took her hand, pulling her back. She met those eyes, so like her own. And she found herself smiling.

'Stay safe, Melissa.'

Her half-sister's eyes met hers. 'You too, sis.'

Amber shook her head. 'No.'

'Too soon?'

'Just no.'

Melissa giggled. 'Hell, yeah. Sis. Sissy? Sissy sis sis?' She started to drag Ray down the hall. 'Angelo, come with?' He got up, and soon the two of them were dragging a protesting Ray down the hall.

Jeanie was laughing. 'Welcome to the wonderful world of siblings, Amber. A whole lifetime of always knowing there's someone out there who will take the mick out of you. How does it feel?'

Amber grimaced. 'It feels—' She stopped. 'It feels...' She took a breath.

Because the truth was it felt bloody fantastic. It was connection, it was recognition. It was family.

But she wasn't going to say that out loud, of course. One step at a time.

Instead, she turned to Jeanie. 'I'm starving. Let's go eat.'

She knew her friends had noticed how she had dodged the question, but she didn't care. Some things were too precious to say out loud.

36

CLIO

Once Lynda and Ray had been shut into two separate storerooms, Melissa joined Clio, Amber and Jeanie in the kitchen.

She clapped her hands together. 'It's slightly later than planned, but time to eat!'

'At last.' Clio opened the casserole dish full of boeuf bourguignon and happily began spooning some of the fragrant meat and sauce into bowls. Jeanie took a piece of bread from the sliced pile that stood next to it and chewed happily. Everything was cold, or stale but it didn't matter. Sauce splashed all over the table, all over their hands and faces, but absolutely no one cared.

Clio tucked in. 'This is the best meal I have ever had.'

Jeanie looked at her askance. 'What do you mean? How could this be better than the Nutella pancakes I make you every single birthday?'

Clio blinked, searching for words, before realising that Jeanie was laughing.

'It's too early for humour.' Clio forked more food into her mouth and groaned with pleasure. 'My blood sugar levels are nowhere near high enough to handle sarcasm.'

'It's so great that none of this has been poisoned.' Jeanie rubbed her belly happily.

Melissa snorted. '*Chateau la Fontaine.*' She held up her hands as if writing a slogan across the sky. '*Where none of the food is poisoned.* We'll win awards for that slogan.'

'It's a great customer guarantee, to be honest.' Amber took a long drink of water, standing up to refill the glass jug.

'I'd come and stay, for sure.' Clio took a sip of the red wine that Melissa had pulled out of the rack at the end of the kitchen and poured into heavy crystal glasses. At last, the weekend was starting to resemble the pleasurable experience Clio had imagined.

Amber reached for her glass. 'It's a five out of five on Tripadvisor from me if I don't get poisoned. Or attacked. Or murdered. I have a very low bar now.'

Clio glanced at her. 'Don't kid yourself, Amber. I know that you will never ever go on holiday again, will you? This has scarred you for life.'

She could tell Amber was considering lying, but she was probably too tired. 'Correct. If you want me, I'll be at home doing crunches.'

Melissa grimaced. 'Crunches? That's so nineties. I need to get you into biohacking and battle ropes.'

'That just sounds painful.' Amber shook her head.

Clio eyed up the wine rack beneath the book shelves in the alcove where their suspects board had been. She had wiped off all their workings out and thoughts, and instead written 'WE GOT THEM' in triumphant capital letters.

Melissa put down her fork. 'So, what was your first clue, Amber?'

Amber didn't hesitate. 'The tattoo.'

'Yeah.' Jeanie sat back in her chair. 'Why do you think she did that? Seems a bit of a giveaway, doesn't it?'

'I think she never really wanted to leave her old life.' Amber nursed her wine glass in both hands. 'I think she always missed Hastings, missed her old friends, her family. She probably had no idea how much leaving her home would cost her, of the hole it would leave in her heart.'

Clio thought about leaving Amber and Jeanie, or her daughter Nina, and had to swallow the lump that rose in her throat.

Amber continued, leaning forwards now. 'So she got the tattoo, to remind herself of who she really was. She passed it off as being about Sacre

Coeur, which was great until her old friend came looking for her.' Amber looked at her friends. 'Because I think Valerie probably tried to deny to Lynda that she had ever been Samantha Cohen, and that maybe she would have got away with it if only she hadn't had that tattoo.' Amber mopped up some more sauce with a chunk of baguette. 'So that was the first clue. A link to a past that didn't fit with Valerie la Fontaine, gourmet chef, brought up in the back streets of Paris. You know?'

'I wonder if it was worth it, for Jocelyn, or Lynda, or whoever she is.' Jeanie twirled a curl around her finger. 'That moment, when she killed her. I wonder if in that moment it all felt like she was finally getting the revenge she wanted.'

Amber took another sip. 'Why? Are you contemplating killing anyone?'

'No chance.' Jeanie shook her head. 'Though Tan would murder me if I left him alone with the twins for more than a weekend. Their main hobby at the moment is punching each other in the face.'

Clio laughed. It felt good to remember that she had a sense of humour, to feel the muscles of her face lifting, rather than sagging in stress.

'So, everyone, time for the big question.' She stretched her arms above her head, feeling exhaustion welling inside her.

'No, Clio, you don't look like Helen Mirren now you have blonde hair.'

'Harsh, Amber.' Clio frowned at her. 'And I know you're right. I look more like Emilia Fox.'

Amber rolled her eyes. 'If you say so.'

'Back to the point, please.' Clio tapped her glass. 'How many marks out of ten would you give our relaxing weekend away?'

'Zero.' Jeanie and Amber said in unison.

'No!' Melissa gulped the last of her wine. 'How can you say so? There was in-house entertainment, after all – a murder mystery weekend, if you will.'

Clio smiled. She was going to enjoy getting to know Melissa, assuming Amber didn't cast her out without giving her a chance. Melissa tried again. 'Oh, come on, this breakfast must be worth a few points. Be fair!'

'It's 5.40 a.m. Does this even count as breakfast?' Jeanie licked a crumb from her forefinger. 'I could do with about thirty hours of sleep.' She yawned.

'It does if we want it to.' Clio thought for a moment. If there was one thing this trip had taught her, it was not to let things fester – to confront them head on. 'Now. Are we all going to talk about the elephant in the room?'

'What elephant?' Amber's eyelids were half-closed and she was slumped back against the wall.

'Well, there are two really. The first is Melissa. And the second is the fact you've been propping up the agency with your savings, Amber.'

Amber jerked upright, sleep forgotten. 'How the hell did you know about that?' She turned on Clio. 'What did I say about never looking at my files?'

Clio put a hand on her heart. 'Why are you assuming it was me?'

'Because it's always you. Jeanie might as well come with a built-in halo.'

Clio thought for a second, then realised she had no choice but to come clean. 'You're right. It was me.'

'See? I knew it!' Amber tutted. 'You always do what I tell you not to do.'

'You were acting weird! And I have no regrets about what I did. You should have just told us that the agency was in trouble. You should have asked us for help.'

'But neither of you have any money either.'

'That's not the point.' Clio drew herself up to her full height, inwardly bemoaning the fact that she was only five foot one. 'The point is that you're meant to tell us everything. To trust us. Not to bankrupt yourself in order to keep paying us our salaries. How would you feel if I did that for you?'

Amber's eyes slid down to her plate.

'See? You wouldn't like it, would you?'

Clio had no regrets. She had seen Amber's drawn expression, her frown as she trawled through the accounting app for the millionth time. When you shared an office with someone it was impossible to miss the signs that something was wrong. 'Amber, you've taught us to do this. You've taught us to ask questions, to never let a lead go, to follow the clues. I knew there was something wrong with you, so I investigated. Just like you taught me. So don't get angry with me now. I meant well. I was trying to help.'

'Okay, okay.' Amber raised her hands. 'But you didn't have the right to go through my files.'

'But you'd never have told me otherwise! You'd just have struggled on, eating Pot Noodles for every meal until you had nothing left.'

Amber snapped. 'I like Pot Noodles!'

Jeanie put her fork down, resting her elbows on the table. 'No one likes them that much. Especially the mushroom one. Always bottom of the list, the mushroom one.'

Melissa nodded understandingly. 'I do hate that mushroom one.'

'Well, I like it!' Amber bristled. 'Get off my case, you lot.'

Jeanie laid a hand on her arm. 'Come on Amber. We're meant to be a team. And, once Clio had told me how bad things were, well, we just wanted to make things easier on you. You've looked after us for long enough, after all. So I've lined up some interviews – junior marketing positions, that kind of thing.' She nibbled her lip. 'I mean, I'd far rather work for you, of course. But I don't want you to have to look after me. I can stand on my own two feet.'

Clio sat up straighter. It was her turn now. 'And I've got some auditions coming up. It seems there might actually be some work for a midlife actress looking to get back into the game. So...' She looked at Amber. 'So yes. That's my plan.'

Jeanie met Amber's eye. 'We're not your responsibility, okay?'

'No, we're not.' Clio echoed her.

For a moment it looked as if Amber might cry. Her lip was actually wobbling. Then she pulled herself together, as she always did, as she always had. 'I'm sorry. I haven't paid you yet. I meant to yesterday, but then I found Valerie and I forgot. You're right – things have been really hard. I thought I could make the agency work, but now there's no money, and not many clients, and...' Her eyes dropped away from theirs. Clio stared as a tear rolled down Amber's cheek. 'Please don't leave me.' Amber held out her hands, palms raised. 'Please?'

Clio took one and Jeanie the other. 'But you can't afford to pay us. The agency doesn't have enough coming in.'

'So we'll figure it out!' Amber took a shuddering breath. 'We'll find a way to get more business happening. I just...' She swallowed. 'I just know we can make it work. And I'm the practical one here. I'm the one who keeps things real.'

'Rude.' Clio shrugged. 'But probably fair.'

Melissa coughed. 'Can I say something here?'

Amber put her head on one side. 'Well, I don't know. It really involves the three of us.'

'Hear me out.' Melissa held up a hand. 'If you don't mind?'

Clio met Jeanie's eye. These two had a lot in common.

'Yes?' Amber played with the stem of her wine glass. 'What?'

Melissa swallowed. 'I could help.'

'How?'

'Well, I have some savings.'

Amber was already shaking her head. 'You mean your inheritance from Valerie? I thought you said there were financial issues.'

Melissa sighed. 'Oh, ye of little faith. Clearly, I am going to have to teach you to trust me. I have savings. Of my own. And I wondered if you might like a bit of investment. And a bit of my marketing expertise, based on a decade of working for the world's finest luxury gourmet retreat.'

Amber was staring at her. 'You want to work for me?'

Melissa shook her head. 'No. I absolutely 100 per cent do *not* want to work for you. I think there would be blood on the floor before I'd even finished my first coffee. But I would like to help you and your very clever friends to continue your work. And I have an eye for a good investment, which is why I would be very happy to put some money into your agency. And, by the way, your marketing sucks. Now, do you want my help or not?'

'Oh, wow.' Clio watched Amber's face. The light that sparked and then went out again. The hope and then the reality.

She beckoned to Jeanie. 'Time for us to go, I think?'

'No need.' Panic clouded Amber's face. 'You can stay here.'

'There's every need.' Clio crossed her fingers and she and Jeanie left the kitchen, leaving Amber and Melissa facing each other across the table.

37

AMBER

Amber and Melissa sat in silence. Amber reached for any number of words, but none of them seemed to fit.

Finally, she broke the silence. 'You know, you don't have to help me.' Amber rubbed the heels of her hands into her eyes. 'I don't need your money. Or your pity.'

'It's not pity.' Melissa heaved a sigh. 'It's an investment.'

'But why would you invest in my business?' Amber eyed the woman across the table. This woman who had opened up the past, revealing all the things that Amber had run from for so long. This woman who, despite all that, Amber felt herself wanting to spend time with, wanting to know better. Melissa. Her half-sister.

Melissa shrugged. 'I have a feeling you're going to go places, sis.'

Amber flinched. 'Just to be clear, you can never call me sis. Never. Ever.'

'So you are planning to talk to me again, then?' Melissa put a hand to her bloody hair. 'Well, that's encouraging.'

'Maybe.' Amber felt a pang of guilt as Melissa's face fell. She found it so hard to open up, to let people in.

Melissa tried again. 'You know, you don't have to worry. If I do invest, I won't be in your face about it. I won't get in your way, or stalk you, or anything. You can just go back to being Amber Nagra, and I'll be Melissa

Lopez and we never have to meet again. I don't want to be someone you regret having met. If you don't want to be my half-sister or whatever, then that's fine with me.'

The tremor in her voice gave her away.

Amber waited a moment, trying to pull her feelings into enough order to speak. Then she let go. Sometimes you just had to try. Given everything that had happened in the past twenty-four hours, she had learnt that, at least.

Amber took a deep breath, which came out more like a sob. 'What was our mum like?'

Melissa exhaled. 'Are you sure you want to talk about Mom?'

'Yes. Totally. Absolutely.' Amber hesitated. 'Actually, I don't know. Maybe a little? It...' She couldn't carry on.

'It hurts too much?'

'Something like that.'

'Okay, keep your hair on. I'll be gentle.' Melissa leant towards her, reaching for her hand. 'Speaking of which, does your hair ever fall out?'

'What?'

'It's just mine is coming out in handfuls and I've tried everything, and...'

Amber felt a surge of relief. Because hers had been falling out – big clumps in the shower every morning. Naturally she hadn't talked about it – instead she had Googled wigs and started buying thickening shampoos that never worked.

She kept her eyes lowered. 'Mine too. I'm blaming the menopause.' She raised her gaze and saw nothing but recognition. Maybe this was what sisters did. Half-sisters, anyway. Maybe there didn't always have to be a goal, or something to strive for, or a plan. Maybe sometimes you just sat in the kitchen and chatted about hair. Amber found she was okay with that. In fact, she couldn't wait for more.

Melissa's deep brown eyes shone, full of hope. Her fingers unclenched, her hands relaxing as her fingers stretched long. A small smile tugged the corners of her mouth upwards.

'Well, Mom's hair fell out too. She swore by coconut oil, but it doesn't seem to work for me.'

'And?'

'And what?'

'Tell me more about her...'

Melissa rested her chin in her hand. 'She was sarcastic like you. Strong, like you. A great singer.'

'Not like me.' Amber sagged. Then she brightened again. 'Though I do like karaoke and "Turn Back Time" is my favourite song.'

'No freaking way.' Melissa's face lit up. 'That is A. Ma. Zing.'

'It is amazing.' Amber nodded. 'That key change. My finest moment.'

'Not that, you egomaniac. It's my favourite karaoke song too!' Melissa was on her feet in a minute. 'If I could...'

Amber couldn't let a singalong of her favourite tune ever go unchallenged. 'Turn back...'

The two of them finished the chorus together, heads thrown back, arms wide. Then they looked at each other and Amber felt something hit her so hard it was as if Ray was shooting at her again. It was like a missing limb returning, or the sound of a loved one's key in the door. It was coffee made just the way you like it or arms reaching for you in the dark.

It was everything. Her heart. Her future. Maybe she could handle sharing the karaoke mic, or her worries or her joys. Maybe she could trust someone new. Maybe she could change. Make space. Take a chance.

They heard footsteps approaching and Clio and Jeanie appeared at the door.

'We were lured by your terrible singing.' Clio beamed. 'She's just as bad as you are.'

'Hey!' Amber threw a piece of bread at her. 'You didn't say that last time I sang that song. You told me I was brilliant.'

'That's because you were in charge of mixing the margaritas, and I needed to keep you sweet.' Clio dodged out of the way as another piece of bread flew at her head. 'Now, have you two done the decent thing and made friends yet? Because I just saw a police launch out of the window, and they're pretty close and I don't want to face them alone. I need you and your police chat, Amber. So let's get out there.'

'All right, all right.' Amber walked over to Melissa. 'After that, do you want to talk some more?'

'Talk, not sing.' Clio muttered. 'There's only so much of that a girl can take.'

'Just talking.' Amber looked Melissa dead in the eye. 'What do you think?'

'I don't think we can commit to that.' Melissa grinned. 'How about we try some Adele?'

'*No.*' Clio put her hands over her ears as Amber and Melissa launched into 'Set Fire to the Rain.' Amber grinned as they joined arms and sang louder.

They kept singing as the four of them made their way down to the jetty, where Amber stood with Clio and Jeanie on one side, hands over their ears, and Melissa on the other. The four of them looked like refugees from a crowd fight scene in an action movie: exhausted, bloodied and hollow-eyed. But Amber didn't care. These were her people. The people she would fight for no matter what.

Clio leant towards her. 'Margaritas later?'

Amber nodded. 'Hell, yes.' And she stood, smiling, as the police launch arrived to take them home.

ACKNOWLEDGEMENTS

Thank you firstly to my readers – I love you all, and I will adore you even more if you spread the word about how much you enjoyed it (if you didn't, then silence is golden). Thanks to Claire Pollard for police insights, to Isabelle Broom for more than I could ever say, to Sarah Turner for solidarity and Bad Girls love and to Aidan, Evie and Max for some of the best cheerleading an author could ever dream of. I am also enormously grateful to One Tree Books for support and inspiration and want to thank my POTPs – Charlotte, Frankie, Roz, Helen and Rosie, I love you all. And Issy, you rock.

A huge thank you to everyone at the brilliant Boldwood Books, especially Amanda Ridout, Claire Fenby-Warren, Jenna Houston, Wendy Neale, Marcela Torres, Grace Cooper, Hayley Russell, Ben Wilson and Leila Mauger. Big hugs to Debra Newhouse and Gary Jukes and to my editor Isobel Akenhead, who really has gone above and beyond on this one. Emily Hayward-Whitlock, thank you, thank you, thank you, and Charlie Campbell, you are truly my agent of dreams. Sam Edenborough, Maria Brannan and everyone at Greyhound Literary, I am so happy to be on your team. Thank you.

Lastly, I would like to thank Maisy, who will not care, but who does make a world of difference every single day by snoozing as I write my stories. I couldn't do it without her.

ABOUT THE AUTHOR

Katie Marsh wrote five romantic fiction novels before turning to crime. Her debut, 'My Everything' was a World Book night pick, and her books are published across ten countries. She lives in the English countryside with her family and loves coffee, puzzles and pretending she is in charge of her children. Her move into crime was inspired by her own bumpy arrival into midlife, complete with insomnia so severe that she once forgot her own name. Her crime debut 'How Not to Murder your Ex', was inspired by the friendships that helped her to get back on track.

Sign up to Katie Marsh's mailing list for news, competitions and updates on future books.

Visit Katie's website: www.katie-marsh.com

Follow Katie on social media here:

facebook.com/katiemarshauthor
instagram.com/katiemarshauthor

ALSO BY KATIE MARSH

The Bad Girls Detective Agency Series

How Not To Murder Your Ex

Murder on the Dancefloor

Murder on the Menu

Poison & Pens

POISON & PENS IS THE HOME OF
COZY MYSTERIES SO POUR YOURSELF
A CUP OF TEA & GET SLEUTHING!

DISCOVER PAGE-TURNING NOVELS FROM
YOUR FAVOURITE AUTHORS &
MEET NEW FRIENDS

JOIN OUR
FACEBOOK GROUP

BIT.LY POISONANDPENSFB

SIGN UP TO OUR
NEWSLETTER

BIT.LY/POISONANDPENSNEWS

Boldwood

Boldwood Books is an award-winning fiction publishing company seeking out the best stories from around the world.

Find out more at www.boldwoodbooks.com

Join our reader community for brilliant books, competitions and offers!

Follow us
@BoldwoodBooks
@TheBoldBookClub

Sign up to our weekly deals newsletter

https://bit.ly/BoldwoodBNewsletter